REFLECTION

A Whitney Steel Novel - Book One

Kim Cresswell

KC Publishing

Copyright © 2014 Kim Cresswell

All rights reserved

Reflection/Kim Cresswell - 2nd Edition
ISBN: 978-0-9920841-4-1

Cover design by KC Book Cover Design

Subscribe to Kim's quarterly newsletter so you don't miss out on exclusive content, deals, upcoming releases, first-to-see book covers, contests, freebies, and more at www.kimcresswell.ca.

For Justin, Carla, Porter, and Peyton
In memory of Mary Beech
Death leaves a heartache no one can heal, love leaves a
memory no one can steal. — From a headstone in Ireland

ABOUT THE AUTHOR

Kim Cresswell resides in Ontario, Canada and is the award-winning author of the action-packed WHITNEY STEEL series.

Her debut romantic thriller, *Reflection* (A Whitney Steel Novel - Book One) has won numerous awards: RomCon®'s 2014 Readers' Crown Finalist (Romantic Suspense), InD'tale Magazine 2014 Rone Award Finalist (Suspense/Thriller), UP Authors Fiction Challenge Winner, Silicon Valley's Romance Writers of America (RWA) "Gotcha!" Romantic Suspense Winner, and an Honorable Mention in Calgary's (RWA) The Writer's Voice Contest.

Kim recently signed a 3-book German translation deal with Luzifer Verlag for the first three books in the Whitney Steel series: *Reflection*, *Retribution,* and *Resurrect.* The popular series will be published in German beginning in 2019.

The Assassin Chronicles TV series, based on Kim's upcoming 4-book paranormal/supernatural thriller series: *Deadly Shadow (2018)*, *Invisible Truth, Assassin's Prophecy*, and *Vision of Fire* was in development with Council Tree Productions.

Web Site: www.kimcresswell.ca

Facebook: www.facebook.com/KimCresswellBooks

Twitter: http://twitter.com/kimcresswell

ALSO BY KIM CRESSWELL

The Whitney Steel Series
Reflection (Book One)
Retribution (Book Two)
Resurrect (Book Three)

The Assassin Chronicles Series
Deadly Shadow (Book One)

The Sum of all Tears Series
Icehaven (Book One)
Liberty (Book Two)

The Raina Storm Thriller Series
Dawn of the Storm (Book One)
Dawn of the Enemy (Boon Two)

Novellas
Lethal Journey

The True Crime Short Story Series
Real Life Evil – A True Crime Quickie
Murder on Sunset Strip (Book Two)
Garden of Bones (Book Three)
Edge of Madness (Book Four)

Chameleon (Book Five)
Backwoods Murder (Book Six)

True Crime Anthologies Published by Grinning Man Press

Serial Killer Quarterly "21st Century Psychos"
Serial Killer Quarterly "Partners in Pain"
Serial Killer Quarterly "Unsolved in North America"
Serial Killer Quarterly "Cruel Britannia"
Serial Killer Quarterly "They Almost Got Away"
Serial Killer Quarterly "Lostmord: Murder in German"

PRAISE FOR REFLECTION

"Holds you captive to the very end." — New York Times Bestseller, Dianna Love

"This was definitely an intriguingly phenomenal read. Cresswell is an amazingly captivating and suspenseful storyteller who is able to switch gears at the flip of the hat." — Pure Jonel Book Reviews

"Cinematic writing, powerful visuals, sleek, fast, utterly sexy, notches above anything we have read before!" — UP Authors

"Action packed from page one...an impressively laid out passionate thrill ride!" — InD'Tale Magazine (www.indtale.com)

"I was looking forward to reading about Whitney and Blake. I anticipated a Booth and Bones relationship (from the Bones TV Series) and I wasn't wrong...this book is definitely worth reading." — Quality Reads UK Book Club

"A brilliant mixture of action, romance and mystery. Well worth a read...a very tough book to put down." — Jeep Diva

"Five-star page-turner! A truly edge-of-your-seat, never-a-

CHAPTER ONE

Mason Bailey gulped down his third Glenlivet. "I didn't kill her."

How many times had Whitney Steel heard those words? Dozens. But never from the mouth of a United States senator. For all she cared, the man could drink himself to Mars, but not until she got what she'd come for. An exclusive.

Under the awning shading the Pink Flamingo Club's patio, she took a sip of her lime daiquiri, and couldn't help notice the way the mid-afternoon sunlight brutally magnified every line on Mason's tanned face.

"Of all the reporters in Panama City, let alone Florida, why me? We cut our ties years ago." *And our losses,* she wanted to say but didn't.

"I know I can trust you." His gaze darted across the street then back to her. "Besides, we were married once. That should count for something."

Whitney straightened. Anger coiled in the pit of her stomach. "Give me a break. For a year and a half, I thought we were married. Too bad your girlfriends didn't know about our little legal arrangement." *Especially, your twenty something assistant.*

"Damn it, Whitney. I didn't ask you here to rehash our past." He yanked a monogrammed handkerchief from his jacket pocket and dabbed the sweat from his forehead. "I need your help. I know why Carmen Lacey was murdered."

Her eyes widened. Now they were getting somewhere. "You have my full attention. Are we on the record?"

Mason shoved his empty glass aside. "Yes."

Her heart thumped with anticipation. This story would be the topic du jour for months. Her ratings at WBNN-TV would soar, and finally her colleagues would take notice and treat her with the professional respect she deserved.

For the past twelve years, her colleagues said she'd had a free ride because of her father, an award-winning war correspondent, and her ex-husband's political connections. This time she'd prove them wrong.

She rummaged through her leather bag, placed her digital voice recorder on the table and gave the record button a firm push. "For the record, Senator Bailey, did you kill Carmen Lacey?"

"No." He leaned back in the chair and loosened his pinstriped tie. "It's true. I was the last person to see her alive. But there's more to this than you think."

Brown eyes that once set her heart hammering now conveyed a chilling, hollow look. Was it guilt? Desperation?

No. Fear.

Uneasiness slid down her spine. She stopped the recorder. "Mason, you're scaring me. What the hell is going on? It's been over three years since we last spoke. Then, out of the blue, you beg me to meet with you today. I know the police don't believe you killed that woman."

"But do you, Whitney? Do you believe I killed her? I

need to know. It's important."

Stunned by the urgency in his voice, she answered carefully. "Of course not. You're many things, but you're not a killer."

"Thank you. That means a lot to me." He reached for his empty glass and tapped his chunky gold ring against the side.

Whitney turned the recorder on again.

"Carmen was a scientist working for a biotech company in Nevada. ShawBioGen. Heard of it?"

"Who hasn't? They were one of the first to clone animals in the eighties. Caused quite a stir. But I don't understand. What does that have to do with Carmen's death?"

He opened his mouth to answer.

The large window behind them dividing the patio from the main restaurant exploded. A storm of glass rained down, showering the patio.

There was no warning. Everything moved so fast, yet in slow motion as if part of a horrid nightmare.

Screams. Rushed, heavy, thumping footsteps.

A few feet away, a male waiter dropped the two plates of food in his hands. He froze.

"Get down!" Mason yelled.

Whitney dropped. She huddled into a ball under the table and squashed the side of her face against the patio stones. Amid the chaos, a gunshot echoed, and the waiter ran for cover.

A bullet ripped through the man's shoulder and spun him around, the force slamming his body against the restaurant door. He folded to his knees and howled out in pain.

More shots rang out. Debris spewed through the air.

Food, glasses, plates. The sickening smell of deep fried food and scorched cordite assaulted her nostrils. She gagged.

Crimson snaked toward her hand. The warm, sticky liquid met her fingertips.

Blood. Lots of blood. But it wasn't hers.

Her gaze snapped to Mason, lying on his back. Dark red blood pumped from a gaping wound in his chest, soaking his white shirt. She held her breath to keep from screaming.

He raised his arm and reached for her. "I swear—I didn't kill her. I swear."

"I believe you." Whitney kept her head down and inched her body closer. She grasped his hand. "I do. Oh, God."

Please don't die. Her pulse roared so loud in her ears she couldn't hear her own words. "You're bleeding so much. Someone help us!"

Another bullet whizzed through the air and slammed into the bottom of the wooden table leg.

Needle-like splinters from the wood slashed through her pants and drilled into her thigh like a hundred slivers. The pain knocked the breath from her. The world twisted and turned yellow. Darkness thickened and threatened to overpower her. *Can't pass out...help Mason.*

He gasped a ragged breath and shoved a key into her bloody palm and curled her fingers closed. "Don't trust—anyone."

She clutched the piece of metal. A knot wedged in her throat, one she couldn't swallow. "I'm going to get help."

"No—stay." Blood bubbled at the corners of his

mouth and trickled down his jaw. "They cloned..."

His eyelids slid shut.

"What Mason? They cloned what?"

Whitney lowered her head to his chest. "Oh, Mason, no."

CHAPTER TWO

George Raines, WBNN-TV's assignment editor, teetered on the edge of Whitney's desk. "I can guarantee an Emmy."

In her spacious tenth-floor office, Whitney sat behind her desk and kicked off her pink leather high heels.

Across the room, she eyed her bronze Peabody statue, the last honor she'd won for an exposé involving three of Panama City's finest and the disappearance of millions of dollars' worth of cocaine.

An Emmy. The only award she hadn't won. The one she wanted the most.

During her career, she'd been punched, censored by authorities, and even carjacked. Hell, she deserved an Emmy for surviving. Nothing had prepared her for Mason's death. The senator was more than a story. He was a man she'd once loved, still loved.

Her eyes stung with fatigue as she fought to suppress a yawn. The savage assault of sleepless nights definitely took a toll.

You weren't there, George. Others died. The waiter... "Look, the funeral was less than six days ago. I know this story is important. I can't do it."

No surprise when his eyes narrowed. "Okay. What did you do with the woman of steel? Remember that feisty woman who'd march into a room and defy any opposition? Where the hell did you put her?"

Whitney managed a weak smile. If only she had the answer.

"Hey, if your father was alive."

She held up her hand to stop him. "You don't need to remind me." As much as she loved her father, she'd spent her career in the shadow of Robert Steel. Celebrated reporter. Peabody winner. Four-time Emmy winner. Executed in war-torn Colombia.

"I've never seen you like this." George sat back down on the corner of the desk, his pudgy face scruffy from a half-hearted shave. "You're going soft on me."

Was she? She was. "I am not."

"Then reconsider. It's not every day a senator is gunned down." He hopped off the desk and smoothed his hopelessly wrinkled shirt. "The committee Mason chaired was working on something huge. Very hush-hush. The man gave his life, and the public deserves to know why. You're the only one who can deliver that. You're the best."

The best? Not today. Not for the past week. She shook her head. "I'm exhausted, drained, stressed to the limit. Give the story to someone else. I don't want it."

"Come on, Steel. You can't be serious. Cliff Peterson will jump at this chance. You know he'll never let you live it down. I thought this was what you wanted. The *Big* story."

The sixty-year-old man was persuasive, but not persuasive enough.

"George. Why is it so hard to believe I need a break?"

"Because I've worked with you for years, kiddo. Whitney Steel doesn't take breaks. She doesn't do vacations. And she sure as shit doesn't walk away from a story."

His raspy growl harbored a touch of impatience. He was testing her slow fuse. She scribbled an address and phone number on a piece of paper and handed it to him. "Oregon is only a phone call away. I'll be back before you know it."

He took the paper from her hand. "Swear you'll come back?"

"Two weeks. Promise." With her pen, she pointed toward his shoes. "And, George—your socks don't match. Gray on the right, brown on the left."

He slipped his hands into his pants pockets and looked down. Knowing George was, in his words, "color-challenged," all she could do was smile.

"Man. I've got to find a woman to dress me in the morning." He planted a kiss on her cheek. "Since I can't change your mind, guess I'll see you soon. Enjoy your vacation."

Long after he'd left the office, English Leather cologne remained, as though the woodsy, moss fragrance had permeated the walls and carpet. George was stuck in a time warp. She'd miss the old fool. In less than two hours, she'd be aboard a flight to Florence, Oregon, sipping a glass of wine.

When she opened her desk drawer, her breath caught in her throat. The crumpled white tissue stared back at her like a gift waiting to be unwrapped, inside a key crusted with blood—Mason's blood. A shiver rocketed down her spine, and Mason's dying words echoed in her head.

"They cloned..."

❊ ❊ ❊

Blake Neely faced certain death. "I don't want to shoot you, but I will if I have to." The beast stood its ground, glaring at him with opaque, marble eyes and razor-sharp teeth. Nothing stood between them except a cool Nevada breeze and moonlight.

The way the monster gawked at him, with perked ears and raised hair, forced his throat to tighten. As if anticipating his next move, the creature crinkled its face and then hissed.

Blake's blood froze. Yup. He was going to die.

He started to reach for the nine-millimetre pistol tucked in the waistband of his jeans when his cell phone rang. The savage monster let out a high-pitched whine and scurried off in the opposite direction.

Thank you. There really is a God.

Relieved, he forced his body to move and answered the call. "Yeah, Blake here."

"Did you find the security breach?" Nathan Shaw asked.

"Yeah—a cat—a God damn cat. It dug a hole just enough under the fence to set off the main alarm."

"What? A bobcat? Did you shoot it?"

Blake raised an eyebrow. He may as well lie. That was what he was trained to do.

"Nope. Scared the hell out of him, though. He took off before I had a chance."

His boss laughed. "Guess he wasn't hungry."

"Guess not. I'll finish up here and be back in ten."

"Keep your eyes peeled. The cat might come back."

Blake spun, the phone gripped in his hand. "I—will." He snapped the cell phone shut, and then slid it into his jacket pocket.

He grabbed a shovel from the back of his truck and

moved the loose reddish-brown earth under the fence and filled the hole. When he finished, he jumped into the F-150 pickup, scrounged up a piece of stale donut and chucked it out the window. In case the "bobcat" was hungry.

Northeast of Vegas, between Alamo and Mesquite, a full moon cast a hovering spotlight over the narrow desert road. In the distance, a thirty-foot-high security fence surrounded ShawBioGen's million square-foot concrete and steel compound. From the air, the place looked like a state super-prison dropped in the middle of nowhere.

Within those walls, Nathan Shaw had successfully cloned a human. Blake had earned a degree of Nathan's trust, but not enough for his boss to give him access to the lab or offer a personal invite to meet the small child.

Outside the main gates of the complex, Blake threw the truck in park. He peered through the tiny opening of the retinal scanning device and kept his eyes focused on the tiny green light. After ten seconds, the device beeped, and the gates opened.

In the past week, he'd gone so deep undercover no one at the Bureau had heard from him. That alone created a situation. If he didn't check in within the next forty-eight hours, the pistol-packin' posse would show up, and his cover would be blown. He wasn't about to let that happen. For two hundred and seventy days, he'd pretended to be a security specialist to the ruthless multi-billionaire owner. He'd even dyed his dirty-blond hair a darker shade of brown. With his hair, now a few inches longer, he liked his rugged new look—might even keep it for a while.

He had a job to do. Something next to impossible. Infiltrate the lab and get the evidence to take Nathan down. And soon. He'd spent too much time and energy to let the Bureau pull the plug on this mission.

Nathan Shaw was another story. Philanthropist. Las Vegas Man of the Year six years in a row. Nevada's largest employer, and until recently, Blake's sister's boss. How does a woman so terrified of water end up dead on a boat?

She couldn't swim, and a boat was the last place she would be. Instinct told him someone wanted her out of the picture. But why?

Recently, another employee was found stabbed to death in her Las Vegas apartment. A coincidence? Not likely. Too many bodies connected in one way or another with ShawBioGen.

He parked at the rear of the security building and shut off the ignition. His cell phone rang again. "Yeah."

"Get back here, pronto."

His boss' voice sounded strained. "What's up?"

"Now," Nathan growled.

The line went dead.

＊ ＊ ＊

On the second floor of ShawBioGen, Blake leaned against the polished stainless-steel wall and cracked his knuckles. The eccentric asshole had already kept him waiting for more than half an hour.

Hopefully, his boss' foul mood would turn out to be nothing more than one of his daily fits.

Not a day passed without Nathan twisted up about something. Like when the cleaning staff hadn't emptied his trash pail, or when his secretary moved the ashtray on his desk from the left side to the right. The man could be downright anal at times. When you're worth billions, you can act however you like. Who cares what anyone else thinks.

The office steel doors spread apart like the parting of the sea, revealing the tangy smell of sweet peppers and woodsy tobacco.

Blake grunted. About damn time. He took a deep breath and sauntered into the massive office.

In the middle of the room, Nathan sat behind his gold trimmed cherry desk, smoking some brand of cigar that Blake more than likely couldn't pronounce, let alone ever afford. Through the billowing smoke, the man raised a hand and pointed to one of the brown cowhide chairs in front of the desk.

As commanded, Blake sat.

Puffing on his cigar, Nathan stood and walked to the floor-to-ceiling window at the east end of the office. "We have a problem."

"Someone employed at ShawBioGen has only been pretending to be part of my team. You know how much I hate a liar."

Blake's heart leaped uncomfortably in his chest. *Remain calm. Your cover isn't compromised. It can't be.*

Nathan turned and put out his cigar in one of the numerous ashtrays scattered throughout the room. "You do understand what I mean, don't you?"

Play it cool. Don't let him get to you. "Of course. No one likes a liar."

"Exactly. So, here's the problem. One of my most trusted employees snuck a video camera into my research lab. Breaches like this are not acceptable."

The heavy weight on Blake's chest lifted. He could

breathe again. His secret was safe—for now. "Really? Who?"

"Her name isn't important. She was a brilliant scientist." Nathan wandered to the fully stocked bar. "Scotch?"

"Sure." Blake watched Nathan pour two drinks from one of the many crystal decanters.

"You make it sound like this woman isn't around anymore."

"Sadly, she isn't. She'd been an important part of my team since I began my research decades ago. I heard she was killed, recently. A real shame."

Carmen Lacey. Yeah, you sound real broken up about her death. Had Nathan bought and paid for her death?

His boss handed him the glass of scotch.

"Thanks." Blake took a sip, enjoying the smooth robust taste.

Nathan stood in front of the window again. He ran his hand through his receding gray hair.

Either the guy liked staring at his reflection, or he loved the distant view of Vegas at night lit to the hilt. Probably the latter. He knew Nathan liked to gamble, and an illegal cloning project was just that. A huge gamble.

"Because of this breach, I want you to beef up security at the lab. Have a retina scanner installed as soon as possible. My research is too important."

Blake gulped down the last of his drink. "Will do. It could take a few days to get the equipment up and running properly. In the meantime, I'll post two guys at the lab."

"We're through here then."

The doors opened behind Blake. Apparently, he was

being dismissed. Before leaving the room, he set his empty glass on the bar. By the time his boots touched the hallway floor, the doors swept closed with a prison-like-lockdown hollow thud.

Lockdown. Just like prison. Get used to it, Nathan. 'Cause that's exactly where you're heading.

CHAPTER THREE

*W*aves crashed and pierced the cool night air. Deep within the shadows gunshots echoed. A body washed ashore and turned the sand into a whirlpool of blood.

Mason—God, it was Mason.

A light breeze whispered. "They cloned..."

Whitney jolted awake, gasping, but relieved to find she had dosed off on the deck in the rattan rocker and wasn't lying on a beach. Another horrid dream. They visited more often, each more vivid than the last. When would they end?

After connecting flights and stopovers late yesterday afternoon, the short flight to Florence, Oregon, had turned into a seven-hour adventure from Florida. She'd finally fallen asleep around four in the morning. Tired and a bit moody, she decided nothing would ruin her first vacation in years.

On the spacious deck, the molten sun blazed against her fair skin. Dressed in white shorts and a loose flamingo-pink T-shirt, she stood and stretched, gazing across the turquoise ocean.

Her long-time friend, Marcus Wheeler, had offered the use of his beach house while he was on assignment in Europe. It was a secluded paradise complete with a fireplace, whirlpool and steam room, but coming home to Florence was bittersweet. The last time she had been here was to bury her father.

Whitney closed her eyes and spread her feet shoulder width apart, ready to begin her daily Tai Chi routine.

She relaxed her body, drew a long, deep breath and found her center. She bent her knees slightly, faced her palms toward her thighs and exhaled even slower. With deliberate fluid movements, she raised her arms shoulder height, turned her palms toward the sky, and lunged her right foot forward.

She repeated the movements until an impatient triple-blast of the doorbell broke her concentration. Whitney stormed through the house and swung open the front door, ready to give some poor door-to-door salesman a good tongue lashing for interrupting her vacation.

"FedEx. Are you Whitney Steel?"

"Yes."

"Sign here." The man handed her the electronic signature pad.

She wrote her name.

He handed her a package the size of a paperback novel. "Here you go."

Her stomach contracted into to a tight ball. She stared at the parcel, confused. *No one knows I'm here... except for George.*

After the deliveryman left, Whitney pushed the door shut with her foot and noticed the name, Trossen, and Meyers, on the corner of the package. Where had she heard that name before? Finally, it came to her. Mason's divorce lawyer. Why would his lawyer be sending her something? On the way to the great room, she kicked off her flip-flops and ripped open the package.

Inside, she found a white envelope with her name scribbled in blue ink on the outside, a hand drawn map, and what appeared to be a videotape. Intrigued, she opened the envelope first.

A shiver traced her spine, despite the heat of the sunlight flooding through the floor-to-ceiling windows. A note from Mason.

Whitney,

Approximately 18 months ago, the FBI received information through its tips website that ShawBioGen had been conducting illegal experiments, which resulted in the successful cloning of a child. Under the direction of the Justice Department, a covert task force was formed to investigate. I was called upon to be the main liaison because of my past involvement with the Justice Department.

The FBI tracked the Internet user, Carmen Lacey, who'd been working for Nathan Shaw. Over the next four months, Carmen and I grew close.

Fully aware of the dangers, she'd gathered the enclosed items because she feared Nathan would use the technology to create his own super-race, sell the technology, or worse, kill the child to hide his devilish deeds.

Nathan is keeping the cloned child, a three-year-old girl, known as Angel024 somewhere in the complex.

Whitney, you must get inside that lab.

Trust no one.

Her jaw dropped open. "For God sakes, Mason, I'm a reporter, not a friggin' commando. What were you thinking?" Her legs trembled. She sank to the sofa, and continued to read...

I can hear you now, Whitney. You're only a reporter,

right? You can do this. You have the brains and the skills to get into that lab. Without documentation or physical evidence, the U. S. Attorney's Office is unable to indict. They need proof, and so far, other avenues have resulted in failure. In return, you'll receive the exclusive of a lifetime.

She paced in front of the coffee table. "What in the world makes you think I can do this? Why? Because I have a black belt in karate? What am I supposed to do, Mason? Karate-chop down the lab door?"

Once you have the evidence, contact Ned Ford at the Justice Department.

Remember Shaw's resources are unlimited, his power colossal.

Trust no one... Mason

Tears collected in the corners of her eyes. Damn you, Mason.

She shoved the tape into the VCR and pressed play. The mammoth plasma screen burst to life with crackling white snow before it erupted into a grainy black and white picture. Whitney squinted, scanning the screen in hopes of seeing something. Anything. The camera jiggled and swung to the right. It was obvious the video was taken with a concealed camera.

A child with long, light-colored hair sat surrounded by toys and stuffed animals. Someone in a white coat bent and scooped the child from the floor.

"Testing time, Angel. Then chocolate ice cream."

The child let out a tortured screech and flailed her tiny fists, thrashing at the man's face. Whitney gasped, wanting to dive through the screen and comfort the child. She felt so powerless. The same helpless misery she'd felt when she had miscarried during her marriage.

The child continued to kick and scream. The camera shifted.

"Carmen, give me a hand with her, otherwise, I'll be forced to sedate her again," the man said.

The camera zoomed in until the screen turned black. Pondering the situation, Whitney stared out at the surf as the water rolled over the sands. Graceful gulls thronged the private beach, searching for scraps. Her vacation had ended before it had even begun.

The odds were against her, big-time. What if she didn't try? What would happen to the young girl? Another shiver drove through her spine. Two people were already dead because of Nathan Shaw's secret world and Whitney could easily be next.

Mason, the man who had always drank too much, believed she could pull this off. Could she? In spite of his imperfections, he always believed in her, supported her driving need to do the right thing.

Shoving her nose where it did not belong was what made her one of the top investigative reporters in the country. But behind closed doors, Whitney still had to prove herself on a daily basis to the men she worked with, the ones who thought she wasn't good enough, and never would be. In particular, her colleague, Cliff Peterson.

Damn it. I can do this. This wasn't the first time she'd been tossed into a dangerous situation and this certainly would not be the last. After searching and finding a notepad and pen, she quickly scribbled a list.

Make copy of tape

Call George-courier key

Call sources in Florida

Make appointment to meet Nathan Shaw

CHAPTER FOUR

L ater that day, Whitney stood outside the thick steel gates surrounding ShawBioGen. She couldn't shake the creepy feeling she was being watched. After landing at McCarran Airport in Vegas, a driver met her, drove northeast for almost two hours, and dumped her here. His only words: "I'm only following instructions."

Standing alone in the blazing desert sun, she flipped a pair of sunglasses over her eyes and pressed the intercom.

The box crackled to life.

"Your name?" a man's voice asked.

She pressed the button. "Whitney Steel."

High-pitched whining from behind startled her. She spun around to find four closed circuit cameras pointing at her. She swore they weren't there before.

The gates opened to reveal a square-jawed, fit man fully clad in cream and brown camouflaged shirt and pants.

"This way." Army guy kept a stern face and ushered her to a yellow Humvee style golf cart.

The grounds sprung to life with cacti, boulders, decorative grasses, and tumbleweed. In the distance, an enormous letter "S" shadowed the main entrance of ShawBioGen. The driver parked the golf cart and then escorted Whitney through tinted revolving doors.

"Wait here," he ordered before disappearing into an area marked "Security."

A circular skylight lit the main lobby and water rushed over a waterfall centered in the room. Highly polished stainless-steel walls created the illusion of a never-ending mirror, but at the same time gave the space a chilling cold feel.

Army guy returned with the same stern look on his face. "This way."

Whitney followed him into what appeared to be a security surveillance area. Glancing around, she counted dozens of security monitors, a flock of people sitting at computers, and one huge screen with a black and white picture that appeared to be a satellite image of the complex.

"Welcome to ShawBioGen, Miss Steel. I'm Blake Neely, the company's security specialist."

Whitney gave him a quick once-over. Dressed in black jeans, cowboy boots, and an open-necked shirt with its sleeves rolled back over his forearms, he was tanned and well-toned.

"Isn't a security specialist just a fancy title for a bodyguard?"

Lines crept across his forehead. "You need to sign in," he said in a firm even tone as he shoved a clipboard and pen at her.

After signing her name, she noticed an x-ray machine at the end of the long counter. If security were this tight here, she'd have no hope in hell of getting into a lab where Nathan kept the child.

Next Blake slid a tray in front of her. "Empty your purse."

"You're kidding, right?"

With his arms crossed in front of his chest, Blake shook his head.

"And I thought airport security was tough." Whitney chuckled and dumped the contents of her purse onto the tray. While he picked through them, she wondered what kind of man lurked behind those deep-set brown eyes.

"Sorry, no cameras. You can pick this up on the way out."

"Fine, but—" She reached toward him, but was a second too late. "Those are—"

He clicked open the gold and black leopard print case. Four foil-wrapped condom packages fell on the counter. Unsure if she should be angry or embarrassed, she felt her face flood with heat. To make matters worse, he took his sweet time inspecting each package, obviously getting her back for the bodyguard comment.

He raised an eyebrow. "Twisted Pleasure. Rough Rider. Must be for cowboys. And this one, Paradise..."

Their gazes collided.

Her body hummed with electricity so intense her heart raced, and her breasts tingled. Raw lust.

She snatched the condoms out of his hand upset he had this effect on her. "Do you mind? Aren't you getting a bit personal?"

"Personal or not, you'd be surprised at what these packages can be used for." He snatched them back, tossed them on the conveyor belt and grinned. "Better safe than sorry."

What a jerk. She remained silent while the contents of her purse inched through the x-ray machine. After having her picture taken, she was rewarded with a laminated visitor's pass.

Blake escorted her back to the main lobby and pointed down an endless stretch of hallway. "Take the elevator marked C2 to the second floor. And hurry, Mr. Shaw doesn't like to wait."

❋ ❋ ❋

In the security room, Blake stared at the main monitor as Whitney entered the elevator. He was completely mesmerized.

She was trouble. Pure trouble, dressed in that skin-tight pink jacket and short skirt, showing off every glorious curve. The slim and leggy blonde had him wanting to highjack a truckload of condoms. He could still smell her perfume, floral, soft.

His body reacted. He felt the tightness in his jeans.

Damn it. It had been a long time since a woman had such an effect on him. Too damn long.

She turned, raised her hand to the camera and waved.

Blake grinned.

No way could he allow anyone to get close to him, especially a woman, a reporter no less.

Dangerous was the word that popped into his mind. He must remain focused. He had a job to do.

Whitney sure had guts, though. If she thought for one second, he hadn't noticed the way she'd scanned the security room, surveying, and cataloguing, she was crazy.

Her visit to ShawBioGen had nothing to do with an interview with Nathan. What was Whitney Steel up to?

❋ ❋ ❋

The second the elevator doors opened, Nathan Shaw greeted Whitney.

"You're late, Miss Steel."

"I'm sorry, Mr. Shaw." She followed the man dressed in a casual gray shirt and black dress pants into a huge office.

Behind her, metal doors slid shut like a tomb.

"I was held up with your—"

"Have a seat."

Photographs Whitney had seen of the billionaire did not do him justice. He looked even stranger in person, with receding salt and pepper hair clipped short around his ears, a longer than usual neck and an odd-shaped, beefy face.

She took a seat across from him and realized he was gawking at her breasts. From the background information she'd discovered, Nathan enjoyed shocking others with unconventional behavior. Well, not this gal.

"Thank you for seeing me."

"My pleasure. Of course, I took the liberty and did my own research on you, Miss Steel. You're top in your field. Pretty impressive for a woman, and a young woman at that. Why are you here today?"

Realizing her legs were shaking, she crossed them. Besides, now Nathan was trying to get a peek up her skirt. What a creep.

"A follow up—because of ShawBioGen's research and development activities into products to treat inflammatory and autoimmune diseases." She tugged open her purse, found her tape recorder and carefully placed it between them on the most ornate Chippendale coffee table she'd ever seen. At least the man had excellent taste when it came to furniture. He sure didn't have much taste in anything else.

He stared at her with wide saucer-shaped eyes. "Miss Steel, you really are quite cute and you do intrigue me, but what you just mentioned is old news." His eyes narrowed. "Why are you really here?"

Her breath caught in her throat and for a second she was speechless.

"Get to the point. I'm a busy man."

"Very well." She pressed play on the tape recorder and prayed he hadn't noticed her fingers shaking.

"In the political realm recently, there has been a lot of debate over the moral issues of cloning humans. Since your company has, in the past, cloned dogs, cows, and other creatures, would you consider cloning humans?"

Nathan stood and slipped his hands into his pants pockets.

"Yes, of course, if it were legal. My focus is on reproductive cloning to allow infertile couples, unable to reproduce via other means, to have a genetically related child."

"There have been some rumors circulating, so I must ask, is your company cloning humans?"

He showed no reaction to the question, instead sauntered across the plush carpet and stopped behind her. So close, in fact, she felt his warm, moist breath down the back of her neck. Gross. She wanted to pounce out of the chair and drop kick him. It took every ounce of willpower not to.

"For a veteran reporter and a woman who has a brain in her head, I'm surprised you'd yield to such gossip." He moved around the chair and stood in front of her.

Don't let him get to you. This is what he does. Gets in your personal space, hoping to scare you off.

"So for the record, these are simply rumors?"

He gave her a withering stare and then burst into high pitched nasal laughter. "First off, I'm sure you are aware that cloning humans in this country is illegal. Second, if it were legal, I'd be sharing that incredible technology with countries around the world. Can you imagine what a person could do with that type of technology?"

Yes, she could, and had already seen the outcome on videotape. A helpless young child trapped in a horrid environment. Determined not to fall apart, Whitney gritted her teeth.

When he bent down and looked at her, for a split second, she swore she saw the devil in his stormy black eyes.

"Do you believe I'm cloning humans, Miss Steel?"

A cold-to-the-bone chill drifted through her body. "Of course not, Mr. Shaw. But as a reporter, it is my duty to investigate such rumors."

"I understand." He settled in the chair across from her. "I'm sorry to say, our time is up. You'll be supplied with a press kit on the way out."

Managing the weakest fake smile, she could muster, Whitney pressed the stop button and tossed the tape recorder in her purse. At that moment, the tomb-like doors slid open. She'd hit a chord with Nathan. Her punishment: being sent home like a child.

"I do hope you have a very safe trip back to Oregon, Miss Steel."

CHAPTER FIVE

Whitney's hands trembled.

The impact of Nathan's veiled threat drove a shiver down her spine. What a creep. Inhaling a deep breath, she ordered herself to settle down.

When the elevator opened on the main floor, she stepped out into the hall to the sound of knuckles cracking.

She knew full well Blake was watching her in the elevator. Electronic eyes were everywhere. He probably laughed his ass off the second Nathan banished her from his office after their short interview.

He sauntered toward her, with her camera in hand. She hadn't noticed earlier he was a good five inches taller than her.

She stopped. "You again."

"Thought you'd want this back." He handed her the camera.

"Thanks."

There was something dark and dangerous that made her heart pound when his hand brushed against hers. He had her attention. All of her.

"Let's get you to the airport."

"You're taking me?"

Why Blake? Either Nathan wanted to keep a close

eye on her, or worse. He wanted her out of the way. She'd barely swallowed the lump in her throat when she followed Blake out the front door of the complex.

The hot desert wind whipped her hair against her face. She glanced at the dark blue pickup truck parked in the driveway.

Blake opened the passenger door. "You going to get in?"

Did she have a choice? To the east, desert. The west, desert. And to the north, desert wasteland and battleship-gray thunderheads hovering over the Ruby Mountains.

We'll do this your way. For now. She nodded and got into the truck.

Blake hopped in and they began the two-hour drive back to Vegas.

Maybe this arrangement could work to her advantage. Who better to talk to about Nathan's secrets than his right-hand man. Suddenly Blake smiled at her as if he had read her thoughts.

She kept her gaze lowered and picked at her skirt. Why did he make her feel so uncomfortable?

"How'd your interview go with Nathan?"

Like he didn't know. "Okay." Lie. "He's quite the charmer, isn't he?" She almost gagged on her words.

Blake rested his arm on the door. "Nathan can be a bit unpredictable. Eccentric."

Unpredictable? Eccentric? The guy is creepy.

Something caught Whitney's eye. "Hey, what are those over there?" She pointed to the right on the other side of the security fence. "Those buildings."

From the quick peek of the satellite image in the security room, she knew ShawBioGen was shaped like a nine-sided polygon. She had missed these octagon-shaped buildings.

"Employee housing. Scientists and researchers live on site six months at a time. After their stay, they head home for a month." He grabbed a folder from the dash and handed it to her. "It's all in there."

"Ah, the famous press kit." She scanned through it, page by page, noting the colorful photograph of one of the homes. There was nothing useful inside that she didn't already know. Twenty-five-hundred employees —award-winning scientists recruited from around the world.

"You live on site as well?" she asked.

"Yup."

"Doesn't sound like much of a life out here in the middle of nowhere." And kissing your crazy boss' ass, she wanted to add. Did Blake know what Nathan was up to? If he did, he couldn't possibly approve, could he?

"Oh, I don't mind. I enjoy the peace and quiet."

"How long have you been working for Nathan?"

"Almost a year."

Being a reporter meant reading people. His answers were too short and vague for her liking. He was hiding something.

Her father's voice flooded her thoughts. *"Everyone has something to hide. You just have to look hard enough."*

Tumbleweed bounced across the road. The wind yowled. A dust devil roared around the truck.

Blake rolled up his window and shot her a sideways glance. "Ever been in the desert during a storm?"

"No." Lightning ignited the sky. She quickly rolled up her own window. "By the looks of it, I'm about to find out."

"Doesn't rain much, but when it does…"

Huge pellets of rain thundered down, so loud Whitney thought her eardrums would explode.

Blake flipped the wipers on high and slowed the truck to a crawl. How could he see the road? All she could see was a curtain of water.

"We'll have to wait this one out," he yelled, steering the truck toward the shoulder and stopped.

After another few minutes of heavy rain, the skies cleared, and the wind calmed. Blake steered the truck back onto the main road.

She reached for the handle and rolled the stiff window back down. A rush of rain-fresh air filled the cab of the truck. "I've never seen anything like it."

Then she noticed something round, at least two feet wide, erupting from the ground. "What the heck is that thing?"

Blake slowed the truck again. "Guess you've never seen a desert tortoise either."

She watched the creature inch its way to the middle of the road and stop.

"They live in burrows in the dirt. The males have horns to combat with other males. And they use them to nudge females during courtship."

He shot her a slow sexy smile that made her stomach flip-flop. She felt her nipples harden. Why did she find this man so damn distracting?

"I'm going to have to move him." Blake put the truck into park and got out, leaving the driver side door open.

While he urged the critter along with a stick, Whitney stared at the glove box. Curious, she flipped it open and rifled through the contents not sure what she expected to find.

Every few seconds she glanced up to make sure Blake was still busy. Gas receipts. A brown suede wallet. The wallet slipped through her fingers and fell under the seat. Shoot. She looked up. Crap, here he comes. She closed the glove box. Think. The camera.

"Would you mind taking a picture of that tortoise? No one back home would believe the size of that thing."

"Sure."

She dug through her purse, handed him the camera and waited until he was far enough away from the truck before ducking and grabbing the wallet.

A quick glance at the driver's license was all she had time for before tossing it back in the glove box. The man in the picture had dark blond hair. Robert Blake Neely. So, the man colored his hair. Didn't everyone these days?

"Find what you were looking for?" Blake threw the camera on the seat, jumped into the truck, and slammed the door shut.

Whitney cringed.

His eyes darkened. "Well?"

She looked down at her lap. "I—was looking for a tissue. I thought you might have some in the glove box." He couldn't possibly believe that one, could he?

"Look, lady, I don't know what you're up to, but nosing around can get you in a heap of trouble."

"I'm a reporter. Nosing around as you call it, is what I do." She straightened in the seat and folded her hands in her lap. "I call it investigating."

"Call it whatever you want. We both know you weren't looking for a tissue. What's the real reason you came to ShawBioGen?"

She looked him directly in the eye. Should she trust him? Could she trust him? He worked for Nathan. Maybe she could tell him a bit to see how he reacts. "I heard Nathan was working on a new cloning project at the complex. I was hoping to get an exclusive."

Blake shook his head and laughed. "You've got to be kidding me."

That was not the reaction she had hoped for. Not even close.

Blake was still laughing. "And I suppose you also think he's hiding aliens there too? Rumors. Nothing more. I'd be checking your sources if I were you."

The man was hard to read and sounded convincing. Maybe he didn't know about Nathan's experiments.

Blake remained quiet until they reached McCarran airport. After parking the truck, he escorted her to the airport terminal.

"Long lineup. Might take you awhile to get through security." He pushed aside a stray hair on her forehead.

The touch of his finger made her heart flutter.

"Now if you're smart, you'll get on that plane and forget about ShawBioGen."

Was that a warning? Sounded that way. Whitney smoothed her jacket over her hips. "Then I guess it's up to me to debunk those so-called rumors." With that, she turned and headed into the airport.

A line of impatient travelers waited to go through the metal detector. Security personnel apparently incapable of smiling strutted about carrying wooden batons coated with glossy black paint. As the procession slowly moved forward, she looked over her shoulder.

Blake was nowhere in sight.

The hairs on the back of her neck rose.

Someone else was watching her.

* * *

Blake had a huge problem. Whitney Steel.

Outside the airport terminal, he punched in the number he had been forced to memorize into the pay phone. On the third ring, Mike Jacobs, his Bureau contact answered the call.

"Hey, Mike."

"Blake. Jesus, man, you had us worried. The boss is in a real nasty mood. Hell, another twenty-four hours and—"

"I know. Chambers would've sent the posse." Blake leaned against the booth. "I should have access to the lab in the next few days."

"Great, I'll let the boss know. Everything's in place. Four rent-a-goons are ready on the outskirts of Elko. Six of ours are in Alamo. The plane is on standby at Nellis Air Force Base. When you get the kid, give the word. And watch your back, buddy."

"Always. I might have a problem, though. A reporter snooping around." A damn sexy one.

"A reporter? Christ. We don't need any complications at this point," Mike said in a raspy voice. "We're too damn close to nailing Shaw."

Blake couldn't agree more. Considering the stakes, nothing could compromise this mission.

"I'll be in contact. Later, man." Blake hung up.

In his line of work, problems sometimes had to disappear to save a life, protect the operation—to shield an agent's cover.

Over a decade ago, while working undercover trying to nab Pablo Sanchez, a top leader of the Sur del Calle cartel, Colombia's largest drug trafficking organization, Blake permanently made a person disappear. Pablo's twin brother, Manuel.

Somehow, Manuel found out Blake and Mike were FBI agents. With his gun pointed at Mike's temple ready to kill him, Blake made a decision. He snuck behind the man and slit his throat, leaving Manuel to die in a pool of his own blood.

Did Blake regret taking a life? No. He didn't have a choice. Would he do it again? If necessary.

He doubted anything like that would happen this time around. He liked the reporter, but he smelled trouble. She appeared to be around thirty-five and gutsier than hell. He shook his head. Shit. The woman was already growing on him.

As Blake walked back to his truck, he struggled to concentrate, eying an elderly couple arguing, loudly. The scene reminded him of his parents. His father determined to have his way, his mother giving in, anything to end a public outburst.

At this point, he would have welcomed an outburst from his father instead of years of silence. When Blake had joined the Bureau thirteen years ago, his father, a stern career Marine, showed his disapproval by never once asking him about his job with the FBI.

Blake shook his head.

Ahead, the airport parking lot buzzed with activity Sin City style. The walking-dead with dark circles under their eyes and the ones who'd drunk too much, lost everything they ever had and thanked God they had bought a round-trip ticket.

Then there were the winners.

The ones with permanent smiles plastered on their faces who'd hit it huge, now ready to head home. Nothing like neon lights, booze and gambling twenty-four-seven. Nothing like Las Vegas.

Through a sea of vehicles packed in the lot, Blake heard the loud rumble of a motor, then a screech.

He turned.

A black Chevy Camaro raced toward him. He bolted down the aisle and jumped on the hood of a nearby car, rolled off the side and hit the pavement with a thud.

By the time he hobbled to his feet, the car was gone. Definitely not road rage. The driver's mission was to take him out.

❋ ❋ ❋

After a long hot shower, Blake's body still ached. He rubbed his shoulder, scraped and bruised from his topple over the car at the airport. Behind him, Nathan paced the length of his office, dressed in an expensive powder-blue jogging suit.

"Interesting story," Nathan said.

Blake wanted to blame Nathan for his recent brush with death, but his observations indicated the man had nothing to do with the incident. When Nathan got spooked, he developed a facial tick. And right now, his left cheek pulsed itself into a major convulsion.

Nathan stopped in front of the window and stretched, preparing for his daily run. He was single, fifty-one, in top physical shape even though he smoked cigars. Maybe it was his unattractiveness, that homely face that women wanted to forget in five seconds or less. Money sure as hell didn't buy love. Nathan Shaw was living proof.

"I believe our Miss Steel may have something that belongs to me." Nathan bent and touched his toes. "Did you know she was once married to a Florida senator?"

"That's news to me."

"She was present during the shooting. Poor girl." Nathan turned his head and shot Blake a self-satisfied grin. "Must have been dreadful—traumatic."

Oh, yeah, I can see you're really choked up about it. Man, you're a sick freak. Blake swore Nathan got off on other people's misery. "You figure someone else is interested in what the reporter might have?"

"That's what I like about you, Blake. You're always thinking. Maybe that someone thought *you* had the tape since you escorted Miss Steel to the airport." Nathan stopped stretching and walked over to him. "Do you?"

Blake's muscles tightened. "Do I what?" Man, he hated when Nathan got in his face. His breath stunk of cigars.

"Do you have my videotape?" Nathan screamed. "Haven't you heard anything?"

"Of course, I don't." Blake shifted on his feet. What the hell was on this tape?

"We can't allow that tape to fall into the wrong hands. Do you understand me? My project is important to the company's future and to the rest of the world."

Nathan finally stepped away from him. "Imagine having the technology to produce super-humans. Organ transplant lists will become a thing of the past. Medicinal methods will be propelled into a new era, all because of my experiments and technology."

And what about the cloned kid you're hiding? Blake stared at him. Think she's thrilled with your so-called experiments? Blake detested him. His muscles tensed. The sight of the man made him want to use the bastard as target practice.

Nathan glanced at his watch. "I want you in Oregon. Be on my jet in two hours."

"What?" Nathan couldn't do this now. No. He needed to stay here. "I thought you wanted the retina scanner operational at the lab. You need to secure the area, especially now."

"I agree. But I need you elsewhere. You're going to get close to our Miss Steel. Real close. Find out what she knows and what she might have. Get packed."

Blake dragged a frustrated hand through his hair. What he wanted to do was strangle the little prick. It took all his strength not to wrap his hands around Nathan's short neck and squeeze.

Nathan patted Blake on the shoulder, a bit too firmly.

"One piece of advice. Turn on the charm, Blake. No one is immune to temptation, especially a beautiful woman."

CHAPTER SIX

T he moon shone bright, illuminating the foaming whitecaps crashing against the shore. Waves crept up the beach, soaking Whitney's canvas shoes.

After a lengthy phone conversation earlier and a barrage of questions, George had reluctantly agreed to send her the key.

"George, please don't give me a hard time. Send me the key. You have the address."

"Hey, you're on the trail of something. I can feel it. Is it big? When are you going to let me in on it?"

She heard the excitement in his voice. "Not yet. You'll be the first to know. Please send the key. I need it, yesterday."

"Why the hurry? Why do you have it wrapped in this...tissue? What's all over it?"

A few beats of silence passed.

"George, you really don't want to know."

"Yes, I do." His voice sounded small, pinched. "What the hell is this about, Whitney? Are you in some kind of trouble?"

She pushed her hair back from her face. After her father died, George had taken it upon himself to become her self-appointed father figure. Most of the time she didn't mind because it felt good to have someone who cared.

"George, I promise, I'm not in trouble. You'll courier the key, right?"

A long beat of silence. "I'll do it. But I want to hear from you once a day. Do we have a deal?"

Whitney smiled. "Yes."

What she was about to jump into couldn't be any riskier than the countless times she'd worked on dangerous assignments in the past.

The difference this time: no camera crews, no assistants, no security. She was on her own.

What about Blake Neely? How did he fit into all this? How much did he know about Nathan and the child? Could he help her? Would he? Could she trust him?

She pushed windblown hair from her eyes and gazed at the sky. The diamond-like sparkle of the evening stars gleamed above. "Wish me luck, Dad. I'm going to need it."

With that, she wandered back to the beach house. A long shadow passed before her in the sand. Another shadow crossed her path. She looked up at the house and felt the blood drain from her face.

Was someone inside or was she seeing things?

After walking up the stairs to the deck, she peered through the living room window. Nothing. Maybe it was her imagination? She grasped the handle, opened the door and crept inside. Her gaze darted about the lit room.

A creak. Footsteps behind her. She turned.

A heavy-set person wearing a black ski mask barreled toward her and tackled her. All she saw before hitting the carpet were green eyes, wide, cold. A heavy arm looped around her neck like a noose and dragged her to her feet. A leather-gloved hand covered her mouth. Her heart rate remained amazingly calm. He waved a large knife in her face and commanded her with the tip of the blade to sit in the nearby chair. She did.

"The tape, bitch." He removed his hand from her mouth.

"Where's the tape?"

She gasped for air. "I don't know what you're talking about."

"Last chance." The man leaned forward. "Where is it?"

His steamy breath reeked of stale beer and cigarettes. The odor almost gagged her.

"You've got five seconds. Tell me where it is, or I slice and dice you just like that other bitch. One—"

Her heart skipped a beat. This was Carmen Lacey's killer. "I swear I don't have it." *Stay calm.*

"Two...three."

She needed to gain control before it was too late. "It's—not here. It's in a safety deposit box at the bank."

He stroked the side of her face and lowered the knife. "You can save your breath now. Tape or no tape—you were dead the minute I walked through the door."

He should never have released his grip on her. The big ape never saw it coming. Whitney whipped her hands at his face and jabbed him in the eyes with two fingers. The Double Dragon. Worked every time.

"You stupid bitch. I'll kill you!" He dropped the knife to cover his eyes and staggered backward trying to regain his balance. When he turned, his shin slammed into the corner of the glass coffee table.

"You're dead!"

Not today. Whitney took full advantage of the situation. She leaped out of the chair and rammed her knee up into his groin with such force she lost her balance and tumbled back onto the floor.

The man squealed in pain and grabbed his testicles. His legs gave out, and he crashed to the carpet unconscious. To make sure he was out cold, Whitney shoved her foot into his ribs. Nope. This guy wasn't going anywhere.

❊ ❊ ❊

Blake arrived at the two-story beach house on Sea Gull Drive at twenty past nine. After turning off the headlights, he parked the rental car at the end of the driveway and shut off the ignition.

Nathan had screwed up everything by sending him to Florence. Now it would be a week or so before he could get into the lab. The entire mission sat in limbo because Nathan was lost in a wild fantasy of ruling the world with clones. As if any sane person would even accept such a notion.

Blake brought a fist down on the steering wheel. He'd been so damn close to ending this operation. He grabbed the binoculars from the passenger seat and focused them toward the house.

A silver SUV was parked outside the double garage, lights were on inside the house. The breeze held a salty tang. It had been a long time since he'd been near any water, let alone the ocean.

Whitney entered the kitchen talking on the phone. Her body language, the way she paced, indicated restlessness. The moment she hung up the phone that was his cue. He dropped the binoculars on the seat, hopped out of the car and headed up the sidewalk to the front door.

He pressed the doorbell.

A few minutes went by. He thought for sure he'd heard movement on the other side of the door. What was she doing?

He rang the doorbell again. "Whitney, I know you're in there."

The outside light flicked on.

"Who is it?"

"Blake Neely."

A long pause of silence.

"What do you want?"

"Can you at least open the door, or are we going to talk like this?"

The door cracked open slowly.

Whitney's jaw dropped. "What are you doing here?"

No way could he pass up this Kodak moment. He stepped back, held up the camera and snapped a picture. "You forgot this in my truck." He handed her the camera.

"God, you're a royal pain in the ass." She blinked, blinded by the camera's flash. "Give me a break. You can't possibly think I'd believe you came all this way to return my camera."

"I had some personal business in town. Thought I'd drop by."

"Business." Whitney rolled her eyes. "Here in the big town of Florence? You're not a good liar and I'm not stupid. How did you find me? Oh, let me guess. Nathan. He can find anyone. He sent you, didn't he?"

She looked cute, dressed in white cotton pants

rolled up just under her knees and a low-cut black top. When she folded her arms, he observed some mighty fine cleavage.

"Are you going to answer me or continue gawking at my breasts?"

If he had a choice, he'd pick the breasts.

"Sorry. I had a few days off and thought I'd visit Florence. Never been here before. Nice place."

She held up her hand. "Stop, now. Okay? Be straight with me. Did Nathan send you?"

He wished he could be straight, but not yet. Not until she trusted him. "No, Nathan didn't send me. I wanted to see you again."

"You're a real piece of work. I don't know what to believe." For a long moment, she stared at him. "Fine, come in. The more the merrier."

Relief washed over him until Whitney pointed to a man lying on the living room floor.

"Meet the thug who tried to kill me tonight. The police are on their way."

"Tried to kill you? Jesus." Blake bent and checked the man's pulse. He was alive. "You did this to him?"

She nodded. "Would you like me to demonstrate?"

He straightened and glanced at Whitney, who may have weighed a hundred and twenty pounds at best. He then stared in amazement at the two-hundred-pound motionless blob on the floor. "Christ, I think I'll pass."

"My father made sure I could take care of myself. A third-degree black belt in karate. It comes in handy."

"I guess so. I'll have to keep that in mind."

Blake had trained in advanced hand-to-hand combat techniques, but nothing like this woman. Most agents with the Bureau would need a gun, a big gun, to take down a man that size. Very impressive.

Several seconds elapsed before Whitney sank into the brown tufted couch. "Your boss sent him to kill me."

Why did she have to smell like baby oil and the ocean? The combination was driving his senses wild. *Focus, man.*

"Why would Nathan do that?" Blake had to admit the idea wasn't farfetched.

At first, she dismissed his question with laughter, and then she sat up straight. "Because I got too close. I know Nathan Shaw's secret. You work for him. You know exactly what I'm talking about."

So Nathan was right. Whitney knew more than she let on. One for Nathan. But did she have the mysterious tape? And if she did, what was on it that Nathan would possibly kill for?

"Sorry, I don't know what you're talking about. Care to share?"

The woman didn't bat an eyelash. "I don't think so."

Her answer didn't surprise him. Why would she trust him? Trust was earned. At this rate, he had a hell-of-a-lot of work to do.

"Look. I don't know what happened here tonight. Someone tried to run me down in the Vegas airport parking lot."

Whitney sprang to her feet. "What? Were you hurt?"

He smiled, somewhat taken back by her genuine concern. "A few scrapes and bruises. I'll survive, but thanks for asking."

She sat back down and fidgeted with the tassel on a pillow, her expression serious. "Whether you want to believe it or not, Nathan sent that man."

Blake took a seat next to her, his arm rested against hers. Her skin felt warm, too warm. Heat prickled to his groin. His pulse shot into overdrive. Shit. This wasn't a good time to be aroused. He shifted on the couch.

Whitney must have felt something too. She bounced off the couch and high-tailed it to the panoramic windows facing the ocean. She kept her back to him.

For a long moment, he imaged her naked. Her long legs...the shape of her hips...

Damn it. Could he be any more uncomfortable? He shifted again, this time crossing his legs to hide his erection. "Do you have proof?"

She turned, pointing to the man on the floor. "He's all the proof I need. That lump made it clear he'd 'slice and dice me like that other bitch.' That woman worked at ShawBioGen. Her name was Carmen Lacey. Did you know her?"

Blake paused a few seconds before he answered. "I met her once. A scientist. A quiet woman." He lied. He'd read that in the newspaper. Finding common ground with Whitney continued to be a challenge.

For a moment, he tossed around the idea of mentioning his sister's death but decided against it at least for now. Claire's death had been ruled an accident. Blake wasn't buying it. Too many things didn't add up.

"Nathan isn't stupid. If he hired the thug, he'd never leave a trail leading back to him. Ever. The guy is a perfectionist."

"Perfectionist or not. I plan to expose his dirty little secret to the world."

Blake got up from the couch and stood beside her. "I

wish you'd trust me. Maybe I can help."

She chuckled. "Trust you? Not a chance. You're in Nathan's camp."

"Well if you're not going to trust me, can I at least make some suggestions to secure the house so you're safe? I'm surprised you don't have a security system installed."

"This isn't my house. It belongs to a friend of mine. I'll be fine once that guy is locked up. Besides, I'm leaving tomorrow night."

That revelation surprised him. "You're heading home?"

"Not yet. I thought I'd spend a week in Las Vegas. My last trip was far too rushed."

The last thing he needed was Whitney anywhere in the state of Nevada. The farther away, the better. "After what happened tonight, I don't think that's a good idea."

"Excuse me?" She straightened like a board. "I'm capable of looking after myself and making my own decisions."

He studied her for a moment. Over the years he had dealt with all types of women. This one was feisty, confident and damn cute. Didn't mattered though, because Blake lived in a different world. A world he created, built of lies. Lie after lie after lie.

"Look, Blake, go back to your boss. Tell him anything you want, I don't care. All I know is I'm going to expose Nathan for the scum he is, and no one is going to stop me."

Like fingernails scraping down a blackboard, Whitney's words put his nerves on edge. He'd have to keep a close eye on her to make sure she didn't screw up the mission, or worse, blow his cover.

* * *

In the spacious loft bedroom, Whitney flicked on the lamp and then flopped into the unmade bed on her stomach. At one o'clock in the morning, any physical remnants of the night's events were long gone. The police parade had finished its job, Blake had left, but mental images slapped her in the face. She survived tonight, but luck might not be on her side next time. Next time would come soon. Too soon. Nathan would make sure of that.

She'd done well during the attack. Kept her calm. Waited for the no-turning-back-moment. No one would know she'd been deep-down-bone-pounding-terrified. She rolled over on her back and stared at the cathedral ceiling.

Blake's unforeseen intrusion into her life left a bitter taste in her mouth. What was he up to? He acted as if he liked her. Did he? That electrical zap she'd felt between them earlier still tingled her skin. The way he flashed a saucy smile at her when he'd asked her to trust him. The last person she had trusted was Mason and look where that had gotten her. Heartbroken, divorced, and now in the middle of a huge mess.

After turning off the lamp, she went to the window and pushed the metal blind to the side, just enough to peek outside.

Blake's car was parked at the end of the driveway, and she wasn't sure if she should feel safe or not.

CHAPTER SEVEN

Blake opened one eye and squinted as the sun touched the horizon and spread across the morning sky. He stretched, smacking both knees on the bottom of the steering wheel.

"Shit."

He'd forgotten about his confined sleeping quarters. With every motel in Florence jam-packed due to the Fourth of July celebrations, what choice did he have? Either the car or the beach. He'd opted for the car, simply to have a better view of the house, in case another intruder paid Whitney a visit.

He rubbed his knees wishing now that he'd rented a minivan instead. The damn thing would've been more comfortable than this cramped space.

Man, he could use a coffee. His lips and mouth felt like wrinkled sandpaper. After raking his fingers through his hair, he got out of the car and inhaled the salty air. The blue waters of the ocean rolled across the sand. Seagulls squawked and circled, waiting for their breakfast to crawl up the beach. If Whitney weren't awake yet, she soon would be.

Out of the corner of his eye, he noticed a vehicle in the distance. Blake slipped behind a large prickly bush and waited. Nathan couldn't have sent someone so soon. Or could he?

The driver parked the gold four-door-sedan in front of the garage, beside Whitney's SUV. A slim man emerged, dressed in black pants, a brown short-sleeve shirt wearing a Florida Marlins ball cap. He didn't appear to be a threat. A friend? Perhaps, a boyfriend? Blake hoped not. What the hell was he thinking?

The man pressed the doorbell and then proceeded to peek in the window to the left of the entry.

Blake continued to wait and watch.

When the man glanced behind him and placed his hand on the doorknob, every hair on the back of Blake's neck stood at attention. He charged out of the bush like a star linebacker, tackling the man to the ground. The poor guy didn't know what hit him.

The front door opened.

"What are you doing?" Whitney asked.

Blake looked up. She stood with her hands on her hips, wearing a long white robe, her hair damp. The sunlight gave her face an angelic, sexy glow.

"Get the hell off of me, you crazy bastard," the man pinned under him said.

"George? Is that you? What in the name of God is going on here?"

"You know him?" Blake rolled off the man and caught his breath.

"Yes. Meet George Raines, my editor, and a damn good friend." Whitney pulled the belt of the robe tighter.

Talk about feeling stupid. Blake helped George to his feet and handed him his hat. "I thought you were trying to get into the house. Sorry about that."

George swiped the hat from Blake's hand and popped it back on his head.

Whitney stepped outside the door. The wind blew her robe open enough to give Blake a glimpse of a shimmering thigh. Her gaze met his and she pulled the robe closed.

"George, you're supposed to be in Florida."

"I was worried about you." George gave Blake the once over. "But it looks like you've got everything under control with He-Man here."

Whitney smiled at George. "This is Blake Neely. He's like a dog that doesn't know *when* to go home."

Blake shot a grim smile and continued to brush the sand off his jeans. "I thought after last night—"

George's eyes widened. "What happened last night?"

Whitney shook her head. "Nothing, George. Nothing. Now that you two are through playing, how about coffee?"

Blake piped up. "I'd love some."

Interesting. With Whitney's editor in the picture, maybe the guy knew where the tape was.

❊ ❊ ❊

While George explored the beach house like a kid on summer vacation, Whitney spun and faced Blake. Their gazes locked. "What did you think you were doing, attacking George?"

Blake shot her a quick grin. "Sorry, the guy was acting strange. Peeking in windows. Checking doorknobs. Crap like that could land him in jail."

Still annoyed, she lifted her chin and narrowed her eyes. "What about you? Parked out front all night, watching the house. That could land *you* in jail. I'm beginning to think you're stalking me."

As she spoke, he inched closer, crowding her until they stood toe-to-toe, her back pressed against the wall. For a moment, the air in her lungs stopped flowing. His finger traced her cheek, stopped at her jaw, then lingered at the collar of her robe. "Why would I be stalking you? Your driveway was convenient."

The deep tone of his voice made her pulse leap like a jackrabbit. Never had she felt such raw physical attraction. Why was she allowing him to do this to her? The man was just as much the enemy as his boss.

She drew a breath. "Okay, so you're not stalking me, but if you think I need protection, you're wrong."

"Hey, no argument there. I've seen first-hand what you can do. I slept in the car because all the motels in town were full." Blake stepped back, looking her up and down for what seemed like forever.

"You expect me to believe—"

"It's true. Not a room anywhere." George reappeared from his one-man tour and wiped his forehead with the back of his hand. "Guess I'm bunking with you, kiddo."

"Oh, goodie," she muttered and marched barefoot into the kitchen, not sure why she was ticked. Had part of her believed, no hoped, Blake wanted to protect her? Or was it because George had shown up and now she had someone else to look after? She had no answer.

George gawked at the Jenn-Air grill. "Sweet kitchen." He sat at the breakfast bar, separating the kitchen from the dining area. "Our old colleague has done well for himself. Never liked him much. Too artsy-fartsy for my liking."

Whitney handed George a cup of coffee. "You don't like anyone, male or female. No wonder you've never married."

"That's not true." George sipped his coffee and then set it down. "I like Blake, here." He slapped Blake on his shoulder. "Any man looking out for you is all right by me."

Looking out for her? She wished she knew for sure if he was or not. Whitney shook her head, poured another coffee and slid the cup across the counter to Blake.

A slow smile crossed his face. "Thanks."

"If you want more, help yourselves. I'm going to get dressed."

Before she left the kitchen, Blake winked at her. Whitney felt her face flush as she dashed upstairs to the bedroom. She'd have to be quick. George and Blake were getting too chummy, and that spelled trouble. She flung the terrycloth bathrobe on the bed, wiggled into a pair of jeans and pulled a white top over her head. They were talking about her downstairs. She could feel it.

After applying black mascara and a bit of pink blush, she finger-combed her damp hair, slipped her feet into a pair of leather sandals, and then headed downstairs.

Back in the kitchen, she poured a mug of coffee and took a sip. "Hope I didn't miss anything."

"Nope." George tapped his fingers on the counter-top. "I told Blake you wouldn't mind if he showered and got cleaned up here. Seems we're both in the same boat. No hotel rooms."

Whitney gritted her teeth. "That's fine." If George wasn't like a father to her, she'd drop-kick his ass right here, right now. When she turned, Blake was staring at her. Drumming her fingernails against the coffee mug, she forced a smile.

Blake slid off the stool. "I've got to get my bag out of the car."

Whitney frowned and glared at him as he left the room. The moment she heard the front door close, she ran to the front window and peeked through the vertical blinds.

George trailed her. "What are you doing?"

"Watching him. He's opening the trunk. Getting the bag. He put his bag down. Oh. Now he's on a cell phone. I'll be right back."

George had barely walked to the front of the house before she tore past him and slid open the patio doors that led to the back deck.

"Where you going now?"

"I'll explain later. Don't tell Blake. Be right back."

At the side of the house, Whitney crawled on her hands and knees, inching along the endless bushes and shrubs until she heard Blake's voice.

She stopped, straining to hear over the seagulls squawking overheard.

"Yeah, I know. The tape. I'll get it."

The conversation ended. She knew it! That lying bastard. All he wanted was the tape. Blake was Nathan's robot, nothing more. Why had she expected any different?

Blake picked up his black bag from the driveway and shut the trunk. It looked like he stuck something inside the bag. What, though?

As soon he was out of view, she hopped to her feet, sprinted around the house and tore up the stairs to the deck.

"Where's Whitney?" She heard Blake ask George.

"I'm out here." She waved from the deck. "Tai Chi."

Blake's eyebrows rose. "I'm going to hit the shower."

She bent and touched her toes. "You do that."

Brushing off the dirt from her knees, she inhaled a long deep breath and then exhaled. Her instincts had been right on. Trust him? Not a chance.

Two could play this game. Confront him, that's what she'd do. No way could he deny what she had just heard.

George poked his head outside the patio doors. "Are you going to tell me what's going on? I'm worried about you."

"I'll explain later. Promise. Give me a few minutes." Whitney rushed past him and ran down the hall to the bathroom. She put her ear to the door. The water was running. Should she? Yes. She turned the brass knob, opened the door and stepped inside.

The misty room smelled fresh, woodsy, and manly. Through the steam, her gaze snapped to the shower stall and the toned outline of Blake's body. Wow! He stood with his back to her, washing his hair.

Hot desire stirred inside her. Too bad he was the enemy.

Eyeing the open travel bag on the ceramic floor, she bent and slipped her hand into the bag. Wrapped between a shirt and a pair of boxers, cold metal touched her fingers. She pulled the item out of the bag. A gun. Her stomach knotted as she stared at the weapon. The truth struck her hard.

Nathan had sent Blake to kill me.

The water stopped. The shower doors opened.

She leveled the gun at Blake's chest. "Stay right there."

He froze. "Guess you found my gun." He stepped out

of the shower stall. Water pooled at his feet. "We both know you're not going to shoot me."

"Wanna bet?" *God, please don't make me.*

It took all her willpower to keep her eyes focused on his face and not on the way his muscular, wet body glistened under the halogen lights. Wonderfully hard... well defined. Her pulse sped up.

He lifted his hands above his head. "Okay. We'll play this your way."

"Damn right we will." With both hands, she gripped the gun tighter to stop her hands from shaking. How could he look so relaxed? And that smirk on his face screamed sarcasm. He wasn't taking her seriously, just like the male reporters she had worked with throughout her career. "How can you be so damn calm?"

"Easy. You've got the gun. I'm just following orders. It's not every day a beautiful woman points a gun at me while I'm naked. Got to say, you're turning me on."

He was turning her on. "Oh, please." She kept her gaze locked on his. "Everything that comes out of your mouth is such crap."

He lowered his hands. "It's the truth. See what you do to me?"

Whitney looked down. Her breath caught in her throat. Mercy. She blushed and forced herself not to stare. With one hand, she snatched a towel from the counter and tossed it to him.

Grinning, he caught the towel and wrapped it around his waist. "I warned you."

"Get dressed and don't try anything stupid. I'll be right outside the door. You and I are going to have a chat."

Whitney backed out of the room and stumbled

over her feet in haste to leave the room. In the hall, she flattened against the wall and let out a breath of relief, praying her heart would stop pounding and her pulse would slow. They didn't. Part of her wanted to feel his naked body beside her. Another part of her wanted to strangle him for lying to her.

Blake emerged with his hair combed back, dressed in a black T-shirt and jeans. Not only did he look good, he smelled wonderful. Spicy, woodsy and clean.

She poked the gun into his back. "After you. Move it."

"Hey, you're the boss."

In the living room, George's eyes bulged as he sprung off the couch. "Holy shit! Have you lost your mind, Whitney? Where'd you get the gun?"

"Ask him." She steadied the weapon at Blake's back.

Of all things, Blake had the nerve to start laughing.

"What's so funny?" she demanded.

He turned, his face relaxed. "You. I'm not going anywhere. Put the gun down."

She straightened, determined to remain in charge. "Not a chance."

"Is the gun really necessary?" George rubbed his forehead. "What the hell am I saying? I have no friggin' idea what's going on. None." He flopped onto the couch.

Whitney pointed to the burgundy chair next to the couch and gave Blake a nudge. "Sit."

She kept her gaze glued to him. "You bastard— you're here to kill me."

❋ ❋ ❋

Blake had underestimated the woman, not only her strength but her guts. By the way, Whitney clutched the 9 mm Glock, she damn well knew how to use it. Another trick her father must have taught her.

Wide-eyed, George huddled in the safety of the couch, beads of sweat shining at his temples. The poor guy probably had never seen this side of the reporter and prayed he never would again.

Blake shifted his attention back to Whitney. "Believe me. If I was sent to kill you, you'd already be dead."

Her eyes narrowed. "Not until you had the tape. Right? Isn't that what Nathan told you? Get the tape, then kill me?"

"What tape?" George straightened. "Nathan who? What does this have to do with the key?"

The sigh and the immediate frown lines that creased Whitney's forehead told Blake she wished George had kept his mouth shut about a key.

Blake rubbed the peach fuzz on his chin and figured he might as well join in the babble-fest. Maybe he would learn something new. "What does a key have to do with anything?"

Whitney kept the gun aimed at him. "You tell me."

Okay, this was going nowhere quick. Blake had had enough. Time to call this woman's bluff. It was too early in the morning to continue this half-assed-going-nowhere-conversation. "Look. It's barely eight, and I don't know about you, but I could use some breakfast." He glanced at the other man. "Hungry, George?"

"Sure am." George fought his way out of the plush couch and proceeded to stretch his legs.

Blake stood. He knew he was risking his ass, but he had to take control of the situation.

Whitney stepped forward. "I'm calling the shots,

not you. Sit or I shoot."

"This is insane," George said, his voice trembling. "You're not shooting anyone."

Blake studied her face. Her eyes held an angry glow, but they said she was losing confidence. He stepped toward her, turned and strolled to the kitchen. A thunderous bang sent him plummeting to the floor.

CHAPTER EIGHT

Blake lumbered to his feet. Whitney did it. She pulled the trigger.

The scorched odor of gun-cleaning fluid lingered in the air. So much for his keen instinct and prediction. Never let a woman get her hands on your gun, and don't for a second doubt she'll use it. Especially when you're dumb enough to push her to the limit. He sure-in-the-hell hadn't liked the whistling sound of that bullet whizzing past his head. He'd made a mistake, one that could have gotten him killed. He knew better than to be blinded by a woman, no matter how charming, skillful...and that pissed him off.

Whitney stood, shoulders back, head high, with the gun lowered at her side. Triumph shone in her eyes, not a speck of remorse. Like a switch on a railroad track, her expression changed to a smirk. The kind of satisfied grin that boasted, I-told-you-so.

The woman was a real pain-in-the-ass. Time to even the playing field. Give Whitney what she wanted. Information. But no one said it had to be the truth.

* * *

"Are you happy now? You've made your point." Blake's cheeks puckered, and muscles twitched in his jaw.

Whitney grinned. She had the gun. He looked mad-as-hell. Good. What kind of man turns his back with a gun pointed at him? An arrogant man she could deal with. But a crazy one?

George, pale and shaking, crawled out from behind the couch and stood. "I should have stayed in Florida. Someone really needs to fill me in on what's going on here."

Whitney placed her hand on George's shoulder. "Sorry, I didn't mean to scare you."

"You didn't scare me." He raised a shaking hand and pointed next to the brass mantel of the fireplace. "Man, Marcus isn't going to be happy about that mess."

She looked at the wall and curled her lips in disgust. "I know."

Maybe her dear friend wouldn't notice the jagged hole in the wall and the missing paint chips on the floor in flakes. Who was she fooling? Three inches lower and Marcus's prized black and white lighthouse photograph would've been destroyed. Her stomach dropped at the thought.

"Now that you've killed the damn wall, do you think we can talk like rational adults?"

Blake now appeared calm. The tone of his voice sounded sincere.

"We'll talk." She couldn't trust him, not as long as he worked for Nathan. "For now, I keep the gun." If the man wanted his weapon back, he'd have to earn it.

"Fair enough. You sure you're not going to shoot again?"

"Only if you give me a reason to." She clutched the gun and cast him a shameless grin before heading to the kitchen.

Whitney turned. "How about we talk while you make that breakfast you promised?"

While Blake searched the cupboards for what he needed to prepare breakfast, George tugged on his right ear.

"Christ, my ear won't stop ringing. I'll probably end up deaf. Why didn't you tell me you knew how to use a gun?"

Whitney glanced at him happy some pink had returned to his white face. "It's not something I go around advertising. Would you?"

"Yeah, I guess you're right," George said.

At the breakfast bar, she sat on the stool and placed the gun in front of her on the counter. "Dad believed strongly in protecting his family. I think even more so after Mom was killed. I remember in the eighties, when he heard that the murder rates in the state had doubled, well, I started karate lessons—"

"You father got his money's worth last night." Blake winked at her.

Hopefully, George had missed that one. Whitney preferred he didn't know about the intruder, otherwise, he would start his fatherly lectures, something she didn't need right now.

"Then in the mid-nineties, the Happy Face killer was on the loose. Since Dad was away a lot on assignment, he figured I should learn how to use a gun. After my twentieth birthday, I took firearms lessons."

"You certainly can look after yourself." Blake opened a drawer, pulled out a large knife and paused, staring at it.

Whitney inched her hand toward the gun until her fingertips touched the steel handle. He grabbed the wooden cutting board, and with expertise chopped a green pepper and onion into small pieces. She exhaled a silent breath.

He looked right at home in the kitchen. He was also, she realized, the first man to cook for her, and she liked the idea. For a moment, she wondered what it would be like to have him dressed only in an apron and serve her breakfast in bed. Where the hell did that come from?

She glanced around the room. "Enough—about me. Let's get back to the why you came to Florence."

George took a seat next to her and continued to fiddle with his ear.

Blake set a carton of eggs on the counter beside the sink.

"You're right about one thing." He cracked an egg on the edge of the metal bowl. "Nathan did send me to get the tape. Nothing more."

Tell her something she didn't already know. When Blake wanted to, the man had a remarkable poker face, relaxed, unreadable. Not even a twitch. "Why the gun?"

"Habit. I've always carried one. Besides, it has saved my life a few times out in the desert. A lot of hungry animals out there."

Whitney didn't buy it. He wasn't in the desert now. Her gaze shifted to George. "And the real reason you are here is—"

"All right, busted." George hung his head. "I was sent to convince you to investigate Mason's death. You're the only one who knows what happened that day."

He was right. She was. But that didn't mean she was going to jump for the top brass at WBNN. The boys' club at WBNN-TV certainly would be kissing her ass after she exposed Nathan's dirty little secret. She smiled to herself.

Blake beat the eggs with a fork and poured them into the frying pan. "I don't know what's on the tape, but I was hoping it might have something to do with my sister, Claire Barnett."

Now we're getting somewhere. Whitney tried not to appear excited. "Okay, you've lost me. What does your sister have to do with Nathan Shaw?"

Blake popped four pieces of whole-wheat bread into the toaster. "Claire worked in the research lab. Fourteen months ago, she turned up dead. I don't have proof, but I'm convinced Nathan was involved."

That explained quite a bit, including why Blake worked for Nathan. He needed answers. Was it possible Nathan had Claire killed too? If he did, the body count just climbed to three.

She watched the muscles on Blake's back tense as he spoke about Claire. She knew how he felt. The feeling of anger, helplessness, and loss.

"I'm sorry about your sister." Her reporter instinct kicked in. More than anything, she wanted to question him about the details of his sister's death, but she decided to hold off, for now. "Has Nathan ever mentioned a scientist named Carmen Lacey?"

"Nope. Nathan isn't real open. He tells you what *he* wants you to know. Which isn't much."

George rubbed his hands together like he'd won a prize at the fair. "So what's on this tape?"

She couldn't help but feel bad that she hadn't filled George in any sooner. "You're going to love this. The tape shows ShawBioGen's secret project, a young girl. The world's first cloned human."

"Holy shit! You've got to be kidding?" George

slapped his hand down on the counter with such force he toppled off the stool. He quickly straightened and pretended he had meant to do that. "You know what this means, Whitney? Guaranteed Emmy. I can see it now. Where's the tape? I've got to see this."

She held up her hand. "Slow down, cowboy. No one is viewing the tape." Her gaze shifted to Blake. "For now, it's in a safety deposit box and that's where it's staying. We've got a lot more work to do before we can break the story."

Unable to contain his excitement, George continued to ramble, because his mouth worked faster than his mind. "I still can't believe this. Are you sure this is for real? This isn't some kind of hoax? Please tell me it's true."

"It's not a hoax." Blake handed Whitney a plate with a western sandwich and two pickles.

"Thanks." That image of him naked dressed in that apron again popped back into her mind. She took a bite of her sandwich and fought to shake the thought away. What the hell was wrong with her? *Get it together, Steel.*

While they ate breakfast, Whitney relived the horror of Mason's death, filling both men in on the details, including how the tape had landed in her hands. After George inhaled his breakfast, he rinsed his plate, while Blake disappeared to the deck with a cup of coffee.

George's expression grew serious. "The more I think about this, Whitney, the more I don't think you should go after Nathan. It's too dangerous."

"You know I have to do this, and you know I'm going to with or without your help. This truly is the story of a lifetime. Every self-centered, egotistical man I've ever worked with, excluding you, of course, will give me the respect I deserve."

Whitney and George moved to the living room. "Is that worth getting yourself killed?" He flopped onto the couch beside her. "Blake told me about last night —the guy with the knife. Whitney, think about this. Enough people have died."

"What has gotten into you?" Disappointment surged through her. George had always stood behind her decisions. The change of heart didn't sit well. "I'm surprised. I figured you'd be on my side. What about that Emmy?"

"Hey, I am on your side, kiddo. Emmy or not. I don't have to agree with you. There has to be another way to get this story."

"There isn't." Blake strolled into the living room with his coffee cup in his hand. "I know Nathan. He's a creature of habit. The lab. Your evidence will be there."

Whitney nodded. "I agree. George, did you know Nathan donates millions of dollars each year to food banks and homeless shelters around the country? Not only that, he dumps millions of dollars into healthcare and scientific research. He was Man of the Year six years in a row and made the cover of *Time* magazine, twice. With a track record like this, we'll need as much evidence as we can get. A video and our word won't cut it. To hang him, we need solid proof."

"Someone did their homework." George turned to Blake. "Have you seen the kid?"

In the kitchen area, Blake poured a cup of coffee. "No."

"Let me get this straight." George's eyes narrowed. "You've never been in the lab. You haven't laid eyes on the kid, how do—"

Blake turned. "You'll have to trust me, George. I'm looking for answers too."

Goosebumps erupted on Whitney's arms, but she wasn't cold. Her skin grew clammy and Mason's chilling words echoed in her head.

Trust no one.

She swallowed the lump in her throat and continued determined to learn more from Blake. "What's the lab security like?"

"Minimal." Blake took a sip of his coffee and set the cup on the breakfast bar. "At the moment, keycards and guards."

Whitney glanced at the clock. Eleven-twenty. She wanted to see what more Blake would reveal, but she had a few errands to do before her flight to Vegas later tonight.

"Listen, I've got to run. We'll talk more when I get back."

"Sure. Whatever you want." Blake slipped his hands into his jeans pockets and shot her a what-the-hell-are-you-up-to grin.

"Oh, just to let you know, I'm taking this with me." She waved the gun in the air, a gentle reminder. With a deep breath, she put her arm around George's shoulder. "Walk me to the door."

As they headed to the front of the house, George raised an eyebrow. "Where are you going?"

"I have a few errands to do and while I have a chance, I want to stop at the cemetery."

She placed Blake's gun in her purse and pulled out her keys. "George, keep a close eye on Blake. Believe me, something doesn't smell right."

CHAPTER NINE

By one-thirty, the overwhelming need to know landed Whitney in an uncomfortable plastic chair at the Ninth Street library, examining microfilm and searching the Internet. She needed to verify Blake's story about Claire. If she could trust the man, perhaps she could convince him to help her get into the lab. Armed with little to go on except a name and possible month, she first explored *The Las Vegas Sun*. Had Claire Barnett even lived in Vegas?

Hushed whispers, quieted footsteps, and the tick of the wall clock collided with the annoying shrill of a cell phone somewhere within the stacks.

Whitney looked up.

A male library assistant busily shelving books stopped, then shook his head in disgust at the noisy interruption.

Hours had passed, and she found herself drumming her fingers on the worn table. Maybe she had the incorrect month? The wrong newspaper? Or had Blake made up the story? She stood and stretched her stiff legs. Then a small headline in the *Las Vegas Review-Journal* caught her attention. She dropped into the chair and read:

MOLECULAR BIOLOGIST FOUND DEAD

Claire Barnett died of carbon monoxide poisoning early Tuesday morning aboard a boat docked at the Mead Lake Marina. Dr. Barnett, a molecular biologist with ShawBioGen, was found alone in the boat's galley. The County Coroner's office ruled the incident accidental after completed toxicology tests showed that Dr. Barnett's blood had a 64 percent saturation rate for carbon monoxide, Coroner Richard Hale said.

ShawBioGen's owner, Nathan Shaw, issued a statement earlier today. "We have lost a brilliant young mind and a valuable member of our close ShawBioGen family. Dr. Barnett will be sadly missed."

Bile rose in Whitney's throat, threatening to gag her. Nathan Shaw emotional? Family? What a load of crap. She wanted to kick herself for doubting Blake. With a couple of clicks of the mouse, she discovered the obituary section hidden within the classifieds.

Claire Anne Barnett, 34, of Las Vegas, died April 10th. She is survived by parents Carol and Frank Barnett of Las Vegas. Visitation will be from 3 p.m. to 7 p.m., Saturday, April. 12th. The service will be held at 11 a.m., Monday, April 14th, at Calm Pines Mortuary, 1425 N. Main St.

She read the notice again. A mixture of sadness and intrigue plagued her thoughts and left her with more questions than answers. Why different last names? Why no mention of Blake? Carbon monoxide poisoning on a boat didn't sound very common. Or was it? And what made Blake believe Nathan was involved in Claire's death?

"Miss, it's four o'clock. We're ready to close," the male assistant said in a hushed voice.

"Oh." Whitney looked around. Other than statue-like security men on either side of the lobby entrance, guarding a celebrity art collection, the library was virtually empty. "Of course. I didn't notice the time." She gathered her purse from the table.

On her way out, she remembered the days when her mother would bring her here for Saturday story hour. The interior of the library hadn't changed much. The wood-planked floor had been replaced with industrial-strength white vinyl, and the walls were painted the same boring beige. For a second, the fruity floral scent of her mother's perfume tantalized her nostrils...

"Mommy, you know what?"

"What, honey?" Her mother sat at the dressing table brushing her long hair.

"When I grow up, I'm going to marry Prince Matchabelli and live in a beautiful castle."

Her mother's eyes twinkled like stars. "Yes, you will marry your prince one day, Whitney, just like I married mine."

At the age of ten, Whitney discovered her Prince Matchabelli wasn't a real prince, only the company that made her mother's favorite perfume. Although saddened by the news, life went on, until the day her mother drove to the grocery store and never returned. For the first time, the fifteen-year-old saw her mother's prince hang his head and cry.

Outside, a salty, tepid breeze ruffled Whitney's hair. She bit back the tears and started the SUV.

It had been seven years since her last visit to Florence and she knew the journey would be emotional. She tapped her fingernails on the steering wheel and drove south on Rhododendron Drive.

Even though angry gray clouds hovered above, the buildings and planter boxes exploded with color, decorated in red, white and blue flowers, in preparation for tomorrow's Fourth of July celebrations. Memories of the waterfront town surged through her mind. Horseback riding along the beach, picnics with her father, and her favorite, whale watching at Otters Rock. Amidst the city's charm and beauty, an old man dressed in ragged clothing pushed a shopping cart filled with his meager belongings past the numerous gift shops.

Her instincts suddenly prickled. She glanced in the rearview mirror. A dark green sedan with tinted windows trailed behind her. Her fingers tightened around the steering wheel. Was she just being paranoid after what had happened last night? She slowed and turned left onto Kingwood. The sedan tagged along making the turn too quickly for her liking. She continued to watch. Then the car turned onto Eighth Street, sped up and disappeared. With a long sigh of relief, she forced her body to relax.

Whitney drove through the open iron gates of the Pine Hills Cemetery. Pristine green grass and Japanese maples complimented red yucca plants that edged the fence of the cemetery. As she parked the car, her pulse skittered and goosebumps skated across her arms. God, she hated cemeteries. After shutting off the car, she grabbed the colorful bouquet of flowers she had purchased earlier from the passenger seat.

❈ ❈ ❈

Concealed behind a thick row of trees at the far end of the cemetery, he shut off the engine, rolled to a stop and parked the green sedan.

He knew the reporter had seen him following her. Christ, he'd watched her check her rearview mirror numerous times. The thought made him smile.

The useless thug Nathan hired to get his videotape had gotten himself caught. Knocked out cold by the woman. What a joke.

Karate isn't going to help you, bitch when a gun's pointed at your head and I pull the trigger.

Eventually, the woman would be his.

Now all he had to do was get Nathan Shaw's tape then he could kill her. In the meantime, he'd keep the reporter constantly looking over her shoulder.

He popped the trunk latch under the dash and got out of the car. Staring in the trunk at the rifle and handgun, he had only one thing on his mind.

Killing her would be an absolute pleasure. Sweet retribution for what she'd done.

❊ ❊ ❊

In front of the double gray monument, Whitney ran her fingers along the elaborate curved top. The cold granite sent a shiver down her spine.

*In Loving Memory Elaine Teresa Steel beloved
mother and wife
Died 14th December 1983.
"Gone but not forgotten."*

*Robert Lucas Steel
Reporter, husband, and loving father
Died 21st October 1997.
"He did his duty and feared nothing."*

She knelt in the grass and laid the flowers on the stone base, hoping to drown the sudden guilt that washed over her.

"I'm sorry I haven't visited sooner. But there isn't a day that goes by that I don't think of you both." As if her throat were filled with cotton balls, she forced the words out. "Hi, Mom. I miss you. I still volunteer twice a month at MADD. I've met so many wonderful people who've lost loved ones."

She clasped her hands together. "And Dad, I miss you too. I just want to say—you did a great job raising me after Mom died. Thanks." After wiping her eyes with the back of her hand, she stood. "I love you both."

She paused for a long moment and stared at the monument before turning to walk away.

In the distance, a dog barked. The top half of the monument exploded, spraying shards of granite around her.

❋ ❋ ❋

If Blake returned to Nathan empty-handed, the little prick would continue to send someone after Whitney. Blake had to convince her to give up the tape, forget the story, and get on with her life in Florida. If he wanted to, he could easily delay her trip to Vegas. Maybe have her pulled from the plane before take-off, or have an officer stop her on a bogus traffic stop. That would buy him a bit of time to decide his next move. Man, that would piss her off. He grinned at the thought.

The woman was driving him crazy, in more ways than one. He liked her a lot but keeping a step ahead of her had become a major sporting event.

"Hey, there's her SUV." George pointed before he

folded in the seat like an accordion. "Whitney isn't going to be happy we followed her. You sure she can't see us?"

Blake glanced at him. "Don't worry, I'm sure." Even though the man had the backbone of a squashed spider, George cared very much for Whitney. Maybe he could talk some sense into her? Dumb idea.

More than likely, George had already tried and failed. "Don't worry. Tell her I threatened to torture you if you didn't tell me where she was going."

George shot him a half-cocked grin.

Thunder rumbled, and rain splattered against the windshield. Behind the graveyard, Blake parked the car and shut off the engine. Weather-beaten headstones crammed the grounds, like an ancient stone maze. He felt at home here. Dozens of times, he'd met informants in the black of night, none of them too thrilled with his choice of surroundings. However, all were willing participants persuaded one way or another that being on *his* side was much better than working against him.

A single gunshot split the air.

Birds scattered.

George grabbed the dashboard. "What the—"

"Stay put and stay down." Out of habit, Blake reached for the glove box. "Shit. Whitney has my gun."

He leaped from the car and sprinted along the iron fence. Adrenaline ripped through his veins. Unable to see Whitney or determine which direction the shots were coming from, he scaled the fence and dropped to the other side. Hidden behind an immense stone angel next to the mausoleum, he bent and stopped to catch his breath.

Where the hell was she?

Another shot rang out. He dove for cover.

Someone was more than a bit trigger-happy. An explosive flare of lightning ignited the sky; a floodgate of rain assaulted his body, dousing him. He wiped his eyes and inched his way on his belly across the wet grass.

Covered in mud, he searched row by row. Where was she? He heard a car door slam, then the growl of an engine.

Blake popped his head up.

A green sedan raced through the graveyard before exiting onto the street and sped out of view.

He sprang to his feet and ran. His waterlogged clothes stuck to his body as he zigzagged in case he had to dodge a bullet. Then he saw her...

Whitney lay on her side, motionless, sheltered by a tall bronze statue of a woman holding a baby.

His gut clenched. *Please be alive.*

He reached her and dropped to his knees, rolled her onto her back and cradled her in his arms. Her breasts rose and fell through the mud-splattered white shirt she wore. Blood trickled from a small jagged gash centered in a quarter-sized bump on her forehead. By the numerous pieces of granite strewn about, it looked like one had walloped her, knocked her out and probably saved her from a bullet.

He ground his teeth. Damn stubborn woman. She could've gotten herself killed—for the second time. If this didn't stop her from going after Nathan, he'd be forced to take matters into his own hands.

❋ ❋ ❋

Moist breath whispered against Whitney's cheek. A low voice urged her to open her eyes. *Blake's voice? How*

*could that be? She'd left Blake and George at the house...
stopped at the library....*

Frantic, she searched the layers of her mind, trying
to remember. The cemetery. What happened? And why
did her head hurt? When she lifted her hand and ran her
fingers across her forehead. "Ouch."

Everything came back. Someone tried to shoot her.

"You'll survive, but you've got a pretty good
bump." Blake held her close on his lap, so close his heart
beat thumped against her arm. "Want me to kiss it better?"

He wouldn't. The guy had to be joking. Besides,
what was he doing here? She opened her eyes.

Blake carefully smoothed the hair out of her face
and lowered his head. Rain dripped from the ends of his
hair and sprinkled onto her cheeks.

A shiver ripped through her the moment his warm
lips caressed her forehead, gentle, loving. "I'm glad
you're okay." He raised his head and looked into her
eyes with an unruffled gaze that took her breath away.

Breathe, damn it.

Less than a second of silence, that's all it took before he cupped her chin in his hand and kissed her.

The feel of his mouth on hers launched a burst of
heat that singed every nerve ending. Her heart flipped.
She wrapped her arms around his neck, kissed him
longer, harder, wanting so much more.

Then instinct kicked in. She pulled away.

He worked for Nathan.

She slowly sat up. Her head felt fuzzy. Was she dizzy
from the bump on her head or from the kiss? "Why did
you do that?"

Blake offered a quick half smile, got up and helped

her to her feet. "Because you wanted me to."

"What? So now you're a mind reader?" Okay, she had wanted him to, but she refused to admit it. "I did not."

That kiss scared the hell out of her. It had been well over six months since she had a date, let alone been kissed. Never had a kiss had such power over her, but Blake worked for a killer. She must remain strong. Even if she could trust him, she didn't get involved with older men. But he wasn't that much older. Maybe a couple of years. But still older. Not after her failed escapade with Mason, younger men and no commitment worked for her. If a man became too clingy or wanted more, she walked away.

"So, why'd you kiss me back?" Blake asked.

"Why are *you* making such a big deal over a kiss? It just happened. It doesn't mean anything." If she could convince herself maybe, she'd convince him.

He ploughed his fingers through his wet hair and smiled again. "Face it, I'm growing on you."

He was. No way would she give him the satisfaction. Stay focused. Get the story. Walk away. "Yeah, like mold."

"Where'd you hide my gun?"

Trusting Blake, trusting anyone, would not be an easy task. Maybe he shot at her to scare her away from the real issue, Nathan. She searched his expression, eager to find the answer. Again, that damn attractive poker face told her nothing.

"Come on, don't give me a hard time. I wasn't the one who took pot shots at you. If you don't believe me, ask George. He's waiting in the car."

"George is here too?" Apparently, a conspiracy had

brewed between the two newfound-men-pals the instant she'd left the house. Not fair. "Under the front seat. You'd better be on the up and up."

"I am." Blake flashed another quick grin before he headed to the SUV. "I'll be right back."

A stiff cold breeze ripped through the gray clouds, making the air feel much cooler. Whitney shivered. Being drenched to the bone didn't help. What she wouldn't give for a hot shower and a cup of coffee. Veins of lightning severed the sky. The rain turned to drizzle and fell from the trees like silent snowflakes. She turned her head to the right.

The top section of her parent's monument had been reduced to rubble. The sight pulled at her heart. She'd had the special granite imported from India because her father had wanted it. She bit her lower lip to stop from crying. When she returned from Vegas, ordering a new monument would be a top priority—if she made it back.

Blake returned, his shoulders heaved beneath his wet shirt. "You okay?"

"Yes." Through moist eyes, she glanced at her watch. Two-ten. "I've got a flight to catch in less than three hours. Let's go."

He snatched her arm and stopped her in her tracks. "Wait. You're still planning on going to Las Vegas? I can't believe it. Woman, you're crazy. If George and I hadn't followed you—"

"Thank you, okay. I'm glad you were here. I really am. But no one asked you to follow me."

"Think about it. Please."

In your dreams, buddy. "Blake, there's nothing to think about. I'm going to Vegas and getting into that lab with or without your help. Nathan started this and I'm damn well going to finish it."

He shook his head. "Even if it means getting yourself killed?"

"Yes."

"Will you at least get that bump looked at?"

"I'm fine, really." He actually sounded and looked as if he cared. "We'll stop and get it checked on the way back to the house."

As they walked to his car in silence, mud sucked at her leather sandals.

The cemetery looked different, strange under the gray skies. She drew a deep uneven breath. Carved gravestones emerged from the green grass like beaten-up yard ornaments.

When Whitney approached the back of the car, she didn't see George. She turned to Blake. "Well, where is he?"

"Probably still hiding under the dash. I told him to stay down. Hey George, you can come out now."

She took another step. "George, stop playing games. I'm not in the—"

"Wait." Blake held out his arm to stop her and whipped out his gun tucked into the back of his jeans. He grabbed her hand and pushed her behind him.

Gun raised, finger on the trigger, he peered through the passenger side window, and then looked back at her.

George had vanished.

CHAPTER TEN

Blake cautiously circled George's rental car before opening the driver side door. "Maybe he got scared and took off."

"George wouldn't just leave." Whitney followed his lead and finally got into the car, grateful to be out of the rain.

"I know George isn't the most courageous person, but…" Then she noticed the Florida Marlins ball cap on the back seat.

No way would George leave without his beloved hat unless someone forced him to go. She reached over the seat and grabbed the hat. Underneath it was a note. Oh, God. She snatched the paper and read the scribbled handwriting.

Meet outside Heceta Head Lighthouse 3:30. Bring the tape. No cops or George dies. Wear the hat.

Fear replaced Whitney's earlier dizziness. If anything happened to George, she'd never forgiven herself. She passed the note to Blake, her gaze locked on the dash. The bluish digits of the clock screamed, taunting her. Ten after two. Time was running out.

"Shit." Blake tossed the note aside and started the engine. "We'll have to postpone that stop to get your head examined. Which way to the bank?"

The hell with her head. This was all her fault. Stupid, stupid, stupid. She prayed George would be okay. But one thought kept nagging her. Something bad always happened when Blake was around. When she'd been attacked at the house, within minutes, Blake appeared at the door. Now here at the cemetery, someone had tried to shoot her, and he appeared to save the day. She didn't like where this was going.

"Whitney, which way?"

Robot-like she pointed. "North on Kingwood then left on Seventh." What if George was sitting back at the house and Blake had set this up to get the tape? She had to know.

"Why did you follow me here?"

At first, Blake didn't answer, just glanced at her, and then laughed. "You think I had something to do with this, don't you?"

How could he read her mind? "You have to admit—"

"You're a real piece of work, you know that?" He flicked the windshield wipers off. "This is your doing, not mine. How many lives are you willing to jeopardize for your damn story? People have died, Whitney. This is *not* a game."

His words bit her skin like millions of tiny teeth. She hugged her purse and stared out the window. Neither said a word until they reached Pacific National Bank.

Blake parked the car in the rear lot and shut off the engine. "Make it quick."

Before Whitney got out of the car, she glanced at the clock.

Two-twenty-four and counting.

❊ ❊ ❊

Although Blake prided himself as a skilled liar, with that talent brought certain circumstances that forced an agent to question his decisions. This was one of them.

His words hurt Whitney, but the woman had left him no choice. Just because he had orders from Nathan to get the tape didn't mean he staged George's disappearance. Actually, the idea was brilliant. Why hadn't he thought of it? And how did that son-of-a-bitch shooter slip by him and grab George? The sedan must have circled back when he was kissing Whitney.

He'd also done exactly what he said he would never do, get personally involved. He'd kissed Whitney because he wanted to, and man had he wanted to. He'd do anything to protect her, anything for her—except help her get into the lab. Why had his boss decided to take matters into his own hands? Where did that leave Blake? He needed to check in with Nathan after the exchange and hoped like hell his cover hadn't been blown.

✻ ✻ ✻

Whitney rounded the corner to the bank and eyed the red and white sign in the window. Her heart sank. *No!* The bank was closed.

She raced to the doors and pounded her fists on the glass until a well-groomed man appeared, clutching a coffee cup. "Sorry, we just closed." He pointed to another sign. "Holiday hours."

"Please." She dug through her purse, pulled out a hundred-dollar bill and waved the money at him. "Here. All I need is a couple of minutes to get something from my safety deposit box. Please. It's a matter of life and death."

The man raised an eyebrow.

No doubt, the guy thought she was a lunatic. Who could blame him? One glimpse at her reflection in the glass said it all. Hair wet and straggly, dried blood on her forehead, dirty, and pathetic looking. Right now, she looked as bad as the homeless man she'd seen wandering the streets earlier.

"Lady, we're closed. Get lost or I'll call the police." He shook his head and walked away.

Whitney crumpled the bill and tossed it in her purse. Her methods were a bit unorthodox but this time she'd reached an all-time low. Trying to bribe a bank employee. *Think Steel. Think.*

Less than a block up the street a group of young boys emerged from a store carrying bottles of pop. Any tape would be better than no tape. Some stores rented movies, right? She took off running.

Inside the store, an old woman was busy inspecting the canned food aisle while a male clerk leaned against the counter.

"Do you rent movies?"

The clerk, short and on the chunky side, pointed to the far end of the store. "At the back."

Whitney scurried to the rear of the store, snatched a movie cover from the wire rack and raced back to the front counter. "I'll take this one."

While the man replaced the cover with actual movie and case, she ploughed through her purse for her wallet.

"That'll be two-ninety-nine." He grabbed a sales slip from under the counter. "I'll need a driver's license and—"

"You don't understand. I need to buy this, not rent it."

"Sorry, we only rent them."

"Not today." She slapped fifty dollars on the counter and removed the tape from the clear plastic case. "That should cover it."

"Yeah, but…"

Whitney tore out of the store and glanced over her shoulder, half expecting someone to stop her. It never happened.

Her feet pounded the sidewalk as she peeled the outer label from the tape.

This had better work. George's life was at stake.

When she hopped in the car, she gasped. "Let's go."

Blake spun out of the parking lot and headed north toward the coast. "Took you a while. Problems?"

"No. No problems." Her voice sounded convincing, even to her own ears. She drew a long silent breath, eager to calm her nerves, but an unwelcome wrestling match with her conscience kicked in. *Damn it.*

Tell Blake the truth. No.

This was her mess, her problem. However, if she decided to tell him, did he need to know before the exchange? Why not wait when George was safe? Technically, they had a tape, just not the right one. What could go wrong?

Crap, everything. She clutched the videotape against her chest. Oh, hell.

"The bank was closed. The tape's fake." There, she said it.

A muscle twitched in Blake's jaw, and he grinned. "I know."

She narrowed her eyes. "What? How? You followed

me again?"

"No. The red sticker that says Moon Striker is a dead giveaway. Not a bad movie, either. Watched it a few weeks ago. Lots of action."

Whitney flipped over the black tape and checked the end. He was right. She quickly scratched off the last sticker with her fingernail.

"And when were you planning on telling me, or were you?" She heard the quiver in her voice and cursed herself. Weakness made her vulnerable and that was unacceptable.

A frown of irritation creased his forehead. "Regardless if you trust me or not, at this point, I'm all you've got." He shook his head. "We'll be there soon."

Encroaching dark clouds hugged the coastline like mist. Above the rugged cliffs, she spotted the brick-red roof of the lighthouse. The numbers on the dash blinked. Three o'clock.

Once they parked at Devil's Elbow State Park, Whitney got out and popped George's cap on her head. A group of thirty or so cheery tourists scooted by, some with binoculars and cameras. Once the crowd passed, Blake shoved his gun in the back of his jeans.

"I'll stay out of sight. I'm with you every step of the way." He slipped his arm around her and pulled her close. "No matter what, don't hand over that tape until George is free. If anything goes wrong, take off the hat. That'll be the signal for me to move in. Got it?"

Whitney nodded, staring at the videotape in her hand. Goosebumps erupted over her bare arms. *God, this had better work. I can't lose George.*

Blake released her and kissed her cheek. "Okay, get going. Be careful."

Whitney drew a deep breath and started the long hike up the unpaved trail toward the fifty-six-foot tower.

❊ ❊ ❊

Crouched in the woods on the west side of the lighthouse, Blake tightened his grip on the gun and waited.

During his years with the Bureau, he'd only met a handful of people with as much courage as Whitney, but sometimes courage hampered sound judgment. This woman was feisty, impulsive, and far too committed. Those qualities might win her friends, but in this situation, they made her a huge liability.

Even if Nathan got his precious tape, the bastard wasn't going to let her simply walk away. Whitney knew too much. She was a dead woman, and Blake wasn't going to stand by and watch that happen. Once George was safe, he had to convince her to disappear for her own good.

❊ ❊ ❊

At the Keeper's house, now a bed and breakfast, Whitney stopped for a moment to catch her breath. People lined the white picket fence to gawk at the three-story, Queen Ann-style home, hoping to catch a glimpse of the ghost that had reportedly haunted the place since the late eighteen hundreds. The thought made her shudder.

The steady thump and thud of feet stampeding from behind prodded Whitney to get moving. When she reached the lighthouse, a lump had formed in her throat, one she couldn't swallow.

On the table of rock, hundreds of feet above sea

level, tourists and a large group of children watched the surf and salty wind hammer the coastline below. Whitney scanned the crowd.

No George.

Her gaze shifted to the dense overgrowth of soaring pine trees. Could Blake see her? God, she hoped so. A shadow materialized in her peripheral vision.

George, and his kidnapper. A large man who weighed a good hundred pounds more than he should with greasy brown hair walked toward her. He kept his right hand under his jacket as if he had a weapon pointed at George.

Whitney took a few slow steps and stopped. George's right eye was swollen and bruised. *Stay calm. It'll be over soon.* The bastard had hit him.

The man huffed and puffed then held out his left hand. "Gimme—the—tape."

"First, let George go." She waved the videotape. "Then you get this."

Sweat bathed the kidnapper's pale face, as he continued to rasp for air. "Right now, I've got a gun shoved in your pal's ribs. Don't piss me off."

She grasped the peak of the hat with her fingers. "Look, you overgrown ape. The second I take off this hat, you'll feel a bullet rip through your back, and you'll drop like bird crap. You want the tape. Let him go, *now*."

Bubbles of sweat populated the man's thick forehead. He opened his mouth, foamy drool dribbled at the corners. A long moment of silence passed between them.

Clutching his chest, he wobbled and thundered to the ground. The gun dropped out of his hand.

Whitney scooped up the weapon before anyone noticed.

George looked at the man, then at her. "I think he's having a heart attack or something."

Regardless how Whitney felt about the kidnapper, she couldn't walk away and leave the guy to die. "Damn it." She bent down and tossed the hat aside. "Someone call 9-1-1! He's turning blue."

CHAPTER ELEVEN

Blake ran to the scene the moment the kidnapper collapsed. What the hell happened? Curious onlookers formed a tight circle around the man. A woman in a yellow raincoat knelt beside the man administering CPR with the help of another woman.

Sirens wailed, battling against the wind and surf below. As the blaring grew closer, Blake noticed Whitney had a gun clutched in her right hand. Christ. They didn't need any unwanted attention.

He grasped her arm, pulled her back from the crowd, then took the gun and slipped it into the back of his jeans next to his own weapon. "We'd better get out of here."

George snatched his hat from the ground and positioned it on his head low enough to cover his black eye.

One nagging thought played repeatedly through Blake's mind.

Why would Nathan send a guy who was so clearly out of shape to get a tape that was worth killing over?

Fact. He wouldn't.

Nathan would hire a pro. Blake needed answers. The sooner he spoke to his boss, the better.

* * *

From the east side of the lighthouse, the shooter adjusted his sunglasses and watched the chaos unfold a few yards away.

He clenched his fists. *What a screw up.*

He'd met Eric days ago at a corner pub across the street from where the man worked. He was an easy mark. The way his eyes lit when the shooter had mentioned he'd pay him cash. Half up front and the balance when the job was completed.

The perfect opportunity had presented itself when the shooter realized George was alone in the car.

Christ. All Eric had to do was a simple exchange to get Nathan's tape. *Fuck.*

He continued to watch two EMT's lift the big guy onto a stretcher and load him into the back of the waiting ambulance. It appeared Eric might survive the heart attack.

But the shooter couldn't have that.

No witnesses. Ever.

Then he spotted the reporter and her sidekicks rushing down the winding trail toward the parking lot.

He smiled to himself. You're dead, bitch. You just don't know it yet. But you will soon. Very soon.

❋ ❋ ❋

Whitney inhaled a deep breath that did nothing to calm her nerves. While they sped north on Highway 101, rain beat the car roof and thrummed against the windows. The full impact of what could have happened to George hit her like a concrete block. The man cared for her like a daughter and she had put him in harm's way. What kind of person did that to someone she loved? A selfish one. Her.

"I'm so sorry this happened to you." She glanced at George in the back seat, his right eye now swollen shut. "Are you sure you'll be okay?"

"I'll survive, kiddo." He squeezed her shoulder as if to offer a bit of reassurance. "Stop worrying. Nothing a bag of ice and a hot, juicy steak won't cure."

Now that made her smile. "In other words, you're hungry."

"You bet. I'm starving."

Blake flicked the windshield wipers on high. "After we grab something to eat, George I want you on a plane back to Florida. You'll be safe there." He glanced at her and back at George. "You're not the one Nathan wants."

"Hey, you don't have to tell me twice. The sooner I pack the better. Then I'm out of here. I've had enough of this town."

The lines around Blake's mouth tightened. "And you're going with him if I have to sit beside you on the plane."

Get real. A babysitter. No way. She stared out the window. "No, I'm not. I've got a flight to Vegas and that's where I'm heading tonight."

"For God sake, Whitney. Listen to him," George said.

"What you two seem to forget is, I still have the real tape and that tape might buy me more time. Time to figure out a few things. Like why Nathan sent that guy. I mean. The man was a walking time bomb." She turned to Blake hoping he agreed. "You know Nathan better than anyone. Don't you find that odd?"

"Okay, it's strange. Maybe he figured by hiring the big guy it would throw the heat off him. I wouldn't put that past him. Nathan's like a snake slithering in the grass. You never know which direction he'll slide away.

I still want you to go back with George."

"Sorry, I can't do that."

Blake shook his head, clearly ticked off by her decision. She had to push her feelings for him aside. This was her life, her decision, not his. After the kiss between them, she thought he felt something, and he'd want to help. But he hadn't. Actions spoke louder than words; his loyalty sat with Nathan and that would never change.

George rustled around in the backseat until Whitney felt his breath against her neck. "What if someone else wanted the tape? Have no idea why. But it's possible. A past business associate or something. I'll look into it when I get back."

"Exactly. Good, check it out." But who? Why? If the kidnapper survived his ordeal, she'd pay the man a visit before she left Florence. With a bit of luck, maybe he had the answers she needed.

❈ ❈ ❈

The large metal sign with painted yellow letters creaked in the wind outside Jo's Steakhouse.

Blake took the last bite of his steak and watched Whitney's slender fingers as she dabbed the corners of her mouth with a paper napkin. He'd never met a woman so stubborn, so gutsy, and so damn beautiful. If she only knew how much he cared for her. But a relationship needed honesty and trust, things he couldn't offer. The mission came first. Always had, always would. The less she knew about the real Blake, the better. If he liked it or not, an agent's greatest tool was being able to separate fact from emotion. Fact. He had a job to do.

Blake looked around the wood-paneled dining room and eyed a pay phone next to the men's washroom.

Whitney's gaze met his. She knew damn well he was going to call Nathan.

Blake slid out from the booth while George shoveled food into his mouth. Man, the guy could pack it way. "Be right back."

After using the washroom, he dialed Nathan's private number.

"What are you doing calling from a pay phone?" Nathan barked. "I told you to use your cell phone."

"The thing isn't working here. I keep losing the—"

"Stop dancing around the real subject. Have you got my tape?"

Typical Nathan. "No. It's in a safe deposit box and the bank's closed for the holiday." Time to feel the weasel out. "The exchange didn't go down."

"What exchange?" A long second of silence. "For Christ sake Blake, you're not making any sense."

"I'll get the tape first thing when the bank opens on Monday. We've got a much bigger problem. Someone else is after your tape."

"What?" Nathan's voice turned cold. "Explain."

Blake's instincts were right on. Nathan knew nothing about the kidnapping and sounded worried. Hell, he should be. Another party wanted a piece of the pie. Too bad he couldn't see Nathan's face right now.

"What about the pretty reporter? Have you wined, dined and screwed her?"

Fearing he'd hang up on the sick bastard, Blake tightened his grip on the phone. "I'm working on it."

"Just remember I hired you to take care of problems. So, take care of her. Of course, not until you have my tape and at least have some fun with the woman first. Understand?"

"Perfectly."

The phone disconnected.

Asshole. Blake slammed down the receiver.

Back at the table, George had just finished downing a piece of pecan pie.

Whitney folded her arms across her chest. "How's your boss?"

"Worried. He had nothing to do with the kidnapping."

"And you believe him? Of course, you would."

"Yeah, I do. Nathan is scared." And you should be too, he wanted to add. Instead, he pulled out his wallet. "Let's get out of here."

By the time they reached the driveway of the beach house, the sun had set over the Pacific and the rain had stopped. Blake parked the car, shut off the ignition and got out.

Whitney followed and leaned against the car.

"George, you mind if I talk to Whitney alone?"

George smirked. "No problem. Looks like I get the shower first."

"Get some ice on that eye." Whitney tossed the keys to him, but he missed, and they landed in the grass.

She and Blake burst out laughing.

"Hey, it's bad enough I'm color-challenged, but I can only see out of one eye. Shit. Give an old guy a break?"

"He's color blind? That's news to me." Blake put his arm around her shoulder and watched the man fumble around. Then he held the keys in the air as if he'd won the World Series.

"You haven't seen him in the morning at work. It's a sad sight. Look, I know what you're going to—"

From the front of the house, George waved. Then he opened the door.

A blinding white flash. The house exploded with a deafening roar.

They were flattened to the ground by the impact. A giant fireball surged toward the sky.

The earth shifted under Blake's body. A wall of heat slammed him and Whitney as they sprawled on the gravel. He rolled her over and tried to shield her body with his from ashes and burning debris that rained down.

She screamed. "G—e—o—r—g—e!"

She wiggled out from under Blake and pounced to her feet.

She didn't get far before he tackled her to the grass. Searing heat touched his bare skin. "Get back!"

"I have to help George." She fought to her feet again and bolted toward what was left of the house.

He sprinted after her and snagged her around the waist, lifting her off the ground. "There's nothing we can do, Whitney. No one could survive that. George is gone."

Another shock wave rocked the earth and sent them hurling back to the ground as a tree next to the house caught fire. This time Blake smacked his head and ate a mouthful of grass. He got to his knees and crawled to Whitney. Her eyes were wide with fear or disbelief. He wasn't sure which.

"Baby, I'm sorry."

She let out a strangled cry. "We have to help. Please help him. Blake, please." Tears streamed down her cheeks, washing away the soot.

Her body went limp and she crumpled to the ground and cried.

✷ ✷ ✷

Five hundred yards away, the shooter lay on his stomach in the cool, damp sand and stared through the night vision binoculars at what was left of the beach house. Smoke and flames light the darkness.

The reporter was supposed to unlock the front door. Not the old guy.

It should have been her. It was supposed to be her. *Fuck!*

He'd set the perfect trap. Amazing what a little flint in a door lock and a gas leak could do. He'd taken out the tumbler, filled it with flint shavings and replaced it. Turning the key created the right amount of friction, caused a spark, and kaboom!

Ingenious and untraceable.

He'd actually gotten the idea from his father. From one of the many stories told around the dinner table while growing up. God, he missed him.

It was all her fault his father wasn't here.

The shooter threw the binoculars down the ravine behind him.

Bitch.

She would pay for what she'd done. He'd make sure of it.

CHAPTER TWELVE

Whitney had no idea how many hours passed, but there was nothing glorious or beautiful about the sunrise on this morning. The lawn looked like a bombed-out garbage dump littered with window frames, shingles and shattered debris.

This had to be a nightmare. It couldn't be real.

Seagulls squealed and circled the charred rubble of the house. Their tortured screams pierced the smoky air as though they felt her loss. As the last fire truck roared out of the driveway, panic nipped her skin.

She couldn't stop the unsteady breath that shuddered from her lips. *George really was gone. Killed in an explosion meant for me.*

Bile rose in her throat, turning her mouth bitter. She doubled over and retched in the grass.

George had never hurt anyone. How could this have happened? She wiped her face on the wool blanket draping her shoulders and took a long, deep breath of salty air that reeked of smoke.

While the state arson investigators continued to comb through the remains of the house, an energetic black Lab sniffed around the scene. Even though the grim-faced fire marshal remained tight-lipped she'd heard the investigator's whispers—suspicious. The more she thought about what happened, the harder she clenched her hands together. A man died. A kind man. It should have been her.

Nathan, you cowardly pathetic weasel. I know you did this. Determined to speak with someone in charge, Whitney trudged a few steps and then stopped.

What would she say?

Oh, I know who killed George. His name is Nathan Shaw and he's a model citizen other than he clones humans. If that didn't buy a one-way ticket to the nearest rubber room, nothing would. As if anyone would take her seriously. She needed solid evidence.

Detective Garrison must have read her mind because he was heading toward her with Sheriff Larkin. Despite how horrid she felt, a spurt of adrenaline ripped through her veins.

Reporter mode kicked in. "Any news on what caused the explosion?"

Garrison, a lanky man with a weather-beaten face stopped and stared through his wire-framed glasses. "Possibly a natural gas leak. Won't know for sure until our investigation is complete."

"Do you think the explosion was triggered by some type of device? Has the ATF in Portland been notified?"

"You're a reporter?" Detective Garrison asked.

She nodded.

"Figures. Just my luck." He rubbed his forehead as if it ached. "Until our investigation is complete, I can't speculate on anything."

The roar of a low flying Cessna made her look up. She knew the plane was snapping photographs of the debris area to give the investigators more information on the intensity of the explosion. After the plane circled twice, it dipped and headed along the coastline.

"In my twenty years, I've never seen anything like this. Good thing this property is secluded. An explosion like this could have taken out half a city block or more." Sheriff Larkin shook his head. "I did need to talk to you. I need to contact Mr. Raines' next-of-kin. "

"George didn't have any family." Emptiness closed around her heart. "His parents died years ago and he never married. I'll look after…"

Not only did she have arrangements to make for George, she still had to call Marcus in Greece. She glanced at the huge pile of rubble cordoned off by police tape. How do you tell a dear friend he's homeless and it's your fault?

Her hands grew clammy and the blanket slipped from her shoulders to the grass. A deep hollow knot twisted in her stomach. She doubled over again, but this time she threw up on familiar black shoes. When she looked up, Blake's lips twitched into a frown.

"God, I'm sorry." How could she look him in the eye after that?

Blake glanced at his shoes. "They're old. I could use a new pair." He put his arm around her and eased her upright.

The sheriff stepped back and kept a steady "better you than me" look on his face. "I told Mr. Neely it took a bit of doing but I was able to snag a hotel room at the Point Inn. Hope that's okay. My deputy will take you both into town first to get some clothes and whatever else you'll need. Sorry for your loss, Miss Steel."

"Thank you."

At this point sharing a room with Blake was the least of her worries because she'd need every ounce of strength to bury George.

* * *

Whitney's eyes were dull with exhaustion. Soot and dirt streaked her face and hair. She looked out-and-out defeated as she closed the bathroom door behind her. Blake heard the muffled hiss of the shower.

When they arrived at The Point Inn, Whitney insisted he shower first so she could make some phone calls. Probably a good thing because he wasn't sure he could handle hearing the sadness in her voice. He would never forget her child-like whimpers and the stab of pain he felt when she finally accepted George was dead. Man, the thought made him feel sick to his stomach.

When his time was up, Blake hoped his demise would be as fast and painless. Considering he'd killed a man in the past. That alone gave the higher force a damn good reason to execute a long and torturous death instead. Blake would go straight to hell because that was what he deserved. He forced his thoughts back to George.

None of what happened at the house made sense. The explosion took planning, surveillance, and timing. No way had Nathan pulled it off, especially when Blake had spoken to him a half hour earlier. The answer lay with the man at the lighthouse, if he was still alive.

Eager to learn more about George's kidnapper, Blake plunked down in a hideous floral chair beside the dresser and dialed information. Once he had the number for the hospital, he lied and stated he was the sheriff. After a rushed conversation with a nurse in ICU, he discovered the big guy's name. Right now, life sucked for Erik Friklin, who had a ten percent chance of surviving the next twenty-four hours. No visitors. Shit. If Blake could sneak away later, he would have someone at the Bureau run the name.

Thank heavens for small town hospitality. Sheriff Larkin had arranged for a local mom-and-pop department-style store to open on the holiday so he and Whitney could buy what they needed. Blake got out of the chair and slipped a new black T-shirt over his head. When the cotton brushed his shoulders, he cringed. Not even a hot shower had helped his aching body dotted with bruises and burns where flaming debris had landed.

He glanced at the new pair of white and neon-blue running shoes at the end of the bed. Not his color or style, but they'd do. His heart went out to Whitney. She had gone through a lot. First her ex-husband, now George. The woman had bloody-well earned the right to puke on someone's shoes. As much as he wanted her to go as far away as possible, keeping her close was the only solution to keep her safe.

He would do anything for her, anything to protect her.

The water shut off in the bathroom. Blake cracked his knuckles and stared at the queen-size bed, covered in a brown and silver bedspread that matched the room's curtains and carpet. Until now, he really hadn't given much thought about the sleeping arrangements. Two people. One bed. His palms grew damp. Looks like he'll be camping out on the floor. Unless...

The bathroom door opened, and a cloud of steam escaped before Whitney emerged. Wow! She'd colored her blonde hair brown. The rich dark color fell in waves over her shoulders and made her blue eyes bright. Striking, beautiful and sexy as hell. His pulse erupted and so did his body. He felt like a high school kid on his first date, all nerves, complete with a throbbing hard on.

Christ, he wanted her.

Whitney crossed the room wearing blue jeans that hugged her hips and a low-cut white top that showed off every magnificent curve. When she sat at the table by the window, she crossed her ankles. He even found her pink painted toenails sexy.

Grateful for the oversized shirt concealing the bulge in his pants, he sat on the edge of the bed. His gaze moved to her mouth. He wanted to taste those beautiful lips again. More than a bit uncomfortable, he shifted. He gritted his teeth, fighting the temptation to either kiss her or toss her on the bed and rip off her clothes.

Their gazes met. Then he saw it. A boundless tunnel of sadness in Whitney's eyes that wrenched his gut. Christ, the woman just lost a man she loved like a father. He had no right to be thinking about sex. Besides, as far as Whitney was concerned, he was just as much the enemy as Nathan.

"Blake?"

"Yeah."

Tears filled her eyes. "Will you hold me?"

He stood and held out his arms, wanting to take away her pain. "Come here."

Whitney rushed into his embrace. He sealed his arms around her not wanting to let go. With her head nestled against his neck, her damp hair smelled like vanilla and spice. Her body trembled against his.

"Why did George have to die? He never hurt anyone. It should have been me. Not George."

Blake lifted her chin and stroked the hair back from her face. "I don't know why. But I do know George cared about you a lot. He was a good guy." He searched her moist eyes, hoping that what he was about to say wouldn't upset her. "Maybe I'm selfish, but I'm glad it wasn't you."

She remained quiet, staring, her gaze roaming over his face as if taking inventory. Then her warm lips melted to his in a kiss filled with such intensity he thought for sure he'd gone to heaven. He couldn't, shouldn't take advantage of her. She was scared. Vulnerable. But he held her tighter, savoring her sweet tasting mouth as she drove her long fingers through his hair, tugging him closer. His erection pressed against her body. A silent plea for more.

❈ ❈ ❈

Whitney couldn't stop kissing him. God, she didn't want to. Blake's tongue danced with hers and sent sparks of electricity charging through her veins. Nothing mattered as long as his arms remained wrapped around her. How could she feel so safe in the arms of a man she barely knew? But she did. Warmth surrounded her, and she needed him.

He skimmed his hand down her bare arm, a soft gasp escaped her throat and her nipples hardened against his chest.

His lips left her mouth and trailed along the side of her neck to her ear. "You're beautiful."

Even though the words came out muffled, she caught every sweet syllable. The roughness of his hand teased her breasts through her thin cotton top.

"Are you sure about this?" he asked.

Her gaze locked on his. "I'm sure." She lifted her arms and peeled off her top, letting it flop to the carpet grateful she hadn't purchased a new bra. One less thing to take off. For what seemed like forever, she stood before him naked from the waist up waiting, mentally begging him to touch her.

He kissed one breast, then the other, circling her nipples with his tongue in such a way that fire shot through her body.

She shuddered, hot, cold, cold, hot.

"No fair." Whitney moved her hands beneath his shirt careful not to hurt him and lifted the shirt over his head. "Now it's fair."

She stared at the numerous small red burns and welts on his shoulders. He had chosen to protect her instead of himself.

His warm breath brushed against her ear. "I think I'm going to like this game."

She ran her hand down his denim-clad hip and found what she wanted. Hard and ready. He was more than happy to help her by unfastening his jeans with one hand while caressing her breast with the other.

He stepped out of his pants, leaving them in pile at his feet. "Don't say a word."

Before wiggling out of her jeans, she chuckled at his black satin boxers covered in red flaming hearts.

He sat her on the edge of the bed, stood between her legs and gently pushed her back onto the silky bedspread.

With a wildly erotic grin, he slipped off her panties and ran his tongue from her breasts to her navel. Lower and lower, his heated tongue and mouth ravished her.

Kissing, licking, sucking...

She arched her back and bit her lip wanting to scream in tortured pleasure. It took every ounce of restraint not to dig her nails into his wounded shoulders. "Blake—I want you—inside me."

"I thought you'd never ask." Breathing hard, he moved over her, nibbling his way up her hips to her breasts. Then he stood. Tall, tanned, naked and hard. "Time for some twisted pleasure."

"Condoms! They're in my purse in the bathroom. I'll get them." She bounced off the bed. By the time she had emptied her purse on the floor and found the condoms Blake had followed her into the room. His incredible body glistened with beads of sweat under the lights. After ripping open the package, her fingers shook as she slipped the condom on him.

He boosted her up onto the counter beside the sink and spread her legs. "Oh, yeah."

The sound of his low voice echoed in her head as she traced his lips with her tongue. Caught up in the moment, she raked her fingernails over his nipples and felt him tremble. He returned to her mouth where his kiss grew more aggressive, desperate. Without warning, he slid a finger into her. She moaned against his lips. Wanting to be closer, she moved forward on the counter and wrapped her legs around his waist.

With one quick thrust, Blake plunged into her.

Breathless, she dug her nails into the taut muscles of his arms, anchoring herself to him. Her sporadic whimpers combined with his ragged panting fueled the fire between them higher and hotter. Harder and deeper he pumped until she swore, she was floating, swirling, sucked into a new world that she never wanted to leave.

"Whitney," he gasped hoarsely, his breath hot against her neck.

Their consuming need gathered in speed and Blake's body shuddered. Inhaling his woodsy scent drove her senses over the edge. She held him tight, moving with him until every ounce of her body shook, exploding in flooded warmth.

For a few moments, they clung together, exhausted and satisfied.

He lifted his head and stared into her eyes. "You okay?"

She had no idea how she would feel in an hour, tonight or tomorrow. But right now felt loved. "I'm more than okay."

CHAPTER THIRTEEN

The last twenty-four hours felt like Whitney's soul had been blown apart in an emotional minefield. First the kidnapping; then George's death. She could still taste the ashy soot from the explosion in the back of her throat. An image of a barbed-wire fence with a guide saying, "Hey lady. Step here," popped into her head. She should never have taken that first step let alone underestimated the risk. The stakes were higher now, and she couldn't turn back. George was dead and she'd expose Nathan for the killer he was or she'd die trying.

However, she couldn't do it alone.

Whitney rested her head against Blake's chest and listened to the steady thump of his heart over the faint murmur of the TV. She also had no business enjoying any type of closeness with Blake, let alone, mindless, savage sex. Definitely a show of weakness on her part, or maybe a mix of self-indulgence and need. Either way, sometimes life-threatening situations led to unexpected intimacy. Damn it. Why couldn't she admit that she had feelings for him?

Because he worked for Nathan.

The warmth wrapped around her heart turned to

ice. Talk about sleeping with the enemy. Regardless of her new-found affection for Blake, she found it hard to trust him completely. He seemed different. Evasive, guarded, almost detached. In her world that meant one thing. He was hiding something. What?

Blake rolled over and his hand roamed her thigh. "Hey, guess I dozed off."

Heat emanated from his body, the firmness of his thighs. Her skin tingled beneath his fingers and there was no ignoring his erection against her hip. Another vision flashed through her head. This time the guide frowned when her foot almost touched the mine. "I'm starved. How about you?"

She edged off the bed when Blake grasped her arm, pulling her back toward him.

"Oh, I'm hungry—for you."

A devilish grin played across his face. She tried to pull away, but his kiss came quick and undemanding. The tenderness of his mouth took her by surprise. Quite different from their uninhibited encounter an hour ago.

She broke the kiss. "Blake, we shouldn't. It's complicated. You, me, the situation we're in."

"A little late now don't you think?" He continued to kiss and nibble her neck. "What's wrong with enjoying each other?"

"Nothing. But...we hardly know each other." That had to be the lamest excuse yet. What was she, a teenager?

"If it'll make you feel any better, I plan on getting to know every inch of you, starting now."

"Blake, please. We need to talk."

He rolled on his back. "Okay, I'm listening."

"Help me nail Nathan." She tried her damnedest not to sound desperate. "You're the only one who can get me into the lab."

"I'll help you."

Did she hear him right? "What did you say?"

"I said I'll help. You look surprised."

"Actually—I am." He gave in too easily. The queasiness in the pit of her stomach quickly confirmed that thought. "Oh, I get it. This way you can keep a close eye on me for Nathan."

The lines at the corners of his eyes deepened. "Do you want my help or not?"

There was no denying the caustic tone in his voice. Had she made a mistake questioning his motives? No. Too many people had already died, and her life depended on Blake's honesty and commitment.

"I do want your help. No, I need your help. I just hope you're doing it for the right reasons. After everything that's happened, how can you blame me for being cautious?"

His bottom lip twitched, his expression tainted with anger. "Cautious is one thing. Untrusting is another. Did it ever occur to you that maybe Nathan had nothing to do with George's death?"

Was he kidding? The question was so ridiculous she chose not to answer.

"Come on, Whitney. Why can't you admit it is a possibility?"

"At this point, I'm not buying it."

"I thought journalists were supposed to be impartial until they had all the facts."

"Damn it." She rolled away from him. "George—is—dead."

Consumed by exhaustion, it took every ounce of strength to force back the tears. "I've bloody-well earned the right to have an opinion without all the facts."

"Hey. All I'm saying is—leave the door open a crack to other possibilities. I said I'd help. But we do it my way." He grasped her hand and kissed her knuckles. "Deal?"

His way? What choice did she have? He knew Nathan better than anyone and knew the security layout of the lab. Whitney closed her eyes for a long moment and then opened them. "Deal."

A voice on the TV caught her attention. She abruptly sat up, grabbed the remote from the nightstand and turned up the volume. "Look, it's the fire marshal."

Blake plumped the pillow behind his head and sat up.

"...a gas leak. But the exact cause will likely remain unknown due to the destruction of the structure," the fire marshal said, with the professional manner of a man who'd seen it all before.

A sour taste rose in her throat. *There goes any proof against Nathan.* She shut off the TV, dropped the remote on the bedspread beside her. While the town enjoyed the Independence Day picnics tomorrow, she'd be finalizing George's cremation. *God, she hated to say goodbye.*

As if sensing her distress, Blake rubbed her shoulder.

"You okay?"

Compared to what? After pulling the sheet over her breasts, she lay back down. "I've been attacked. Shot at.

The kindest man I've ever known was kidnapped, and then rescued, only to be killed in an explosion meant for me. Am I okay? No. I'll never be the same." Her eyes turned misty. "I still can't believe George is gone."

"I know you miss him. He cared a lot about you."

"Yeah, he did." She managed to smile. "I remember last year when I set him up on a blind date. George convinced me to drop by his apartment early and double-check his wardrobe choices. Thank goodness I did. When I got there, he looked like a giant eggplant sautéed in butter. A shimmering purple shirt from the '80s, which he claimed was black, and a pair of off-white, wrinkled golf pants. What a sight. He was always a cheery soul and a good friend, especially when my marriage ended."

"How long were you married?"

"A year and a half." *Too long*. "Mason wanted more than one woman in our marriage. His twenty-something assistant, and a few other playthings." Why was she telling Blake this? "How about you. Ever married?"

"Nope. Not my style."

His short and vague answer didn't surprise her. He seemed like a bed-them-love-them-then-leave-them kind of man. Exactly the type of men she'd dated since her marriage fell apart. No commitment, no complications. She propped herself up on one elbow and changed the subject. "We have a lot to discuss about Nathan."

Blake slipped his arm around her and snuggled her close. "Not now. We've got more important things to do."

"What could be more important than—"

He kissed her again, a deep, soul-searching kiss that

exiled her breath from her body and left her boneless, floating. The shrill sound of the phone ringing snapped them back to the real world.

"I need to answer it."

Blake kissed her forehead before he rolled off the bed with a groan. "I'll be in the shower."

As he walked naked to the bathroom, Whitney blindly reached for the phone. Nice ass. Full and shapely.

She sighed. "Hello?"

"Steel. I got your message."

It was her boss, Matt Wildell, calling from Florida. The second he mentioned her pain-in-ass co-worker Cliff Peterson, her blood boiled.

"You can't send Cliff here. It's not safe. Don't you understand? George is dead."

"I'm aware he's dead. Now don't be getting all emotional on me. You're a reporter first. This cloning story is huge."

She swung her legs over the side of the bed and sat up. "How—?"

"George let the cat out of the bag. The guy couldn't keep his excitement contained."

"He told you?" *More like you threatened George, which is one of your typical tactics.*

"Listen, if you're not up to the challenge, Peterson is."

Asshole.

"Steel. You still there?"

She forced her anger to a rolling simmer. "Yes."

In a cold, flat voice, he made it clear. "You've got forty-eight hours or Peterson becomes your new best friend. Get it done."

A short beat of silence, then a click on the other end.

Whitney slammed down the phone.

What a heartless bastard. Not one shred of empathy for a loyal twenty-year employee. The money-hungry head of WBNN only cared about ratings. Ratings equalled money. Dear God. Who was she fooling? Was she any better?

When Whitney had started at WBNN, her career had been at a standstill. Matt Wildell had personally groomed her in hopes to boost the station to the top. And she did just that. Whitney Steel was Matt's shooting star, complete with bleached blonde hair because Florida's viewers preferred blondes. He also claimed she was the only one who could keep the station at number one. Not true. Months ago, Cliff Peterson came on board and she knew Matt was preparing Cliff for a top spot. Her job. It appeared women reporters had a shorter shelf life at WBNN than men, like many other TV stations.

Peterson was an arrogant jerk, whose vulture style investigating techniques impressed the hell out of WBNN's top brass. A storm of emotions blasted through her and threatened to zap the last bit of energy she had left. Regret, guilt, sadness.

Forty-eight hours. Impossible. Whitney grabbed a pillow from the bed and heaved it across the room.

Blake stood in the doorway of the bathroom dressed in jeans, no shirt, and his hair screamed for a comb. His gaze shifted to the pillow on the carpet.

"Pillow fight? Or is something wrong?"

Whitney held his stare. The last thing she needed was Cliff Peterson nipping at their heels.

"We have a huge problem."

* * *

Blake sat at the rectangular table by the window and ran his fingers through his damp hair. "Any chance you can convince this Peterson guy to stay put until the end of the week?"

Whitney laughed, the kind of bark-like laugh used to make a point.

"Not a chance. You don't know Cliff. He'd sell his mother's kidney to be here yesterday. Anything to make my life miserable."

"Guess you two don't get along."

"Now that's an understatement. Don't be surprised if he shows up early. Nothing that man does surprises me."

"That's all we need. We'll have to figure out a way to delay his arrival."

She puffed out her cheeks in frustration. "How? It's not like we can cancel his flight."

No, but a delay of some sort. "Don't worry. I'll come up with something."

What began as a one-man undercover operation had turned into a friggin' circus with him as ringmaster slash babysitter. It was one thing to protect Whitney because he...cared about her. Shit. He was falling for her. Of all the dumb-ass things to do. Thirteen years as an agent and not once had he allowed himself to get close to anyone. Why now? Why Whitney?

It is not as if they could have a real relationship in the future. Once she learned that he's not who he claimed to be, she'd drop kick him, hard. Whitney deserved someone she could trust.

"I'm starved." She rose to her feet and draped the white bed sheet around her body toga style. "Could you order us something to eat while I shower, again?"

He noticed the dark circles etched under her eyes and the way her shoulders slouched when she spoke. "Sure, what do you want?"

"Anything, except shellfish. I'm allergic." The sheet trailed behind her like flowing fog as she walked to the bathroom and closed the door.

Blake scanned the room service menu. Little by little, he was learning more about Whitney, but not enough to know what she liked. Did she prefer salads? Chicken? Beef? Everyone loved French fries. Or did they? Frustrated, he settled on the gourmet burger, a grilled chicken sandwich, fries, a side salad and two beers.

After he ordered, he picked up his gun, checked the ammo, and then placed the SIG back on the table. Following the explosion at the house, he had tossed the kidnapper's gun, a .38 calibre Smith & Wesson into the ocean. Definitely an informed choice for a revolver and plenty effective. His gun was registered. The kidnapper's probably wasn't. He hoped like hell that Erik Friklin survived the night and was able to give them the answers they needed.

Blake had a more urgent problem. Before heading out into the hallway, he grabbed his cell phone and double-checked that the shower was running. He didn't need this Peterson character showing up, poking around. The guy would end up like George. Dead.

When had he developed a conscience? The moment he saw the pain in Whitney's eyes after George died. He shook his head and called his Bureau contact's private number.

"Hey, Mike."

Mike Jacobs sucked in a breath. "Christ man, where have you been? Chambers is pissed."

"Complications."

"Your cover hasn't been compromised, has it?"

Blake sure as hell hoped not. "Not that I know of." He gave the short version of the last twenty-four hours.

"Jesus. The old man is going to have a bird. He's been asking me every hour on the hour if I've heard from you. He wants to pull the plug on the mission."

"Cover my ass, Mike. I need a few more days. Just tell Chambers you haven't heard from me."

"I don't know, man."

"Look. I'll get the evidence against Shaw. I've worked too long on this to walk away now. Besides, Chambers won't pull the plug until I'm out."

Blake wanted to hear the cold steel click of his own handcuffs around Nathan Shaw's wrists. "I need a couple of favors, though."

"The old man will have our balls for breakfast. What do you need?" Jacobs asked.

"Run this name. Erik Friklin." Blake proceeded to spell out the last name. "Find out what you can. Also, a reporter, Cliff Peterson, will be heading to Vegas any-time within the next forty-eight hours. Have a sky mar-shal pull him from the flight and detain him. Be cre-ative. But believable."

"For how long?"

"As long as possible." Blake froze in mid-step. He didn't hear the shower running. "Gotta go."

"Be careful."

Blake shut off the phone, and stepped back into the

room, closing the door quietly behind him. He heard Whitney take a breath and smelled the sweet floral shampoo she used.

"Checking in with Nathan?"

He turned and faced her. "No. An ex-marine buddy of mine." That much was true. He and Mike Jacobs had spent time in the Marines before joining the Bureau. "He'll look after Peterson."

Her brows creased with worry. "What do you mean —look after? This guy isn't going to hurt Cliff, is he?"

"Of course not. Just slow him down enough to buy us more time."

CHAPTER FOURTEEN

D usk had thickened into darkness. Whitney dipped another French fry into the puddle of ketchup on her plate and took a bite. "Why'd you leave the Marines?"

"Too much death and destruction." Blake shoved his empty plate aside, and leaned back in the chair, draping his arm across its back. "My buddy, Jacobs, the guy I was talking to earlier, and I were stationed in Beirut in '83. Part of the multinational peacekeeping force. We watched a truck smash into the building where three-hundred Marines were sleeping. Then the driver detonated two-and-a-half-tons of explosives."

As Blake spoke, anger flickered in his eyes, and his tone hardened.

"I remember that." She recalled her father's disgust with some of his colleagues who'd wanted to use photographs of dead soldiers as shock treatment, hoping to discredit then president, Ronald Reagan.

"If I remember correctly, the Lebanese Shi'ite militants claimed responsibility. It must have been dreadful to be there." Probably the same sickening revulsion she'd experienced in New York covering the horrors of September 11th.

"It was worse than hell. Our headquarters collapsed, trapping dead and wounded soldiers under heaps of cement and cinder blocks." He picked up his bottle of beer and took a gulp before continuing. "Hundreds of men and women died. Many good friends. It wasn't supposed to be like that. When my time was up, I got the hell out."

Survivor's guilt. Whitney had seen it many times. Despite the sadness she felt for him, she was happy he opened up to her. So far, this had been the most she'd got out of him about his personal life.

He eyed her empty plate and grinned. "Have enough to eat?"

Whitney swallowed the last bite of her chicken sandwich. "More than enough, I'm stuffed." So full in fact, that now she wished she'd bought a pair of pants that at least had a bit of give to them.

They sat at the cramped table in awkward silence as if they were on a first date. Whitney should know. She'd been on enough of them over the years. She glanced at the clock. Eight-fifty-five. If this had been a real date, sometime in the next few hours she'd be deciding whether to see Blake again. Under different circumstances, she would.

Blake stood, peeled off his T-shirt and tossed it on the dresser.

Whitney watched, incapable of moving. Her pulse quickened.

He sauntered to the bed with the top button of his jeans unsnapped like a model in a Calvin Klein commercial. The man definitely had a built-for-action body, from the defined muscles of his chest to his firm ass.

Her heart galloped. Heat tingled between her legs.

"You're shredding that napkin."

"What?"

He stretched out on the bed with his arms folded under his head. "The napkin."

She was. Embarrassed, that the sight of him sent her common sense spinning, she balled the remnants and placed the paper wad next to her plate.

"You know, we should try to get some rest."

Rest? Not likely. She needed something to keep herself occupied, keep her mind off...sex. Time to discuss Nathan, come up with a plan, whether Blake liked it or not.

Whitney got up from the table, gathered her purse from the back of the wooden chair.

After dumping the contents on the bedspread beside him, she handed him a crumpled hand-drawn sketch. "What is this?"

Blake sat up. His jaw dropped open. "A map of the main lab area." He flipped the paper over examining every detail. "Where did you get this?"

"It was with the videotape in the package from Mason." She took a seat on the edge of the bed. "Is it accurate?"

"Yeah, it is." He picked up the plastic card. "Carman Lacey's security keycard. She reported it missing a month ago." He tossed it back on the bedspread. "It's useless now."

Whitney eyed the shiny silver card. "Why?"

"Once a card's reported missing, new cards are issued to all employees. Then the facility's security system is reset."

"Do keycards go missing often?"

"Nope. You mentioned back at the house, Mason

gave you a key. Can I take a look at it?"

Whitney's gaze snapped to the folded tissue next to her phone book. The idea of touching that key with Mason's blood on it felt like a boxer's right jab. Her skin prickled hot and she thought for sure her chest would cave in. The room's beige walls closed in. Colors fused together. The silver pile carpet melted into the burgundy curtains. "I—need some air." She hopped off the bed and rushed to the balcony doors.

Outside, the wind howled like a cyclone against the glass, but she slid the doors open anyway. Hot, muggy air flooded her lungs and whipped her hair across her face. *Breathe. Just breathe.*

"Are you okay?" Blake asked.

"I am now." Had she experienced a panic attack or was she just exhausted? Either way, she didn't want to feel like that again. After two more deep breaths, she felt calmer.

Lightning flitted, shooting fiery lances across the night sky. Below the second story balcony, trees swayed and dipped, shadows tap-danced like stick people around the swimming pool.

Something moved behind the dense foliage on the other side of the fence. She squinted.

Her breath caught in her throat.

It wasn't something. A person looked right at her.

What the hell? She shrank back into the room and flattened her body against the wall.

Blake's eyebrows raised. "You look like you've seen a ghost. What's wrong?"

"Someone's out there."

"What?" He jumped off the bed, grabbed his gun from the table. "Get back."

"In the trees behind the lounge chairs." A nasty shiver zipped down her spine. "Be careful."

Blake stepped slowly out onto the balcony. He returned, closed and locked the door.

"Well?"

"I didn't see anyone." After he pulled the curtains closed, he put his arm around her shoulders. "Look, you've been through a lot. You're exhausted."

She backed away from him, shaking, half with fatigue and fear, half with anger. "You don't believe me."

"I never said that." He set his gun next to the lamp on the nightstand. "All I said was—"

"You didn't see anyone. I know what I saw. Probably another one of Nathan's henchmen."

"Let's not jump to conclusions." Blake lay on the bed and gave her a deadpan look. "Could've been kids messing around. You're safe. Come get some rest."

For some reason, he loved to keep her wondering. Charming one minute—concerned the next, and then detached. As much as Whitney wanted and needed to feel safe, she didn't.

✳ ✳ ✳

Behind the inn, the wind roared off the ocean and whipped through the trees. Rain slashed and bit at his face. The shooter pulled the hood of his waterproof jacket tighter to shield his face. He wiped the moisture from his eyes with the back of his right hand. In his left hand, he clutched the .22 caliber rifle loaded with copper jacket steel ammunition.

Accurate and deadly. He should have been ready. No more mistakes. He couldn't wait to blow the bitch's head off.

From his vantage point deep within a row of cedar trees, he eyed two silhouettes in the second-story window.

He smiled.

The front desk clerk had been more than happy to divulge the room number, especially after the shooter had flashed his irresistible thousand-watt smile and a pair of one hundred-dollar bills. An easy mark— a young woman making minimum wage working the graveyard shift. But the girl talked too much, made him late.

Nothing would keep him from success now. Adrenaline bubbled through his veins and his heart pounded against his chest wall.

Before raising the weapon, he wiped the rain from his face one last time.

"Bye, bye bitch. This is for my father."

With his target in sight, he held his breath and squeezed the trigger.

Nothing happened.

He lowered the gun. The damn thing was jammed. The shooter glanced up at the window. He checked and double-checked the weapon again. Still jammed. *God damn piece of crap.* A burst of wind almost knocked him off his feet. The light in the room was off now. If he couldn't have her now, he'd send a reminder to make damn sure she knew he was a step behind her—watching, waiting for his next chance.

✳ ✳ ✳

Blake didn't lie. He hadn't seen anyone outside, but every nerve ending vibrated and told him differently. He eyed his gun on the nightstand. Other than Whitney's boss and the sheriff, no one knew they were at the hotel. Not even Nathan. Who was out there?

Beside him, Whitney had fallen asleep quickly dressed in one of his black T-shirts. He smiled as he watched the gentle rise of her chest with each steady breath.

His new partnership with her would test his patience to the limit. He'd bet his soul she hated giving up control when it came to going after Nathan. The woman was used to getting her own way. Not this time.

A window-rattling crack of thunder vibrated through the room and the balcony glass doors shattered to the carpet.

CHAPTER FIFTEEN

At two-twenty in the morning, Whitney wanted to lie down, close her eyes and block out the world, but she couldn't, due to the remaining police presence occupying the hotel room.

Earlier, she'd watched a technician pluck a bullet from the doorframe with a pair of oversized rubber-tipped tweezers, followed by a snap-happy photographer preparing to calculate the exact angle the shot was fired.

At least she wasn't crazy. She hadn't imagined someone by the pool earlier. Exhausted, but not crazy. Why hadn't the shooter taken a shot then? It made no sense, like a tickle of something unwanted crawling over her body. Why?

In the hall, Whitney sat on the gray-brown carpet with her back to the wall, her arms wrapped around her knees. Snippets of conversations flanked the whine of a vacuum cleaner kicking up dust and hint-o-lemon carpet deodorizer, the odor nauseating.

"You look dead tired." Blake crouched next to her holding a can of cola. "Did I miss anything?"

"You're looking pretty baggie-eyed too. Not much, just the hotel manager. The man couldn't stop apologizing for the 'huge' inconvenience. He even gave us a gift certificate for a free two-night stay."

"Hmm. Two nights." She felt his smile against her cheek, the heat of his breath on her neck. "Imagine what I could do to you over forty-eight hours."

Her skin tingled. An erotic image flowered in her mind. His hand wandered between her legs, his finger slipped inside her...

Damn it. "We both know that won't happen. Once we get what we want from Nathan, we'll be heading our separate ways." Why did she hate how final that sounded?

"Are you sure about that?"

Not at all. "Of course, I'm sure." He moved away from her. Relieved? Disappointed? Why was he so hard to read?

"How much are you going to tell the cops?"

"Not any more than I have to."

Blake looked down the hall. "Good, 'cause it's show time."

"What?" Whitney looked up at the man dressed casually in blue jeans, instead of his black, BDU-battle dress uniform.

Detective Garrison's expression changed. "Trouble certainly seems to follow you, doesn't it, Miss Steel."

More than you know. "It does appear that way."

Back in the room, Whitney sat at the end of the bed next to Blake while a cleaning woman finished shining the new glass balcony doors, and then left.

"Interesting choice of ammo, though." Garrison's eyes narrowed. "Winchester Silvertip."

"Used for long-range accuracy. Probably from a .22 caliber rifle. In this case, not very accurate taking into account the high wind and rain tonight. "

Garrison's bushy brows rose. "You've done some shooting?"

Blake cracked his knuckles. "I've done my share while growing up."

"I see." The detective's gaze shifted, settling on her.

"Now, are you going to tell me what's really going on?"

Whitney pushed a loose strand of hair behind her ear. All she had were a bunch of puzzle pieces, an undeniable gnawing in the pit of her stomach, and no hard evidence against Nathan Shaw. None. "I don't know who would do this."

The detective leaned back in the chair and crossed his feet. "Want to hear my theory?"

"Sure," Whitney said.

"You've pissed someone off. Done a story on them. Someone real important. Maybe a high up official."

She had definitely ticked Nathan Shaw off. "I've reported hundreds of stories over the years. Some might have painted a negative image, but that's what investigative reporting is about. An occupational hazard. That's not much of a theory."

"You must take me for a fool, Miss Steel." Garrison pulled out a small notebook from his wrinkled shirt pocket and flipped through the pages. "Let's see. Since you arrived in Florence, you've been...one, attacked at knife point. Interesting thing about that incident, the perp's DNA matched a crime scene in Las Vegas. Exactly where you two are headed tomorrow."

He gave his glasses a nudge, pushing them higher up on the bridge of his nose. "Either of you know a woman by the name of..." He flipped a page in his notebook. "Carmen Lacey?"

This time she didn't need to lie. She'd never met the woman. Whitney looked at Blake, but he didn't say a word. Instead, he rested his hands on his knees as if to stop from cracking his knuckles again. What was up with that? Why was he stalling? "Not me, but—"

Blake finally piped up. "Carmen Lacey was a scientist at ShawBioGen. The company I work for."

"What do you do there?"

"Security. Guys like me usually don't hang out with the academic crowd. I've never met the woman."

The detective gave Blake the once over before continuing. "Okay. Next. The house you were staying at explodes killing your co-worker, George Raines."

He remained silent for a long moment, studying her. "Three. Had a call from Pine Hills Cemetery. Your parents' monument was vandalized the same day you arrived in town. Reports of gunfire. Know anything about that?"

Blake jumped to his feet. "She said she didn't know."

An officer guarding the door stepped toward Blake. "It's okay." Garrison waved him away. "Sit down, Mr. Neely."

A few beats of silence passed. Blake popped his knuckles again and sat.

Whitney cleared her throat and fixed the steadiest gaze she could muster. "I was informed of the vandalism when I made the arrangements for George. I was shocked to hear about the damage done to my parents' gravesite. Totally sickened."

Did he believe her? His silence was answer enough. Not a chance. Okay, a partial lie. But still a lie. What choice did she have? He'd never believe the truth anyway.

This time the detective's gaze traveled to the door where the uniformed officer stood caressing his trimmed beard as if he were stroking a pet. "What do you think, Officer Hardy? A whole bunch of coincidences?"

The young officer straightened to attention. "No, sir."

"My thoughts exactly." The detective leaned in toward her. "Have I missed anything?"

Yes. The incident with the kidnapper at the lighthouse. Something Whitney needed to check into before leaving town. "Not that I know of."

Now that she'd heard the detective's list, something her father had said before he'd left for his last assignment in Colombia trickled through her mind.

"Honey, you can't choose your fate. Fate chooses you."

Was this her fate? Running scared? Being hunted like an animal?

Hunched over, she dragged a hand through her hair. With any luck, she'd pass out from sheer exhaustion and not have to think or answer any more questions. Not have to lie.

"Can't you see she's on the verge of collapse?" Blake put his arm around her shoulders. "The woman needs rest. She's been through a lot."

Detective Garrison nodded to the other officer. "I think we're done here for now." He stood and shoved his hands in his jeans pockets. "One thing's for sure. If the jail wasn't full tonight with holiday drunks, I'd hold you both in protective custody for a couple of days, just to see how my theory pans out."

She mentally weighed his threat. He had no legal grounds to keep them in Florence and he knew it.

On the way out, the detective patted her shoulder. "Enjoy the rest of your vacation, Miss Steel. Have fun in Vegas tomorrow."

A blast of icy cold seeped into her. A bone-chilling cold. Leaving Florence was like exiting one hell and walking into a nightmare worse than anything she could imagine. Nathan's turf.

❋ ❋ ❋

The phone rang, rattling Blake out of a deep sleep. He snatched the receiver from the nightstand in the middle of the first ring. "Yeah."

"Good morning, this is your seven-fifteen a.m. wake-up call," a spunky, pre-recorded female voice said on the other end. "Today's weather forecast calls for temperatures in the mid-eighties with lows in the seventies. Our red, white and blue continental breakfast is being served in the dining room. Thank you for staying at The Point Inn."

He stretched. His body howled with stiffness, his mouth dry as sawdust. A holiday breakfast? He hung up the phone. What were they serving? Blue scrambled eggs, red toast, and white bacon? Didn't sound appetizing. Actually, green eggs and ham came to mind, sitting on his grandmother's lap when he was a boy, and reading Dr. Seuss.

He stared at Whitney curled next to him, sound asleep. Her skin glistened, bathed in a golden stream of sunlight from the window. Her dark hair spread fanlike across the pillow. Man, she was beautiful. Immediately he was hard, and couldn't resist touching her breast, causing her to stir.

He wanted her. His body craved her, but he

shouldn't bother her. Today would be tough enough with George's cremation. He knew she was strong, but over the last two days, he'd watch that strength being stripped away, layer by layer, leaving her fragile and worn. Instead of touching her again, he forced himself to think about soggy blue pancakes and burnt red toast.

Nathan expected him on a flight back to Nevada with a videotape Blake didn't have in his possession. At least not yet. Before heading to the airport, a quick stop at the bank would remedy the problem.

He looked at Whitney again. He'd never felt like this before and wondered what it would be like waking every day seeing her face? What a stupid thought. Unrealistic and impossible.

He was a professional liar. He had deceived her from the first day they'd met at ShawBioGen. That was his job. Even if she forgave him for his lies, what about his other demon, a secret he'd rather keep hidden. If he decided to tell her he had killed a man to protect his cover, would she understand or walk away?

She'd walk away. Damn right she would, bucko.

Regardless of his feelings for Whitney, the job came first. He couldn't wait to see Nathan Shaw where he belonged—in an orange jumpsuit, behind bars. There had to be another connection between the wide-eyed weirdo and his sister, other than she had worked at ShawBioGen. And what about the small child in the videotape? He wasn't convinced that such a child existed. How could he? He'd never seen her, and he couldn't risk asking any of the employees.

Careful not to wake Whitney, Blake slipped out of bed, grabbed his cell phone and hobbled to the bathroom. With any luck, the kidnapper, Eric Friklin miraculously recovered and was willing to talk. He punched in the hospital's number. A minute later he heard the news.

"I'm sorry, sir. Mr. Friklin passed away early this morning."

CHAPTER SIXTEEN

L ate that afternoon, after a three-hour drive to Portland International, they boarded their flight to Las Vegas on time. Inside the aircraft, female heads shifted, their gazes trailing Blake down the aisle, especially the blonde little-pop-star-wannabe with her mouth gaping open. Whitney tightened the grip on her purse. How could she be jealous? They weren't together, not like a couple. Only partners.

Blake stopped at their assigned seats. "Aisle or window?"

"Window."

As she inched past him, his woodsy, musk scent drifted around her. Her heart beat faster. Why did the man have to smell so good?

Once Whitney snapped her seatbelt in place, a stewardess announced there would be a short delay. Fighting the lack-of-sleep hangover, Whitney rested her head against the seat and closed her eyes. The sugar-laden coffee she'd downed in the rental car sloshed in her stomach like dirty wash water and did nothing to help her fatigue.

Partners.

Her "so-called partner" never volunteered any information. He revealed only what he wanted her to know. Nothing more. Why hadn't he mentioned he was a volunteer sky marshal? Instead, she learned that tidbit the same time as the redhead making googly-eyes at him from behind the check-in counter. Between leaving the hotel and stopping at the bank to get the videotape, Blake revealed George's kidnapper died during the night. Why hadn't he told her this first thing this morning?

The mystery behind Blake that had intrigued her was getting old. Real old. They didn't have any real intimacy. And he wanted her to place her life in his hands. Do things his way. How could she?

If Blake wouldn't play fair, neither would she.

Once the plane finally took off, Whitney unfolded the Oregonian and noted the headline on top of page two.

HOUSE EXPLOSION KILLS FLORIDA MAN

Underneath, in smaller letters, the details. Details she already knew.

That morning, Blake had made breakfast for her and George. She left for the cemetery. Blake and George were alone at the house. What if Blake had something to do with the explosion? He had the opportunity. Hell, he was Nathan's, right-hand man. She tried to force the thought from her mind, to dismiss it as too unreal. She folded the paper and shoved it between the seats.

"Anything interesting?"

She glanced at Blake. "What?"

"In the newspaper."

"Not really." Something in her sagged. Saying goodbye to George had been difficult, felt dreamlike. Reality would hit hard after the memorial service for him in Florida—if she made it back alive. So far, the odds didn't look good. The sick game of cat-and-mouse had frazzled her nerves.

Across the aisle, two rows up, a man with brown wiry hair stared at her. Feeling strangely vulnerable, she turned away. Then it occurred to her. The shooter could be on the plane looking right at her.

* * *

Three hours after landing in Las Vegas, Blake checked the rearview mirror, confident that no one had followed them from the airport. Neon lights winked a chaotic rainbow against the windshield. It was good to be back in Vegas. He glanced at his silent passenger in the front seat of his pickup truck.

"Feeling any better?"

Whitney rolled the window up halfway. "How could I? I made a complete jackass out of myself."

"Hey, stop beating yourself up. How were you supposed to know that creepy guy on the plane was a major sponsor of WBNN?"

"I'm not supposed to assume. I let my emotions— no, my exhaustion and fear dictate my actions. Damn it. FloAgra Foods is the station's number one sponsor. I am so screwed."

"You're human. You made a mistake." He patted her knee and noticed the white-knuckled grip she had on her purse. "Everything will work out."

Did he believe that? No. After Whitney's outburst on the plane, she'd be lucky to secure a job as a weather girl's gopher.

"You make it sound like it's not a big deal. Don't you understand? I yelled at an innocent man, stuck my finger in his face and shouted, "What are you going to try next? Shoot me on the plane in front of all these witnesses?" She shook her head. "My God. I acted like a raving lunatic by accusing the head of FloAgra of being the shooter. Way to go, Whitney. Real professional. I'll be lucky to have a job to go back to."

Stopped at a red light, Blake envisioned Whitney on the plane, wide-eyed with anger when he'd grabbed her arm for a second time and threatened to restrain her. He'd calmed her just in time to ward off a male flight attendant ready to tackle her in the aisle. Man, he knew she was feisty, but he had never seen this side of her.

A couple beats of silence passed before she spoke again. "And why didn't you tell me you're a sky marshal?"

"You never asked."

Her expression turned to stone. "Get real, Blake. Why do you have to be so secretive?"

He grinned at her questioning tone. She was smart, too damn smart. "I'm not secretive. Like I said, you never asked. You should be thanking me for saving your ass with airport security. If I hadn't intervened, there's a good chance you'd be sitting in jail right now."

"Would you have really restrained me?"

"Yes. With pleasure." He winked, hoping to put her in a better mood. One thing was for sure, tonight after he delivered the videotape to Nathan, they needed to sit down and pound out a solid plan to get into the lab. Time was running out.

She stared out the side window, her hands still clutching her purse. "Thanks."

"You're welcome."

Not much truly scared Blake. But when that bullet had whizzed past him in the hotel room in Florence, he was terrified for the first time. Scared he'd lose Whitney.

He needed to keep her hidden, away from the main strip, and this looked like the perfect place.

Blake parked the truck outside the Fiesta Garden, a single floor, out-of-the-way motel doused in chipped terra-cotta paint.

"Well." He shut of the ignition. "It's not Caesars Palace, but you'll be safe."

❋ ❋ ❋

After Blake paid for the room, Whitney slammed the truck door with a grunt of irritation. In front of her, a neon sign idiotically blinked *VACANT ROOM*. Of course, they were vacant. Who the hell would want to stay here?

Blake grabbed her hand. "Let's go. Room five."

She opened her mouth to protest. Before she could say a word, the sound of men arguing came from the other end of the motel next to the gas station. This wasn't the time to complain.

Blake unlocked, opened the motel room door and turned on the light. "After you."

A wave of hot, musty air greeted her when she stepped inside. She froze, staring at the discolored blue carpet, not wanting to think about what those stains were. Her gaze shifted to the faded, hot-pink and orange-paisley bedspread, then to the matching curtains hanging from a bent rod. Were the walls really pink and...bumpy?

Whitney touched the wall and a piece of stucco crumbled to the carpet. "Really nice place."

"The main thing is that no one knows you're here.

Especially the guy with the gun." Blake locked the door and headed to the air conditioner. He turned the machine on. For a few moments, it coughed, changed to a loud buzz, and shot out a stream of cooler air.

When Whitney had first started out as a reporter, she'd stayed in some shabby motels, but this place won the award for disgusting. She walked beside the double bed and set her purse on the tiny wooden desk. Ironic that the battered desk had a small hole for a lock.

The key! A rush of adrenaline replaced exhaustion. Why hadn't she thought of it before? "The key Mason gave me."

"What about it?" Blake sat on the edge of the bed and stretched out his legs.

"The key belongs to a desk. When I interviewed Nathan in his office, I remember seeing two desks."

"That's right. But there's no way anyone could get his keys, though."

"Why not?"

"Because he keeps them on him."

Whitney grabbed her purse and stopped. She still didn't trust Blake. The way his eyes held untold secrets, the way he kept things from her, important things. What choice did she have? She didn't. After dumping the contents on the bedspread, she took one long, deep breath and handed Blake the key, still wrapped in white tissue. "I bet this is a copy."

He unfolded the tissue, exposing the blood stained, silver-colored key. "Looks like one."

"What ifs" bounced through her mind. She plunked down on the bed beside him. Someone close to Nathan had borrowed the master, copied it, and put it back. Carmen Lacey? Had Mason's girlfriend seduced Nathan to get the key? For some reason, she doubted that. "Has Nathan ever mentioned the key?"

"Nope. Just the tape of the kid. Which I need to get to him soon."

Perhaps Nathan didn't know about the key. Or he did, and that was why Carmen was dead. What about Blake's sister, Claire? Where did she fit in all of this? Whitney didn't like what she was thinking but couldn't stop herself from asking.

"Is it possible Nathan and your sister were lovers?"

Blake slapped his hands together and laughed, so hard, he slid off the slippery bedspread onto the carpet with a thud.

"I'm serious. Someone extremely close had to get that key from him. Close, as in naked."

"Shit, Whitney. You're way off. Claire had more taste than that. Nathan, the wide-eyed weirdo? You're nuts."

"You could be wrong. Maybe Claire simply chose not to tell you. Did you discuss with your sister every woman you've slept with?"

He crawled back up on the bed. "Of course not. All I'm saying is I would've known."

"Sometimes a woman tells a man what he wants to hear, even if it's not the truth." She noticed the twitch in his jaw, a sign for her to change the subject. "Are there cameras in Nathan's office?"

"No. The guy's paranoid about his privacy. Section C is his home and office."

"You're kidding? The man's worth billions and he lives on site?" In a sick and twisted way, that made sense. If Nathan lived on the premises, he could keep an eye on his cloning project. "We need to find what that key unlocks."

"We'll have to talk later." Blake stood and flattened out his jeans. "After I fill the truck with gas, I need to get the videotape to Nathan before he thinks I've double-crossed him. How about a late dinner when I get back, say around nine?"

Whitney checked her watch. Only quarter to six. Past the point of exhaustion, the last thing she wanted was to sit in the psychedelic motel room from hell and wait. With Blake's pickup parked outside, she could hide between the blocky toolboxes behind the cab and hitch a ride without him knowing. "Nine sounds perfect."

CHAPTER SEVENTEEN

Shadowy, silent desert stretched for miles on either side of the paved road. Blake leaned his stiff neck against the headrest and tried to ignore the lingering, faint powdery scent of Whitney's perfume. His hand tightened around the steering wheel. This time the woman had gone too far, suggesting that Nathan and Claire were lovers. "The hell they were."

Not his kid sister. Not the same girl he called "Nerdo" growing up. Impossible. Claire had more sense than to get tangled up with Nathan Shaw. Carmen Lacey probably copied the key, not Claire.

So how does a terrified-of-water, molecular biologist end up dead, on a boat, her death ruled accidental with no evidence to prove otherwise? Carbon monoxide poisoning. The words haunted him. He'd never believe Claire stepped on that boat of her own free will. Even though Blake had only seen his younger sister a dozen times in the past two years. Could she have changed that much, her fear of the water suddenly vanishing? Not likely.

According to the coroner, a boat's exhaust contained almost two hundred times more carbon monoxide than the average emissions from a car. Anyone standing, sitting or swimming near a boat's running engine risked being poisoned. There was no evidence that Claire died anywhere else other than inside that boat. Blake was convinced someone had lured her to the marina. Perhaps blocked the exhaust outlets, or tampered with the boat's engine, allowing gas to accumulate inside the cabin. Had that same person caused the explosion at the beach house that killed George?

Like all high-level employees at ShawBioGen, his sister had signed a confidentiality agreement and lived on-site. Blake had no clue what Claire was working on. Pharmaceutical research or something more sinister? Had she been aware of Nathan's cloning project? The child? Had she threatened to reveal Nathan as the demon of the decade? Blake wished he had the answers.

If the key that Mason gave Whitney unlocked a desk, which one? One of the two in Nathan's office, or in one of the other dozen executive suites at the facility? He would start with Nathan's office, and go from there. Not an easy task with eyes everywhere, human and otherwise.

Two miles from the concrete compound of ShawBioGen, the moon peeked from behind a mass of clouds, lighting the road ahead. Clusters of prickly pear cactus and rocks spattered the outer limits of the high security fence encasing the facility. Knowing desert creatures made a nightly stroll across the road, he slowed the truck. He didn't feel like scraping up roadkill tonight. Unless of course, the roadkill was Nathan Shaw.

Blake glanced at the videotape on the seat. The wide-eyed weirdo should be happy to have his precious tape back. Not that it would stop the attacks on Whitney. For now, she'd be safe at the Fiesta Gardens.

His cell phone rang. The hairs on the nape of his neck prickled. He hoped like hell the call wasn't from his Bureau contact, saying that Whitney's co-worker had arrived in Las Vegas and was causing a ruckus. He snatched the phone from the dash. A few seconds passed with nothing but crackling static. "Damn cell phones." He fought the urge to toss the piece of crap out the window.

Then he heard Nathan's voice.

"Got my tape?"

Blake leaned to the right as he negotiated a tight bend in the narrow road. "Yes."

"Where are you?" The phone cut out. A long beat of hollow, airy silence followed.

"A mile or so from the entrance. Can you hear me?"

"Just getting back in town. Meet me—heliport in—an hour."

The call disconnected.

Blake dropped the phone on the seat. Too bad he hadn't known Nathan had been out of town. The perfect opportunity to search his office, missed.

He stopped outside ShawBioGen's main gates and flicked on the truck's interior light. Why could he still smell perfume? It was as if Whitney was in the truck. After he checked the cab of the truck, he shook his head and shut off the light, convinced his lack of sleep was playing tricks on him.

Once inside his living quarters, he gave the thumbs up to the so-called hidden camera in a fake plant above the abstract painting in the living room. Eyes were everywhere, except the bedroom. He'd hoped those prying eyes would offer some insight into his sister's life at the facility. But the tapes had been mysteriously erased as if Claire had never existed.

Knowing his boss' obsession with punctuality, Blake quickly undressed and ran a hot shower. The last thing he needed was to be late.

✳ ✳ ✳

Whitney poked her head out between the chunky black toolboxes lining the sides of the back of the pickup. Stars winked in the night sky, and a cool desert breeze ruffled her hair. She shivered and zipped up her fleece-lined sweatshirt.

What a ride. Her butt was cold and probably bruised. Her back and legs ached from being confined in such a tight space for the two-hour trip.

Traveling in cargo wasn't something she normally did, but she needed to know what Blake was hiding, like a deep itch she couldn't scratch. She had to be extra careful. Her curiosity had already played a role in George's death and probably Mason's as well. But if she didn't take the chance, who would?

She slowly stood and stretched. Her feet felt heavy as if they no longer belonged to her. After a minute or two, the circulation returned in her legs. She hauled her body over the side of the truck, welcoming the steady ground beneath her feet. This had to be the craziest idea she'd ever come up with.

The facility looked desolate at night, except for floodlights in the distance, freezing everything under a ghostly haze. Outside the octagon-shaped bungalow, a lamppost illuminated a cement walkway intersected with multi-sized rocks, junipers and a variety of colorful cacti. *Stay low.*

She crouched below the front window camouflaged

with horizontal blinds and took off in a bent-kneed run to the back of the house. Through a partially open window, she heard the shower running. A quick search inside was all she needed, then back in the truck for the long ride back to the motel. No one would know she'd ever been there.

Whitney peeked around the corner. As she turned the doorknob, her pulse raced in anticipation. It wasn't locked. She slipped inside.

The only light in the kitchen came from a low-watt bulb above the stove. The stale air felt ten degrees warmer than outside. She scanned the small, but cozy dining area. No dirty dishes in the sink. Oddly spotless for a man. An answering machine rested on the counter. No flashing message light. Whitney had no clue what she was looking for. Something. Anything that would offer some insight into Blake the man.

The shower stopped.

Her pulse flickered somewhere in the back of her throat. If Blake caught her...

She clutched her purse and sprinted along a narrow hallway that opened into the dimly lit living room. Skidding to a stop behind a couch, she dropped and curled into a ball.

His fresh, clean scent caught her attention first. His socked feet came into view. She swallowed the lump of fear in her throat.

On the opposite side of the room, she watched him slip on his shoes. The lamp clicked off. A door opened and then shut with a thud. Blake's truck revved, and the grumble of the engine disappeared into the night.

Whitney sat up, slouched against the back of the couch, and searched her bag for her keychain light. The concentrated LED beam would be perfect for snooping. She stood and turned on the compact light. A soft red glow projected across the room. Above an entertainment center housing a flat screen TV and mini-stereo system hung an oil painting that looked like a swirling, splattering mess of regurgitated baby food. Carrots and peas to be exact. No wonder she never liked abstract art. It made no sense. Hmmm. No newspapers, books or music CDs. Whitney ran her fingers across the oval shaped coffee table. Not a speck of dust. Either Blake was a neat freak, which she doubted, or ShawBioGen supplied a cleaning service. Another way for Nathan to spy on his workers.

In the bathroom, the air hung heavy with dampness and the scent of deodorant soap. She picked up an open bottle of cologne from the bathroom counter. The woodsy scent made her skin tingle. Her thoughts touched on their sexual encounter at the hotel in Florence. His hands, his mouth, exploring her body. She jammed the brakes on that line of thought and opened the medicine cabinet. Shaving cream, toothpaste, eye drops. No over-the-counter medications. Did the guy ever suffer a headache or a hangover? Apparently not. Strange.

Further down the hall, she aimed the light inside the bedroom. Darkness shrank into the corners of the room, revealing a double bed made with tight hospital-type corners. No way had Blake made the bed. She crossed the room to a wooden highboy dresser and grasped a slip of paper with a phone number and the name "Nancy" scribbled on it. Probably a woman he'd met in a casino. A showgirl or stripper. Whitney grinned, crumpled the paper and stuffed it in her pants pocket. Tough luck, Nancy. Not tonight.

* * *

Blake arrived at the core building's heliport with ten minutes to spare. A silver helicopter with a white "S" on the side, veered left, stopped in mid-air, hovering over the well-lit roof. The machine lowered, the landing skids bounced on the large red X then rested with a loud thud. The downdraft of the blades roared a blast of hurricane-force air in Blake's direction. He shielded his eyes from the dust and pelting debris.

The helicopter door opened. Nathan appeared with his briefcase in one hand and his coat over his arm. He strutted toward Blake with his back bent under the wind from the blades. As the helicopter's engine slowed and quieted, Blake handed Nathan the videotape. Nathan's smug expression revealed an arrogant air of conquest.

Blake followed his boss down a dozen steps into the waiting elevator. In the polished steel walls, Nathan's face looked distorted, like a bird with mumps.

"How is our beautiful Miss Steel?" A sneer curled Nathan's lips. "Alive and well I presume."

You know damn well she's fine. Blake paused. "She's okay. A bit shaken after the explosion."

"She'll get over it. An unfortunate accident, I hear. I do know she's in Vegas."

What didn't the bastard know?

"I wouldn't expect anything less from a reporter of her caliber." Nathan's voice dropped a fraction lower. "Tell me, whose side are you on?"

Blake's gut twisted. "I wasn't aware there were sides, Nathan. You sent me to Florence to get your videotape. I did that. She gladly handed it over."

"Of course." Nathan grinned. "Was that before or after you screwed her?"

Blake's muscles tightened. *Creep.* It took every ounce of willpower not to flatten the little prick's face into the floor of the elevator. "Does it matter? You've got what you wanted."

Nathan set his hand on Blake's shoulder. "I do hope you enjoyed every inch of her because I have a feeling our Miss Steel won't be with us much longer."

❋ ❋ ❋

Blake's cell phone rang again. "Yeah."

"It's Emerson. We've got a Code Five."

Code Five? An unauthorized person on site? It must be a mistake. Unless someone dropped in from the sky, no one could penetrate ShawBioGen's security. "Morgan, are you sure?"

"Quite. A woman."

A woman? Blake clutched the phone so tight he nearly crushed the damn thing. Whitney. That dumb… "I'm on my way. I'll look after it."

"Too late. According to protocol, I just deployed Bravo team."

Blake's gut clenched. Christ, those guys would kill her. Whitney had no idea the trouble she'd unleashed by sneaking into the facility. How the hell did she do it?

The elevator came to a halt on Level C. The doors opened. Nathan took a step then stopped. "Is there a problem?"

"Looks like another security breach. Nothing I can't handle."

Blake noticed a slight flicker of uncertainty in Nathan's eyes, and his mouth twisted into a shifty grin. "If it's that bobcat again, this time shoot it between the eyes. I'll be in my office."

The elevator doors slid closed.

That damned woman. This could cost him his job. His cover. And if he didn't get to Whitney before Bravo team, it could cost him her life.

❋ ❋ ❋

Blake would not underestimate Whitney again. Obviously, she had given him the slip at the motel. His first reaction had been shock and anger, his second, her survival. He'd successfully halted Bravo team before they burst into his house. These guys were trained to contain security breaches before the problem escalated. They were tough, retired Marines and rogue ex-cops, highly skilled in weapons and hand-to-hand combat. One wrong move from Whitney and they'd shoot to kill.

Blake checked himself mid-thought and wiped the sweat from his forehead with the sleeve of his jacket. Five hundred yards away, he sat in the Humvee and squinted through a pair of night vision binoculars, watching the green-hued twelve-man team scramble around his living quarters.

At least this way, Blake was in control.

The two-way radio snapped to life. "Team leader. Perimeter established. Target in sight."

Blake picked up the radio. "Roger, that. Wait for my order."

"Roger."

Whitney had put him in a tricky position, forced him to protect months of undercover work. With all eyes on him, Blake needed this public display of force to continue to show his allegiance to Nathan. He cracked his knuckles and grabbed his gun from the seat. "Showtime."

* * *

What if she were caught? Whitney envisioned being arrested, thrown in jail amid prostitutes and drunks. Get a grip. What if Blake came back? She shook off the unsettling thoughts and continued to poke around.

What was wrong with this picture? Nothing suggested Blake lived here. No photographs. Nothing personal. A ghost lived here. What type of music did he enjoy? What kind of food did he love or hate? Where did he live before working for Nathan?

Disappointed, she drew a deep breath and opened the top drawer of the dresser.

A tall shadow raced by the window, and Whitney froze.

CHAPTER EIGHTEEN

Something creaked.

Whitney's heart slammed against her chest. She didn't know what she'd heard but getting caught wasn't part of the plan. She turned off the flashlight and set the keychain in her purse as quietly as possible. She could hide. In the closet. Under the bed.

The room exploded with light. Rifles clicked in unison. The scent of cologne and cigarette smoke surrounded her.

"Hands up where I can see them!"

The harshness of the man's voice made her cringe. She raised her hands and fought to keep her purse from sliding off her shoulder.

"Put the bag on the floor. Then turn around, slowly."

Not wanting to give the man a reason to harm her, she did as he ordered.

Four men, dressed in brown and cream camouflage gear, stood in front of her like skilled hunters with their assault rifles aimed at her chest.

Her breath caught in her throat, and she tasted bitter fear.

The tallest man, with a jagged scar on his right

cheek, stepped forward. His eyes narrowed. "On the floor. Now."

"Okay. Okay." She lowered to the carpet and sat cross-legged. What would happen to her? The vibration of approaching footsteps seized her attention.

Please let this be Blake. He'd help her. Wouldn't he?

Blake strolled into the room with his jaw clenched. Blue veins at his temples pulsated, reinforcing the seriousness of her actions.

He spoke low and fast. "If she moves, shoot."

For a moment, Whitney was too stunned to react, mouth open, gasping in disbelief at Blake's stinging order. What was he doing? Had he lost his mind?

"I'm—sorry." She struggled to retain a steady voice. "I—shouldn't have—"

"You're trespassing on private property." Deaf to her words, Blake marched behind her and dragged her to her feet. When the steel handcuffs clicked around her wrists, the other men lowered their weapons, stepped back and huddled in the doorway.

"Let's go." Blake snatched her purse from the floor and nudged her toward the hall.

Where was he taking her? She wanted to ask but bit her tongue in fear of making things worse.

Another man, with hair similar to rusty steel wool, held the door open while Blake ushered her out of the house. Stopping under the lamppost, Blake let go of her arm and spoke to the tall man. "Good work, Sawyer."

The man turned, and spit on the ground. "Sure you can handle her?"

Blake didn't miss a beat. "Easily."

"Who the hell is she? How'd she get past security?"

The men circled Sawyer and Blake as if they were

around a raging campfire, waiting to hear a scary story.

"You guys will love this." Blake dug his foot into the gravel. "She's a reporter who thinks ShawBioGen is cloning humans."

To Whitney's irritation, the men roared into a chorus of laughter, except for Blake. He grinned, somewhat amused by their reaction.

A skinny man with buckteeth edged toward her. "Holy shit. If that's true, could the boss clone another one kinda like her? Maybe two inches taller with bigger boobs."

Jackasses. Who was she dealing with? A bunch of immature frat boys with guns?

"Apparently she hid in the back of my pickup." Blake gave her arm a shake. "Didn't you?"

"Yes."

Even though her reply was scarcely audible, Sawyer shook his head. "Smart woman."

"Not smart enough. She got caught." Blake stared at her. "Missed the cameras inside."

Why hadn't she been more careful? Her skin crawled at the thought of unseen eyes watching her. Were Nathan Shaw's employees aware their sick and twisted boss observed their every move? Probably not.

"You want Russell here to interrogate her?" Sawyer leveled his gaze on the shorter man beside him. "He's been brushing up on his skills."

Interrogate? Whitney looked at the pint-size man picking his teeth with the edge of his thumbnail. An imperceptible note of pleading flooded the man's face.

God help me.

Blake caught her elbow and pulled her hard against him. "Nope. I'll take it from here."

Sawyer slapped Blake on the shoulder and then nodded to the others. "Move out."

Whitney watched the group, one after another, load into a black Humvee and speed away.

A chill crept over her skin. Her stomach jumped. She peered into the shadows, intent on hearing the slightest sound. Lights were on in the nearby houses. Why hadn't anyone come out to see what was going on? They had to know something was up. Strange.

Blake's voice sliced her thoughts. "What the hell were you thinking?"

She shriveled at the hard tone of his voice. "I understand you're upset—"

"For Christ sakes, Whitney. Those guys could've killed you. That's what they're trained to do." His eyes darkened. "Come on." His fingers clamped around her forearm and he hustled her toward another Humvee parked four houses away.

Whitney could barely keep up with him. Her feet dragged in the gravel. "Will you slow down? You're hurting me."

Blake stopped next to the vehicle, his expression deadpan, and his eyes hard. He flung open the passenger side door. "Get in or I'll put you in myself."

Her spine stiffened in defense. She shook his hand free from her arm. "Let go of me."

After stepping up into the Humvee, Whitney lost her balance and plunked down into the seat. The handcuffs pinched her wrists again, but she never said a word. Blake yanked the seatbelt over her shoulder and locked it in place. He slammed the door, went around to the other side of the truck and hopped into the driver's seat.

She'd never seen him this angry. Regret stabbed at her heart. Her reckless curiosity had caused another complication. All she had wanted to do was learn more about Blake. Why he evaded her questions? What he was hiding, and could she trust him?

"Where are you taking me?"

He jammed the key into the ignition. "To Nathan."

For a second her heart stopped. "Are you kidding?"

Whitney interpreted his long beat of silence as a no. Her body trembled. The man she'd slept with, the man she had feelings for, was about to deliver her into the hands of a killer. He had lost his mind.

"Thanks to your dumb-ass stunt, you've left me with no choice."

"But you can't. Nathan will—"

"Damn right I can." He started the engine and floored the gas pedal. "And you'd better be prepared to give the Academy Award performance of your life. Otherwise, we're dead."

❃ ❃ ❃

During the short drive back to the complex, Blake glanced at Whitney. Every curve of her body spoke defiance. Her arms had to be sore and heavy from being held behind her back. Tough. He gritted his teeth. He didn't give a rat's ass why she snuck into the facility. Damned nosey woman. She had no idea the trouble they were in.

The motion-activated lighting at the rear of the security building cast a golden glow. Blake squeezed the Humvee into a parking spot next to the entrance and shut off the engine. As the head of security, he had a hell of a lot of explaining to do. To Nathan. A tight knot formed in his gut. He stared out the window for a long moment and cracked his knuckles. This had better work.

Whitney's voice sliced the silence. "Has anyone ever told you that's a really annoying habit?"

He looked at his fingers then at Whitney. "Can't be any more annoying than finding the woman I thought I'd left in a motel room back in Las Vegas rifling through my underwear."

"I'm sorry." She wiggled in the seat. "I made a bad choice."

He removed the keys from the ignition and shoved them in his jeans pocket. Obviously, it wasn't in the woman's nature to be cautious. Whitney leaped without looking and left a long trail of trouble. "Seems to me you've made more than one bad choice lately."

She frowned, and he caught a glimpse of indignation in her eyes.

"That was low. I didn't kill Mason and George. Your boss did. Now how much longer are you going to make me wear these handcuffs?"

"However long it takes. We're playing this charade by the book. Following protocol."

"Which means?"

"The cuffs stay on. You'll be searched and questioned inside."

She raised her chin and shot him a cool stare. "Does Nathan know I'm here?"

"He will." Blake peered into the rearview mirror. "It's my job to notify him." He stretched his arm across the back of her seat and laid his hand on her shoulder. "Look. We had a deal. Remember? I'd help you get into the lab, my way when the time was right. All you've done is complicated things."

"You're still going to help me, aren't you?"

Faced with the direct question, he wanted to teach her a lesson, make her squirm. He reached for the door handle. "I don't know."

"Please, I'm sorry. I can't do this alone. You know the ins and outs of the complex. And you know Nathan. I need you."

She lowered her head, and for a second Blake almost believed her.

He wasn't getting suckered in this time around. "If you want my help, you're going to march inside and convince everyone that you did this on your own. Got it?"

Her eyes widened. "Yes. Anything."

Blake spied Norm Camaron, one of his security guys, lighting a cigarette outside the entrance. "We'd better get going."

Blake grabbed Whitney's purse and hopped out of the vehicle. A sharp wind bit through his jacket. Damn cold desert air. After opening the passenger door, he undid the seatbelt and lifted Whitney by the waist out of the vehicle.

Norm rose from the shadows. A halo of cigarette smoke followed. "So, this is our breach." He scrubbed a hand over his face and surveyed Whitney from head to toe. "Hard to believe a woman made it inside."

"She did. Guess there's a first for everything." Blake gave Whitney a gentle push in Norm's direction. "Put her in the interrogation room. I'll be there in a few minutes."

"Will do." Norm tossed his half-smoked cigarette to the pavement and stomped the butt with his shoe.

"Let's go."

Without a backward glance, Whitney strolled ahead of the man and through the automatic doors.

Her performance so far was believable. The real test would come soon.

While Norm was busy with Whitney, Blake ducked into the restroom, the only private area of the facility. Luckily, it was deserted. He chose one of the dozen stalls, locked the door and searched through Whitney's purse.

He retrieved the key Mason had given her, the hand-drawn maps of the lab she'd shown him on the flight to Vegas. He discovered something else—a letter from Mason. Information Whitney had failed to mention. She kept things from him, the same way that he hid his identity. She didn't trust him. And he didn't trust her as far as he could throw her.

The restroom door swooshed open. Boots clicked on the glossy white tile floor.

Blake stuffed the items into his jacket pocket, waited a minute or so, flushed the toilet, and then left.

At the rear of the main security hub, he peered through the square two-way window of the interrogation room. Whitney sat forward awkwardly at a rectangular table with her ankles crossed, staring at the stark walls. The camera anchored in the ceiling corner moved slightly, catching every breath.

What would Nathan do with her? Blake shook off the unsettling thought.

Behind him, the atmosphere transformed, charged with chit-chat, employees itching to get sneak a peek of the woman who'd breached their boss' multi-million-dollar security system.

Blake's nerves tightened. The last thing he needed was a bloody freak show. He slipped inside the interrogation room and closed the door.

"Let's get this over with." He wrenched the blind down over the two-way glass.

Whitney shot him a bewildered look, unsure of what to do next. He tilted his head in the direction of the camera, reminding her they weren't alone. "Stand up and I'll remove the handcuffs."

Whitney stood.

He fished the key from his jeans pocket and unlocked the handcuffs. She rubbed her red wrists.

"Now I have to search you for weapons." He knew damn well she didn't have any. All part of the show.

He moved in front of her, so close he felt the heat from her body. Their eyes met. While she stood with her hands clenched at her sides, Blake unzipped her sweatshirt, his arm brushed against her breast. The blood zoomed to his groin. He wasn't supposed to enjoy this.

He explored the soft lines of her back, waist, hips and down to her ankles, then up both legs. How could searching a woman who pissed him off on a regular basis be such a turn on? God damn it. Another minute or so he wouldn't be able to hide his hard on.

When he checked the back pocket of her pants, he pulled out the piece of paper scribbled with Nancy's phone number, a waitress he'd met in one of the casinos.

Now he understood. That reporter brain of hers never quit. Whitney snuck into the complex to learn more about him. If she only knew he had put the number in plain view to make his cover more believable, to show he had a life outside of ShawBioGen, because the housekeeping spies reported to Nathan, guaranteed.

This could work to his advantage. Blake tossed the crumpled paper on the table. "Want to enlighten me?"

A momentary look of discomfort crossed her face. "Not really."

Come on, Whitney. You're going to have to do better than that. An odd sensation descended over him, and he felt Nathan's presence long before the door opened.

CHAPTER NINETEEN

When Blake's large hands finished gliding over her body, their gazes locked. For a moment, Whitney forgot where she was. She hated the way he made her feel. The butterflies that fluttered in her stomach, the way the room grew so hot.

He stepped away from her, staring at the door as if in a trance.

"Blake, what is it?"

Before he could respond, footsteps and muffled voices sounded outside the room.

Nathan.

She shivered. The door opened.

Nathan stepped inside, impeccably groomed, with crease-free, oxford gray pants and a stiff white shirt. The door closed behind him with an unsettling clunk.

He stared at her. His eyes hard, black marbles.

Rapid thoughts fired through her mind. She could try to escape. She'd never make it out of the facility alive. For now, she appeared trapped in a room with a killer.

Her gaze snapped to the ceiling. He wouldn't dare try anything with Blake present and the camera rolling.

Would he? No, that wasn't his style. He was a coward; he had others do his dirty work. She remained on her feet, steeling her nerves to face whatever might happen.

Nathan waved his hand in the air. "Blake, leave. Wait in my office."

Blake's jaw tightened, clearly not happy by the dismissal. Before he left, he glanced at her with a flash of reassurance in his eyes. Blake had the key. He could check Nathan's desk. A certain satisfaction rippled through her.

Nathan angled his head and stretched his neck. "Now sit, Miss Steel."

His emotionless voice and eerie calm chilled her as much as the sterile room. Refusing to be treated like a puppy in obedience class, Whitney folded her arms over her chest. "I'll stand."

"I'm not asking." Nathan swiftly sidestepped the table, grabbed her shoulder and squeezed, forcing her body down onto the steel-framed chair.

The man is insane. "Don't touch me again."

Nathan bent over her, his bony face inches from hers. "Remember where you are, Miss Steel. You're in my house, uninvited."

His moist, cigar-laden breath almost gagged her. "And what are you going to do if I misbehave? Shoot me like you did Mason? Or blow me up, like George?"

He straightened. "I have no idea what you're talking about. Unfortunate accidents I presume."

"You mean orchestrated accidents, planned by you. Your hands might not be covered with blood, but that doesn't mean you didn't pull the trigger. You can hide behind your billions, but you won't be the first or last so-called genius to get caught. You'll make a mistake and when you do—"

"If I were you, Miss Steel, I'd spend your time more wisely, looking deep into your past." A mocking sneer cut across his face. "The past has an interesting way of coming full circle."

A sour taste rose in her throat. Her past? What the hell did that mean? The sinister bastard would do anything to throw her off track.

He's a lunatic.

Nathan slipped his hands into his pants pockets. "I must applaud you, though. Very ingenious hiding in the back of Blake's truck. You're the first human to penetrate my security system." He slammed his fist on the table. "And the last. If I didn't know better, I'd think my trusted employee helped you out."

"Come on. Do you really believe that? Blake's nothing more than your puppet. He works for you. So let's get down to why I'm here. You're hiding a cloned child somewhere in the facility."

"You have quite an overactive imagination. I can see why you chose a career in reporting, Miss Steel. But need I remind you, real journalists deal in facts." He laughed; a vicious, nasal sound that bounced off the white-tiled walls.

She wanted to leap out of the chair and strangle him. Instead, she laced her hands together atop the table. "I deal in facts."

"I disagree. I don't kill. In fact, I help others by developing medications that cure diseases and improve lives. In particular, genetic illnesses and recessive disorders that devastate families, such as Menkes Syndrome. Apparently, you didn't read the press kit you were given."

From the background information Whitney had gathered on Nathan, she remembered his sister died in infancy from Menkes Syndrome—the cells' inability to absorb copper. The disorder caused severe cerebral degeneration and arterial changes, resulting in death.

The hell with your press kit.

"Give me a break. We both know ShawBioGen is nothing more than a money-making front to conceal what you're really doing. Cloning humans."

The man showed no reaction. Not even a twitch.

"Rumors like that rise like dust storms in this part of the country, Miss Steel. You're chasing a ghost."

Her stomach soured then her body flooded with resolve. With her elbows on the table, she leaned forward. "Then consider me a ghostbuster. I will expose what you're doing."

For a long moment, they stared at each other engaged in a potent but silent battle.

"Do you believe in God, Miss Steel?"

Where on earth was he going with this? "My religious beliefs are none of your business."

"Such a young woman to have so many losses in her life."

"Don't you dare pretend to know me."

His mouth twisted in ridicule. "Hit a nerve, did I? I know more than you think."

He pulled up another chair, and sat across the table, watching her face like a hawk. If he wanted a reaction, she refused to give him one.

"Now let's see. You're an only child. When you were thirteen your mother was killed by a drunk driver. You lost your father to militants in Colombia. Very sad. Your marriage to the senator ended in infidelity, on his part. And your inability to carry a pregnancy has left you lonely and childless."

Whitney's nerves stretched to the breaking point. Emotion and action twisted together. She raised her arm to slap him across the face. "You bastard."

Nathan didn't so much as blink. He snatched her wrist in mid-air. An angry flush crept up his scrawny neck. He smashed her arm onto the table, releasing her.

His eyes widened, and his voice came at her like a cannon shot. "Keep your nose out of my business."

He stood, shoving the metal chair aside, and stalked to the door. "Go back to Florida, Miss Steel or the next funeral could be yours."

✻ ✻ ✻

Blake's abrupt discharge from the interrogation room turned into an unforeseen opportunity. Ten long months and he'd never been alone in his Nathan's office. A setup? Maybe.

He hoped Whitney was okay. She was far tougher than she looked. Still, worry gnawed at his gut. He'd heard a faint undercurrent of fear in her voice, something Nathan wouldn't pick up, but a seasoned agent would.

They wouldn't be in this situation if he hadn't messed up at the motel. He was guilty of the oldest mistake in FBI world. He'd dropped his guard.

In the elevator, Blake turned his cell phone on. "Yeah, Norm. Is the boss still busy with the woman?"

"As far as I can tell. Thought it was a bit odd, though, he told me to kill the video in the room. Guess he wanted some privacy."

Christ. Not a good sign. If that asshole laid one finger on her...

Blake might not have been able to help his sister, but he would do his best to protect Whitney. "Let me know when he's done."

"Sure thing."

Blake ended the call and tucked the phone into his jacket pocket as the elevator stopped on the second floor.

In the corridor, he punched the seven-digit code in the electronic keypad. The double steel doors clicked and opened. Nathan's inner sanctum reeked of wealth and the spicy smell of imported cigars that hung in the air in spite of the spray deodorizers the cleaning staff used.

Blake snatched the key from his pocket and hurried across the carpet. In the middle of the room, he stopped in his tracks. Which desk? The small antique one? He'd better make the right choice because he wouldn't get another chance. After deciding on the oversized mahogany desk next to the bookshelves filled with leather-bound books, he eyed Nathan's appointment book. A notation scribbled in red ink stood out.

Man of the Year Award Dinner-tomorrow-8pm.

His attention shifted to the gaudy, frosted glass statues gleaming under the recessed lighting. What a joke. More like Madman of the Year. Blake couldn't wait for the wide-eyed weirdo's fan club to learn the truth.

Blake searched the unlocked drawers first. He discovered pens and paperclips, a handful of lighters, and dozens of meaningless documents filed alphabetically in the right bottom drawer. Nothing interesting or incriminating. Every muscle, every nerve stilled as he eased the key into the top middle drawer's lock and turned.

Click.

He hadn't realized he had been holding his breath until he flexed his fingers around the brass handle and pulled open the drawer. Scribbled on a piece of company letterhead was a name.

Andrew West, June 30th, Northwestern Flight 244, 2:25pm.

Who was this guy? A business associate? The guy trying to kill Whitney? The name was important, otherwise, why lock it up?

The elevator dinged.

Blake looked up. Shit. Why hadn't Norm called?

Time seemed to stop. Footsteps. Heavy, pissed-off-footsteps.

Blake didn't relish getting caught. He closed and locked the drawer.

By the time Nathan entered the room, Blake was sitting on the loveseat pretending to be absorbed in a genetic engineering magazine. Sweat pooled under his arms and his heart thumped in his chest. That was close. Too friggin' close.

Nathan glared at him, his eyes on guard, like a pit bull ready to attack. A nervous tic twitched above his right eye. Whitney had the man fuming.

Blake set aside the magazine. "We need to re-evaluate the facilities' security needs immediately."

Nathan pressed the panel to the right of his desk. A fully stocked bar swung out. Annoyance rippled over his face. "Tell me." He removed the lid from the crystal scotch decanter and poured a drink. "Why did you bring that woman here?"

The words spilled out with the jerky quickness of

a person high on sugar. The question hadn't surprised Blake. It was expected.

He'd learned long ago, years before joining the Bureau, how to control his responses and reactions in any given situation. Besides, he still had a trump card to play, a gesture that would reinforce his loyalty. At least he hoped.

Blake stood. "I didn't know she was in my truck." He dug into the breast pocket of his T-shirt. "But when I searched her purse, I found this."

He chucked Carmen Lacey's missing security card on the desk next to a black marble ashtray. Was the card enough to demonstrate his trustworthiness?

Appearing uninterested, almost bored, Nathan pulled a cigar from the velvet humidor box on his desk. He trimmed the end, lit the hefty roll of tobacco puffing hard four times. Smoke billowed like a steam engine. He glanced at the card and then shot Blake a satanic grin.

"Not good enough, Blake. I want *you* to kill our Miss Steel."

CHAPTER TWENTY

Did the man really believe he would kill Whitney? Blake's pulse ratcheted up two notches. He cracked his knuckles to stop himself from reaching for his gun and shooting the freak between the eyes.

Nathan tilted his head and sent a lungful of cigar smoke spiraling toward the ceiling. "The only question now is how you'll take care of the woman."

Blake's mouth turned as dry as the desert floor. His mind spun. Somewhere in the complex were a little kid and hopefully answers to his sister's death. One way or another he'd succeed, even if he had to play along with the sick bastard. He needed to buy some time.

"You think it's wise to get rid of her right now? What if there's a screw up? It wouldn't look good for Vegas' Man of the Year or his company to be mixed up in another death."

Nathan took slow puffs on his cigar, always thinking three moves ahead. He hungered for control. Through the choking gray smoke, button-black eyes stared hard at Blake. Christ, the guy had the face of a stuffed squirrel

Seconds dragged on, and moisture settled along Blake's hairline. "Late tomorrow night I'll dump her in the desert—let the animals have their way. It'll be weeks before the body's found, if ever. If anyone asks, she escaped after we caught her trespassing."

"Ah, that's what I like. A man with a plan." Nathan straightened in his chair and squashed his cigar in the ashtray. "Just make sure there aren't any complications. I hope you won't disappoint me."

Blake would take care of the problem all right. While the wide-eyed weirdo was getting his ass kissed at his award dinner, he and Whitney would break into the cloning lab and find the kid.

His boss gave him a dismissive wave. "Now get that nosey woman out of my life. She's caused enough problems."

The office doors opened, Blake's cue to get lost. A small victory for now. As he walked out of the office, his gut twisted with worry.

Men like Nathan always had a backup plan. If Blake was plan A—who and what was plan B?

* * *

Whitney leaned her head against the door and listened. What was happening on the other side? Was Nathan plotting her death? What about Blake? Had he searched Nathan's desks? Had he found anything? The waiting was driving her crazy.

Her shoulders ached, and she was thirsty. Exhausted, she pounded her fists on the door. "Let me out of here. You're holding me against my will. I'll have you charged with false imprisonment."

When no one answered or came to the door, her tone grew more petulant. "I know you can hear me!"

What was she thinking? Wasn't she the one caught trespassing on private property? Still, Nathan Shaw had no business keeping her locked up like a caged animal. She turned and paced the length of the small room.

His direct threat shocked her. Quite out of character for a man who used thugs to deliver his messages. Clearly, she'd hit a nerve, the same way he'd shocked her with intimate details about her marriage, especially the miscarriages. She wrung her hands. Damn him. How dare he dig into her life? It had taken her years to shelve that heartache.

She stopped pacing and squeezed her eyes shut, fighting the images flashing through her mind—images of babies.

Months after she'd married Mason, the first miscarriage happened three weeks into the pregnancy. A year later, five and a half months into her second pregnancy, something was wrong. The baby had stopped moving...

Doctor Spencer sat on a stool beside her and gently patted her hand.

"Unfortunately, the ultrasound confirmed what I feared. I know this is difficult, Whitney." He paused and lowered his head. "You've experienced what we call a missed miscarriage, a type of spontaneous abortion. In other words, your body hasn't expelled the fetal tissue."

The baby was dead.

The floor felt as if it had collapsed under Whitney's feet. "We need to perform an emergency D&C today. I'm very sorry."

After grieving for the tiny girl she'd named Isabella, Whitney gave up hope of ever having another child. The price was too high, the anguish too great.

At the time, throwing herself into work made perfect sense, and eventually, the loss became bearable. She even believed at one point that she had driven Mason to other women's beds. But deep down she knew that wasn't true. Mason loved women, something he couldn't control, nor could she.

Whitney opened her eyes. How did Nathan get his slimy hands on her confidential medical records? He had to have bribed someone at the medical center in Panama City.

Damn him. She plunked down in the chair and waited. Waited for what, she had no idea. Each second passed with the echoing tick of the wall clock. Fear clawed at her throat. If she ever left this room, would she be dead or alive?

✻ ✻ ✻

Blake rushed out of the elevator, curious to know if Nathan had asked other employees to do "special jobs" for him. In particular, if someone Blake worked with could be the person taking pot shots at Whitney. Another uneasy thought tangled Blake's nerves. Why hadn't Norm called him back? He had said he would.

Blake needed to get Whitney away from this complex, back to the motel where she'd be safe. He sensed a stir in the corridor, a wrinkle of movement that caught his gaze. It was only the cleaning staff.

His cell phone squawked, halting him. He snatched the phone from his pocket and checked the caller ID.

C. Baxter, a.k.a. his FBI contact.

Thanks to technology, calls were communicated through a labyrinth of Bureau electronics to avoid detection. Still, he couldn't risk answering the call under the closed-circuit camera above him. He shut off the ringer and slid the phone back into his pocket.

Since he hadn't heard if Whitney's co-worker had been detained at the airport, he feared the worst. Another nosy reporter roaming Vegas equaled double-trouble. Hell, he couldn't keep one reporter out of trouble, let alone two.

He swiped his keycard through the magnetic reader. Electric bolts clicked. The steel security room doors slid back to reveal a hub of nightshift activity. Around him, monitors flickered black and white images, and fingers tapped against workstation keyboards.

Blake weeded through the sea of employees' faces, searching for Norm. The man was nowhere in sight.

"Hey, Jackson, where's Camaron?"

"Eh, Norm? Down in the mailroom, I think. Something about one of the bomb detectors malfunctioned again. The boss wanted the problem resolved ASAP."

Blake noted that the man refused to make eye contact with him. "Damn it. Why wasn't I notified? Hell, I am the head of security."

Jackson shook his mop of hair and kept his gaze targeted on the monitor in front of him. "Dunno, man. You'll have to ask Norm."

Blake would definitely make a point to catch up with Norm, but not now. He eyed monitor number fourteen—the interrogation room.

Whitney sat hunched over the small table with her head down. She looked fragile and exhausted.

Blake stopped at an unmanned workstation, leaned over the keyboard, and punched in his password. Three screens in, he double-clicked the interrogation room icon to unlock the door.

As he hoofed it down the back hall, a feeling came over him as if hundreds of eyes were watching his every move. He forced himself not to glance over his shoulder. Whitney must have known he was coming because she was standing by the door when he opened it.

Blake grabbed her hand. "Let's get out of here."

She heaved a huge sigh of relief against his shoulder. But relief would be short-lived, especially when she learned that he'd agreed to kill her for Nathan.

CHAPTER TWENTY-ONE

Outside, Whitney sucked in a deep breath of chilly night air, grateful to be free. Thank God she was no longer a prisoner in Nathan's demented world. When she'd heard the brisk click of the interrogation room door, words had failed her. Who would be on the other side? She'd never been so thankful to see Blake.

Whup-Whup-Whup!

The company's helicopter passed overhead, kicking up a swirling blast of grit. The bird hovered before descending on the rooftop helipad, like a gigantic insect. No way would Nathan let her walk away this easily.

The next move was his.

A numbing dread filled her veins. She tried to move her feet, but they wouldn't obey. Images of Mason and George played vividly through her mind. The sooner she got away from Nathan's grasp the better.

Blake tugged her hand. "Keep moving."

They scurried across the security parking lot and piled into his truck. The pickup's headlights carved a path through the suffocating darkness obscuring the desert road.

Blake glanced in the rearview mirror, then the side mirror as if anticipating a tail.

Whitney peered over her shoulder. Only miles of lonely darkness. "Expecting company?" What did he know that she didn't? He met with Nathan. What did they discuss?

"Just a precaution." He loosened his grip on the steering wheel. "Nathan didn't hurt you, did he?"

She detected real concern in Blake's voice, and that touched her. It had been a long time since a man truly cared about her.

"No." But she hated the fact Nathan knew about her life, how he used those details to intimidate her, upset her. Whitney looked past Blake and out the window. "Did you find anything in his desk?"

"Not much. A name; Andrew West. Anyone, you know?"

She searched her mind and came up empty. "No, I don't think so. The name isn't familiar."

Fighting off the fatigue of hardly any sleep, she leaned her head back on the headrest. Her eyes closed.

"Wait." Whitney popped her eyes open. "Nathan said something about the past has a way of coming full circle. Perhaps Andrew West is connected to a story I've done. If I had a computer with Internet access, I could check my files at work, and the legal and news division databases."

"There's a Cyber Hub on the main strip across from the Boardwalk Casino, but it doesn't open until seven. Whoever this guy is, he flew into Las Vegas last week. And I'm betting he was in the helicopter when we left the complex."

Whitney shuddered. Could they be wrong about

Andrew West? "Maybe he's a business associate of Nathan's."

"Not a chance. A man with nothing to hide doesn't keep a name and flight number under lock and key. If my gut is right, Andrew West boarded a flight in Oregon, which makes him—"

"The man who's trying to kill me."

"Exactly."

She didn't like feeling vulnerable. Being hunted was not a game she wanted to play anymore. If Andrew West was the shooter, he needed to be stopped. But how?

She felt the warmth of Blake's hand on hers. "Look, we still have a long drive ahead. Why don't you try to get some rest? I'll wake you when we get to Las Vegas."

"What about you? You must be exhausted too."

"I'll survive." He lowered his window a few inches. Cool desert air seeped through the truck.

He was right. Whitney leaned her head against Blake's shoulder. The faint woodsy smell of Nathan's cigars still lingered on Blake's clothes, reminding her of the battle ahead.

Icy blue digits of the dashboard clock blurred for a second. She blinked, and the numbers focused. Twelve-twenty in the morning.

How many hours, minutes, would she have before Nathan made his next move?

The plan was perfect.

There would be no room for failure this time. The hunt would end tonight, in Las Vegas.

Andrew West had seen the bitch standing like a

statue in the parking lot. Man, if he'd only had a rifle handy, he could've picked her off with a single shot. Pow!

He stared through the windshield. The cockpit's lights cast an eerie green and white glow against the window.

He rubbed the short stubble on his chin, satisfied the end was in sight. Within hours, Whitney Steel would be dead. A gurgle of laughter bubbled up his throat. Pure justice.

His justice.

The helicopter landed on the roof with a hollow thud. Andrew covered his ears from the snarl of the turbo-shaft engines. A short time passed before the rotor blades slowed to a low whine. The female pilot opened the door. The downdraft from the blades blew her ginger-colored hair across her face. Andrew shot her a smile and stepped out of the helicopter.

A man with a well-used face rushed to meet him, dropped his half-smoked cigarette, and ground it out with the toe of his boot.

"Mr. West. I'm Norm Camaron. The boss is waitin' in his office."

Andrew followed the man down the stairs into a waiting elevator. As the doors slid closed, Andrew eyed his reflection in the glistening steel walls.

When Andrew had answered a telephone call months ago, the last thing he figured he'd be doing was chasing the woman responsible for his father's death from state to state. But the man on the other end of the call seemed understanding, compassionate about the recent loss of his father, a nineteen-year veteran of the Miami-Dade police department. The man had also offered Andrew an extraordinary opportunity. An opportunity for revenge. One he couldn't turn down.

The elevator bell dinged. The doors stretched open to the second floor.

Norm escorted him into a spacious office. The smells of stale tobacco, flowery cleaning solution and money surrounded him.

"Ah, Mr. West. Welcome." Nathan Shaw greeted Andrew with a firm handshake. "Please. Have a seat."

Andrew chose the leather high-back chair and sat.

Nathan was much shorter than he'd envisioned. His white shirt and tan dress pants were sharply pressed. Too neat, considering it was after midnight.

Nathan gave Norm a dismissive wave. "Wait outside."

The man nodded and left. Towering steel doors closed guaranteeing precious privacy.

Nathan crossed the room to the bar and snagged two glasses. He removed the stopper from a crystal decanter. "Scotch?"

One only. Andrew needed a clear head tonight. "Sure."

After Nathan handed him the drink, Andrew tossed back the shot, felt the sting as the copper-colored liquid slid down his throat.

Nathan sat behind one of two desks in the room, set his drink beside him. His expression stilled and grew serious. "There'll be a slight change of plan."

Andrew nearly inched forward on the chair. "What change?"

"You'll wait until tomorrow night to kill the woman." Andrew sloughed off a wave of disappointment and struggled to control any outward emotion.

He wasn't stupid. Crossing Nathan Shaw obviously would prove deadly.

"May I ask why?"

"It would be beneficial to me if her death happened while I attended a social engagement. I'm sure you understand."

The man needed an alibi. "I do."

"Where's the reporter now?" Andrew asked.

Nathan flipped open the laptop on his desk. "Come. See for yourself. Technology these days is quite amazing."

Andrew moved to the ornate desk, studied the detailed map on the laptop screen. He might not be computer savvy, but he knew what he was looking at.

His heart pounded with joy. The woman had no clue she was being tracked.

"You mentioned the man with her. What about him?"

Nathan leaned back in the chair. A long beat of silence passed before he spoke. "Let's just say that when a bullet strays and kills him, no great loss."

"I thought the guy worked for you?"

"The first rule in business, Mr. West. Employees are always replaceable."

Andrew was even more curious to know why a man, who appeared to have the world, wanted Whitney Steel dead and his own head of security? What did she have on Shaw?

Probably a bunch of lies. His hands twitched as he clenched and unclenched his fists. Lies. Like the ones, she had fabricated about his father.

"I know you're disappointed by the delay, but patience, Mr. West. You'll have your chance." Nathan grinned. "I do have something to cheer you up. A little surprise for our Miss Steel."

A bubble of excitement exploded in Andrew's chest. He couldn't wait to hear more.

* * *

No hum of an engine. No vibration. They weren't moving.

Whitney opened her eyes.

She looked at the empty seat beside her. Where was Blake? He'd said he'd wake her when they arrived in Las Vegas. She unsnapped her seatbelt, and then wiped the moisture that had accumulated inside the windshield with her hand.

The side of the parking lot wasn't well lit, but a hundred yards away, under an oval pink and blue neon sign that read Ned's Blast-o-Burgers, Blake was talking on his cell phone.

He couldn't be speaking with Nathan, not after the way he had rushed her away from the facility. Her tongue felt thick, her mouth dry as cotton. Whitney rummaged through her purse and found a mint. She unwrapped it and popped the candy in her mouth.

The truck door opened. "Hey, you're awake." Blake snagged the keys out of the ignition. "Bad news. Cliff Peterson landed at McCarran an hour and a half ago. He's threatening legal action if he isn't released immediately by airport security. He can't be held much longer."

"Great. How long do we have?"

"Two to four hours, tops."

Even though Whitney couldn't stand Cliff, the last thing she wanted was to see the man dead. "We need to stop him. Cliff has no clue what he's getting into. What are going to do?"

"Not much at two o'clock in the morning. So right now, we eat. We haven't had a decent meal in hours."

Decent meal? Whitney peered through the windshield at the ostentatious sign of a cartoon character clinging to a rocket. She was thinking scrambled eggs and bacon. "You want a hamburger—from here?"

"Don't knock the place until you try it. Trust me. The best burgers in Vegas." Blake closed the truck door.

Whitney got out and followed him. Her stomach twisted and churned. From hunger? From the thought of eating at a place called Blast-o-Burgers, or the fact that Cliff Peterson might end up dead like George?

CHAPTER TWENTY-TWO

Whitney shifted in the booth's hard vinyl seat, taken back by how busy the '50s style restaurant was in the middle of the night. In the corner of the crowded dining area, a jukebox wailed, *Wake Up Little Susie*. How fitting.

After their bubblegum-chewing waitress brought their orders, Whitney plucked a French fry from the plastic meal basket and nibbled on it. "What did you and Nathan talk about while he had me locked up?"

Avoiding her gaze, Blake took a long drink of his chocolate milkshake. He appeared to be weighing the question.

"Are you going to tell me?"

He set his glass down. "You sure you want to know?"

Putting it that way only intrigued her more. "Yes, I do. We're in this together, remember?" She took a bite of her burger, savoring the tangy burst of garlic and oregano.

"He wants me to kill you."

She gulped hard once, then twice, forcing down the partially chewed chunk of meat that had lodged in her throat. Finally, able to swallow, she set the burger on her plate.

"I feel like I'm on death row, having my last meal." She looked at the black and white checkerboard floor, then at Blake. "What did you tell him?"

Please say you told the creep to go to hell.

If only the situation were that easy. Blake couldn't. He needed answers as much as she did because so far, he'd come up empty linking Nathan to his sister's death.

He shrugged. "What could I say? I said I would."

Her appetite withered and her stomach churned. "The man asked you to kill for him. How can you act so calm?"

Unless...

"Has Nathan asked you to do things like this before?"

Blake devoured the rest of his cheeseburger before answering. "No."

What a relief.

"I'm calm because I'm not killing anyone." He grabbed the saltshaker and sprinkled his fries. "Actually, I bought you some time."

"Oh, that makes me feel a whole lot better."

Did she want to hear the details of her demise? No, not really. Yes, she did.

"What's the big plan? You shoot me in the back—the cowardly way?"

"Nope." Blake leaned across the table, his voice low. "I suggested that we dump you in the desert for the animals. A much cleaner kill. Little to no evidence."

Her body went rigid. Chills crept up her spine.

"You look pale. You okay?"

No, she wasn't. Whitney pushed her plate aside,

surrendering any pretense of finishing her meal. It was tough to hear facts about your imminent death. "I'm fine. When's this animal feast supposed to happen?"

"Tonight, while the wide-eyed weirdo is at his Man of the Year shindig. With Nathan away from the complex, we have an opportunity to get into the lab. This might be our only chance."

"But how? Nathan isn't a fool. You can bet he's beefed up security since my impromptu appearance."

"I'm sure he has." Blake popped an onion ring in his mouth and washed it down with his chocolate milkshake. "Ever done any hang gliding?"

"A couple of times when I first moved to Florida. You're not thinking...?" By the huge grin on his face, he was. "Are you crazy?"

His grin widened. "Look. The only way into the complex is by air. After Nathan leaves, we'll hang glide to the helipad. There's a service entrance on the south side. No alarms or cameras. Still, have the map Mason gave you?"

She opened her purse and pulled out the crinkled piece of paper. "It sounds like you've given this plan plenty of thought."

"I have." Blake unfolded the map and flattened the paper on the table between them. "Okay, you see here, behind this main corridor, that's where the emergency stairs are. They run along the south side of the complex. My sister worked here." He pointed to a small triangle on the map. "Carmen Lacey worked here in A23, the main genetics lab."

"And that's where you think the child is being kept?"

"In theory, yes."

She raised an eyebrow. "What do you mean in theory?"

"I've got to tell you. In ten months I haven't seen or heard a whisper about the kid. It's as if she's a ghost."

"She's not a ghost. She exists, Blake. I saw the videotape. Besides, what other reason would Nathan have to kill, other than to keep his secret hidden?"

Whitney turned the map sideways. "What's this room behind the lab?"

"Have no idea. I don't have access to that area or the lab. Only technicians and scientists."

That had to be where Nathan was hiding the child. "Isn't that a bit odd? You're the head of security."

"Hey, nothing is odd with Nathan at the helm." His brows furrowed. "I'm also sure that Norm Camaron is working for Nathan in more ways than one."

"That's the guy who took me to the interrogation room?"

"Yeah." He folded the map. "I need you to do something."

Her muscles tensed. She couldn't wait to hear this. "What?"

"As soon as Peterson is released from airport security, set up a meeting with him tonight at the motel, say, around seven."

She shook her head. "No way is Cliff going to meet with me unless I divulge what I know about the cloning project."

"Then dangle the carrot. If that's what it takes to get him there, do it. I want any possible complications far away from the complex. We can be in and out before the guy realizes he's been scammed."

Their waitress appeared at the table with her pink

poodle skirt swaying from side-to-side. She leaned her hip against Blake's arm and rested her hand on his shoulder. "Getcha anything else?"

Whitney rolled her eyes and shifted her attention to a black and white poster of James Dean on the wall. *Why don't you climb on Blake's lap and lick his face?* The woman drooled like a dog in heat.

"No, just the check. Thanks."

"You got it, honey."

Whitney heard the waitress snap the wad of gum in her mouth and leave. She faced Blake.

His gaze met hers. "Now your face is flushed. You sure you're feeling okay?"

"I feel just fine." She toyed with her fork beside her plate.

A long beat of silence. Blake smiled. "You're jealous."

"I am not."

He reached across the table and grasped her hand. "Is it that difficult for you to admit you are?"

For the first time since sixth grade, when Janice Mayer stole her boyfriend, Whitney was jealous. She pulled her hand away quickly and brushed an annoying strand of hair from her forehead. "It's not difficult, because I'm not jealous."

Blake leaned back in the seat and shot her a pleased smile. "I really am growing on you."

Whitney felt heat rush to her cheeks. Blake was right. She changed the subject. "Okay, so let's say everything goes as planned and we get into the lab, find what we're looking for. How do we get out?"

"The same way we left the complex earlier. Through the back door to the security parking lot.

We'll borrow a company truck and scram."

"But won't we get stopped at the main gates?"

"Not likely. Everyone will be busy trying to figure out why the satellite went down and what's causing the breach along the perimeter of the property. Don't worry. Leave everything to me."

Whether she liked the plan or not, at least they had one. Her gaze traveled to the entrance and her stomach knotted. She had a nasty creepy feeling they were being watched. Maybe she was still spooked after hearing about her own death.

After the waitress flirted with Blake one last time, he paid for their meals and they left the restaurant. Under the dim lights of the narrow stretch of the parking lot, a rustling noise caught Whitney's attention.

She stopped. "What was that?"

"Probably the wind." Blake draped his arm around her shoulder. "We should try to get a few hours of sleep before the Cyber Hub opens at seven."

Meowwwwww.

His arm fell from her shoulder. Whitney walked ahead, trying to ignore the disgusting mixture of sour garbage and greasy food that swirled in the air. A scrawny calico kitten scurried out from behind an overflowing dumpster and rubbed and purred against her pant leg.

"Hi, little fellow." She picked up the ball of tangled fluff and glanced around the parking lot. "Look, Blake, the poor little guy's out here all alone."

She held the kitten to her chest and walked toward him. "I'm not leaving him here. He's hungry. Look, there's a store across the street. I'll get him some food and we'll take him back to the motel."

No. Blake rubbed the cat's head. The kitten meowed and pushed against his hand. "We can't bring him with us. I'm having a hard enough time keeping you safe let alone a kitten along for the ride."

"I know, but he's too small to leave here. He'll starve to death or get hit by a car. He has to come with us. Please?"

He saw the sadness in her eyes. Damn it. He had to give in. "Okay. Okay."

Whitney smiled and kissed him on the cheek. "Thank you." She slipped the kitten into her shoulder bag. Its head poked between the straps as if he belonged there.

"See? He won't be any trouble. I'll be back in a flash. Meet you in the truck."

He watched her hustle across the street, and enter the store next to Donut Junkie. He went to his truck and waited for Whitney to return.

CHAPTER TWENTY-THREE

I n the donut shop, Andrew West sat on a hard stool at the end of a worn Formica counter and ordered another coffee, this one to go. Cinnamon collided with the sharp tang of bleach as the waitress wiped the counter beside him.

Outside, traffic built up. While a half-moon poked through the clouds, he eyed the woman heading into the store next door. Anticipation nipped his skin.

She'd be dead by sunset. Sweet retribution.

Thanks to Nathan's unlimited resources, including the use of his helicopter, Andrew could keep a step ahead of the reporter. Of course, knowing where she'd be every minute came in handy. He couldn't bring himself to say her name. The thought of her was like vomit on his tongue.

How could a jury have believed her lies? Her bullshit helped put his father behind bars. Her lies had forced his father to kill himself.

She'd said his old man was a dirty cop, implicated him in the theft of millions of dollars' worth of cocaine from the Miami-Dade evidence-storage facility, and accused him of selling the drugs on the street.

His father had been set up. He wasn't a thief or a

drug dealer. He was a hardworking man who'd dedicated his life to protect others.

Andrew heard she had gotten a friggin' award.

Bitch.

And his father? A wooden box.

From the get-go, Andrew's plan was simple. Take out everyone the woman cared about. Make her suffer, experience loss like he had. Worked like a charm when he'd shot her ex-husband. Funny how things work out. The old guy, George had been a bonus, a two-for-one deal.

She was next.

His palms itched. He couldn't wait.

The woman crossed the street, carrying two plastic shopping bags. Andrew shot to his feet. Once she was on the other side, he tossed two dollars on the counter, grabbed his coffee and left Donut Junkie with a smile on his face.

Tucked inside his rental car, he clutched the PDA Nathan had given him and turned on the handheld device. It felt good to have such control. The Palm Pilot beeped. The small LCD screen burst to life. On a miniature green and blue street map, a red light blinked.

The bitch would be moving soon.

In the semi-darkness of the alley, Andrew started the engine and waited.

❋ ❋ ❋

From Blast-o-Burgers parking lot, Blake watched for Whitney to exit the convenience store across the street. A pair of seedy looking characters lingered outside the entrance. One of them didn't look old enough to smoke, let alone be out in the wee hours of the morning.

Whitney hurried past the two males who eyed her up and down with a lurid whistle. She was certainly worthy of a double-take. A car honked, weaving around a trio of orange traffic cones placed near a manhole cover a few yards from the intersection.

She crossed the street. Blake hopped out of the truck and opened the passenger side door.

"Let me take those." He took the heavy bags from her hands and placed them behind the seat. "Looks like you bought the store."

"Just a few necessities. Cat food, litter box, litter."

Determined not to allow himself to get attached to the kitten, he kept the distance between him and the critter with its head flopped over the side of Whitney's purse.

Whitney met his gaze. "I have good news, though. Well, good news for you."

The only news he wanted to hear was that cat wasn't coming with them, and that didn't look likely. "Yeah, what's that?"

"The clerk at the store offered to take the kitten home with her."

He glanced at the furball, its eyes closing. "Then why do you still have him?"

Shit. She couldn't part with the cat. A frustrated groan slipped through his clenched teeth. She had to. "Look, we—"

"The clerk can't take him until after her shift ends at six. I asked her to pick him up at the motel." Whitney climbed into the truck and closed the door. She stuck her head out the window. "Happy now?"

"Yeah, thanks." He slid behind the wheel and

started the engine.

Red taillights and headlights blurred with the city's colorful flashbulb glow and hurt Blake's tired eyes. As they drove away from the strip, traffic coasted and thinned.

Pockets of people on the sidewalks dwindled to the odd courageous few who didn't mind taking their chances in this less fortunate part of town.

Whitney leaned her head back on the headrest with her purse on her lap. The kitten was asleep half hanging out of her bag. In the Fiesta Garden's L-shaped lot, Blake parked the pickup in front of their motel room.

Once settled inside the stuffy room, Whitney had fallen asleep exhausted after a long day. The cat curled up beside her.

Blake cracked open a cola and took a big gulp, and then set the can on the battered dresser next to him.

He flopped down in the chair and knew damn well he'd get little rest wondering when Nathan would make his next move.

***

His mouth touched her skin, leaving a wet trail over her breasts. His hand inched down her stomach and stopped at the top of her thigh.

She wanted him. As if he'd read her mind, he moved his body over hers, and slid between her legs....

A thump woke her. Whitney opened her eyes. The early morning sun sent light blazing through the room's flimsy curtains. She squinted and blinked at the particles of dust floating in the air. Her skin still tingled from Blake's imaginary touch. It was a dream, wasn't it?

In the corner, next to the bed, Blake was asleep in

the chair with the shabby bedspread tangled around him. The kitten slept in a ball on his lap.

Whitney sat up. The dilapidated mattress sagged under her. She pushed back the thin sheets and got dressed. After pulling on jeans and V-neck top, she carefully transferred the purring kitten to the bed.

Satisfied the cat would stay put, she padded to the bathroom for a drink of water. A loud rap on the door stopped her in her tracks. Blake woke, flung aside the bedspread and scrambled to his feet. The ball of fluff bounced off the bed and high-tailed it under the dresser.

Whitney had her hand on the doorknob, ready to open the door when Blake came up behind her and grabbed her arm.

"Wait." He pushed the curtain to one side and peered outside. "Okay."

Warm breath tickled the back of her neck. Her nipples hardened. What was wrong with her? Her attraction to him more powerful than ever. She wished things were different, less complicated between them. But they weren't. He had his goal and she had hers.

"Are you going to answer it?" His words whispered against her hair before he backed away.

"Yes." She swallowed a lump in her throat and opened the door.

The store clerk stood on the threshold, dressed in black Capri pants and a pink top. Quite a change from the unflattering brown uniform she wore the night before.

"Hi. Remember me? I'm here for the kitten."

Whitney stepped back and opened the door. "Come in, Trish. I'll get the kitten's things together."

The teenager stayed put, leaving the door open. "Is it okay if I stay out here? I don't really know you all that well."

"Of course." Whitney smiled. The girl obviously had street smarts. "I'll be just a couple of minutes."

After the cat popped out from under the dresser, he ventured to the door and brushed against his new owner's leg. Blake vanished to the bathroom, the door shut behind him.

The girl picked up the kitten and cuddled him to her chest. "He's so cute. I promise I'll take good care of him."

"I'm sure you will." Whitney finished gathering the kitten's food and water dish. "I'll walk you to your car."

After saying goodbye to the clerk, Whitney returned to the room. Blake was still in the bathroom.

Another knock at the motel room door. This time louder. Thinking Trish had a question or forgot something, Whitney answered it.

Two Las Vegas Police officers stared at her.

Her knees threatened to buckle when the male officer said, "Whitney Steel. We have a warrant for your arrest."

CHAPTER
TWENTY-FOUR

Whitney couldn't believe her ears. *Arrested?* A nip of fear sent her heart pounding. This was nothing more than a game to Nathan. Of course, he'd press charges. Walking out of the complex had been too easy. She should have known this was coming. Nathan would do anything to keep her out of his hair until tonight when Blake was supposed to kill her. She gritted her teeth to control her anger.

"Step out here please." The male officer, slight in stature and with thinning hair motioned to the sidewalk next to the motel room.

She glanced at her bare feet. "Can I at least put my shoes on?"

The officer guarded the doorway. "Make it quick."

Whitney slipped on her running shoes and snatched her purse from the dresser.

Blake rushed out of the bathroom with a puzzled look on his face. "I heard voices. What's going on?"

She looked him straight in the eye. "I'm being arrested." He stared at her in silence as if he couldn't comprehend the situation.

Outside the morning sunlight assaulted her face.

Whitney shielded her eyes with one hand. "What am I being charged with?"

"Burglary and trespassing." The officer handed her a copy of the warrant.

She lowered her hand and scanned the document. According to the scribbled signature, one of Nathan's connections included a Judge Myers, who issued the warrant in the middle of the night, and in record-breaking speed. She'd have a record. Tightness gathered in Whitney's chest. Yards away, a bearded man with a camera perched on his shoulder darted out from between two parked cars.

The media? Oh, God. This can't be happening.

Her stomach pitched with nausea. Her face would be plastered all over the evening news. Not her finest moment.

The cameraman didn't seem distracted by the skeleton-thin female officer doing her job.

"You have the right to remain silent. If you give up the right to remain silent, anything you say can and will be used against you in a court of law. You have the right to speak with an attorney and to have the attorney present during questioning. If you so desire and cannot afford one, an attorney will be appointed for you without charge before the questioning begins."

The woman took a breath and continued. "Do you understand your rights as I have read them to you?"

Whitney's lower lip trembled. "Yes." Her gaze shifted to Blake speaking to the male officer. What were they talking about?

"Do you waive and give up those rights?" The officer removed a set of cuffs from a black nylon holster attached to her belt.

"No."

"Hands behind your back."

Whitney did as ordered. Cold steel snapped around her wrists.

"Any guns, knives, drugs, needles?"

Whitney fought to keep her knees from shaking long enough to squeak out an answer. "No."

The officer proceeded to conduct a quick body search. The cameraman stepped in for a close-up. Whitney turned her face from the lens.

An arrest record would kill her career, a career that she'd worked so hard to build. That bastard. Nathan knew exactly what he was doing. Another perfectly orchestrated show of power to humiliate and destroy. She couldn't do much about the trespassing charge. Unfortunately, the taped evidence didn't lie, but she'd fight the burglary charge with her last dying breath.

Blake raked his hand over his face. "Where are you taking her?"

"Downtown. North Ninth Street." The male officer removed his sunglasses from the pocket of his khaki-colored shirt and put them on.

He led Whitney by the arm to the police car and opened the back door. She ducked her head and awkwardly climbed into the car. The door slammed shut.

Inside the car, the male officer started the engine. Whitney tried to stretch her legs in the cramped back seat. "How'd you know where to find me?"

The female officer glanced over her shoulder and smiled. "Anonymous tip. Happens all the time."

Right. How convenient. There was something creepy about the woman's smile. Fake and mocking. A shiver tingled up the back of Whitney's neck.

Only one person knew which motel, and she was looking right at him as the police car pulled into traffic.

❊ ❊ ❊

Blake couldn't get the hurt on Whitney's face out of his mind. The way her eyes had darkened with pain. She believed he'd set her up, which he hadn't. The whole scenario reeked of Nathan.

Of all the motels in Las Vegas, how did the cops know where to find her? He slapped his palms down on the dresser. He'd been careful. They hadn't been followed. Sweat rolled down his forehead. "Lousy damned air conditioner."

His cell phone rang, diverting his attention. He grabbed the phone off the bed and answered the call.

"Man, you're one tough son-of-a-bitch to get a hold of."

"Can't be helped, Mike." Hearing his Bureau contact's voice didn't make Blake feel any better. All he wanted to do was wrap his hands around Nathan's scrawny neck and squeeze the life out of him. "What's the bad news? Chamber's pulled the plug on the mission?"

"Nope. I convinced 'Rambo Robot' to hold off for another forty-eight hours."

Blake chuckled at the way Mike used their boss' nickname. "How the hell did you manage that?"

"Man, don't ask. Believe me, you owe me big-time."

"What about the reporter, Peterson?"

"Airport security released him hours ago. He's got a room over at the Golden Gate. I tried to contact you."

"I know. I couldn't answer the call." Somehow, Blake had to keep Peterson away from Nathan for his own good. "Anything else?"

"The rundown on Erik Friklin produced zilch. He's nobody. For the past twelve years, he's worked at Cheap Auto, a car rental place in the north end. No priors. Not even a parking ticket."

Blake walked to the window and peeked outside. The parking lot was empty except for his pickup. How does a nobody get tangled up in a kidnapping-murder scheme? There had to be a connection. "Have Blanche cross-reference Shaw, Friklin and a new piece to the puzzle. Andrew West."

"Will do. We still on for tonight?"

Hopefully. Nothing would give Blake more pleasure than to see Nathan's face when he arrested him. But he needed to get Whitney released first. Or maybe she'd be safer locked up? "Mike, hang tight until six. I've got a couple of things to look after. I'll call you later."

"Stay safe, man."

"Yeah." Blake stared at his truck and ended the call. His instincts screamed. One question kept burning his gut. Why hadn't Norm called him back when Blake was searching Nathan's desk?

With Norm's expertise, he could've....

Shit. Blake flung open the motel room door and marched to his pickup. Lying on the pavement, he tucked his head under the front of the truck and ran his hand along the bumper.

He felt something.

Small. Rectangular. The size of a deck of cards. Something that sure as hell didn't come standard on a Ford F150.

"God damn it!" He yanked out the black box, a Global Positioning System device, and chucked it across the parking lot.

Nathan had been tracking them all along.

❊ ❊ ❊

At the police station, Whitney couldn't stop the anger boiling within her. How could she have been such a fool to trust Blake? He'd told Nathan they were staying at the Fiesta Gardens. What other explanation could there be? What else had he lied about?

Amidst the hustle and bustle of phones ringing and keyboards clicking, she was booked, fingerprinted and posed for a set of unflattering mug shots. To complete the experience, a female officer shaped like an over-sized egg conducted another body search.

Stripped of her personal belongings, and her dignity, Whitney sat on a wooden bench with her hands cuffed in front of her. She stared at the scuffed floor, terrified to make eye contact with any of the four female "criminals" in the holding cell nearby.

*I'm a criminal, just like the*m. Could she feel any lower?

A hulk of an officer stalked by the cell. One of the women, tattooed in heavy makeup, shoved her face against the metal bars and batted her fake eyelashes. "Hey, little sweet thing."

The other women giggled.

"Quiet down, ladies." The officer stopped beside Whitney.

"You've got three phone calls." He pointed to a wall phone located in an alcove across from the holding cell. "There's a list of lawyers posted above the phone."

She definitely needed a lawyer, a damn good one. WBNN TV had one of the best in Florida. Whitney dialed her boss' number.

After three rings, he answered the call. "Matt Wildell."

"Matt, it's Whitney. I kind of got myself into a bit of trouble working on the cloning story."

"What kind of trouble?"

"Trespassing." She decided not to mention details or the burglary charge because by the growl, in his tone, he didn't sound impressed.

"Johnston can't help you from here."

"I know. But since he's the station's lawyer, he could recommend a reputable lawyer in Las Vegas."

"After your crazy stunt of accusing the head of FloAgra of being some kind of hired hit-man, you need a shrink, not a lawyer."

"I'm sorry." Whitney wondered when her wee slip of reality on the plane would come back to haunt her. "When I get back, I'll fix everything. I promise. It was a stupid—"

"You're off the story. Peterson's on."

"No way." Whitney realized she was yelling. She forced her voice down a couple levels not wanting to draw any attention. "I've put my life on the line more than once."

"Save it. I don't want to hear it. We've decided to terminate your contract."

Shock widened her eyes. "What? After all, I've done for the station, you're cutting me loose? You can't do that."

"It's a done deal. Come on Whitney, face it. You'll never be as good as your father."

The harshness of his words bit through her skin down to the bone. She visualized the cocky nerd sitting behind his desk with a smirk on his face. "You ungrateful little twit—"

Click. The line went dead.

Stunned, Whitney slowly hung up the receiver. Just when she thought she couldn't feel any lower. She'd never been fired from a job in her life. Nathan didn't need to kill her, she already felt dead inside.

Knowing she needed to do something, she called two other lawyers from the wall list and left messages on their answering machines.

As minutes twisted into hours, Whitney sat in a corner of the cell, avoiding eye contact with the other women who chatted back and forth.

"Steel."

She raised her head.

"Your lawyer's here." The officer unlocked the holding cell door.

He held her tight by the arm and ushered her into a room outfitted with a metal table and two chairs. In one of the chairs sat an elegant looking woman in her forties with an upswept hairdo. She rose when Whitney entered the room.

"Miss Steel. I'm Joyce Banks."

The woman handed Whitney a raised print business card. "Blake Neely hired me."

"You're kidding." Why would he hire a lawyer? Out of guilt? Or to spring her before Nathan's award dinner and then kill her?

"How do you know Blake?"

"I'm a friend of his parents." The woman opened her briefcase on the table and pulled out a file folder.

"Blake said this would explain everything." The lawyer slid a folded paper across the table. Whitney grasped the paper and unfolded the note.

Joyce Banks is the best in the state. She'll help you. I found a GPS device planted under the truck. That's how the cops knew where to find you. Nathan was tracking us.

With mixed feelings, Whitney looked across the table at what might be her new best friend. The sooner she left this hell-hole the better. "Okay. Work your magic and get me out of here."

The woman smiled. "Let's get started."

CHAPTER TWENTY-FIVE

*D*iscipline and patience are the keys to success, Andy.

That's what Andrew West's father had always told him.

He rubbed his hands together. A perfect day for revenge.

Not wanting to draw attention to himself, he left the air conditioning off. Dark hair clung to his forehead and the back of his neck from the sun's heat beating through the car's window.

Parked in the fourth row of the police station's parking lot, Andrew popped the last bite of his roast beef sandwich into his mouth. Too bad Neely had discovered the GPS. Now Andrew would have to follow him and the reporter the old-fashioned way. Kind of reminded him of when he was a teenager, how his father allowed him to go on the occasional ride-along. A muscle flexed in his clenched jaw. Man, Andrew missed those days.

He couldn't remember much about his mother, except round green eyes. One day she was in his life, the next a brain aneurysm had taken her away from him. Forcing away the memories, Andrew gulped down the rest of a soda and tossed the can in the back seat.

As he glanced in the rearview mirror, a wild idea flowered in his mind. He laughed, the sound oddly loud in the confines of the rental car. Were Neely and the woman involved? It wasn't as if Nathan gave a rat's-ass about the security man. Make the bitch suffer a bit more before the grand finale tonight. Sweet.

He checked his watch and grinned. Three-thirty. Six hours and counting.

Nothing would give him more satisfaction than watching the bitch fight until the last signs of life were drained from her body.

* * *

While the judge studied the records presented to him by the bailiff, Whitney straightened in the chair, hoping to relieve the pain between her shoulders from being handcuffed earlier. Her lawyer sat beside her, gaze fixed on the judge's face, waiting for the next word to spill from his lips.

Even though Whitney hadn't told her lawyer the real reason she'd snuck into ShawBioGen, she was confident Joyce would do the best to represent her. The judge, though, was a different story.

How much pull did Nathan have in Las Vegas? Probably a lot. From where she sat, the thought didn't stomach well. Would the judge be fair? Her body tensed. God, she hoped so, because she needed to get to the Internet café. Her life depended on it. If she could figure out who Andrew West was, maybe she could stop him before he made another attempt to kill her.

"Your professional conduct is despicable, Miss Steel. Aggressive, reporting can be honorable and even courageous, but *does not* give you a free ticket to break the law." Judge William Montoya lowered his balding head. "Just so we're clear, I'm also issuing a Harassment Restraining Order." His mouth tightened. "Stay away from Nathan Shaw and ShawBioGen. This includes telephone calls, emails, and letters."

As if a piece of paper is going to stop me from going after the man responsible for Mason's and George's deaths.

"Is that understood?" The judge peered through the top portion of his bifocals and gave her a stare that felt like a knife in her stomach.

Whitney took a quick, shaky breath. "Yes, sir."

An hour crawled by, and thanks to her clean record, the burglary charge was dropped. Feeling a huge wave of relief, she gratefully pled guilty to trespassing, a misdemeanor with a five hundred dollar fine. A small price to pay for her freedom.

After paying the fine, Whitney pushed open one of the heavy glass doors in the front lobby and strolled out of the police station a free woman.

Then she saw him, leaning against his pickup, waiting for her.

She felt like a heel, thinking Blake had set her up, but a speck of doubt still lingered in the back of her mind, and she didn't know why.

Blake gave her a smile that sent her pulse racing. She clutched her purse to her chest and walked toward him. He met her halfway.

As much as Whitney didn't want to admit it, she'd missed him. They stood face to face, the balmy afternoon air ruffling her hair. He pushed a strand from her eyes with his finger. "Glad to have you back."

His gentle touch went straight to her brain. Her

heart thumped.

She hugged the purse tighter. "Definitely not something I want to experience again. Can we get out of here?"

He nodded. "Sure."

When they sped past the sprawling Las Vegas Convention Center, Whitney couldn't help but notice the large sign, its message taunting her.

Man of the Year Award Dinner.

She glanced at Blake. For a moment their eyes met. "Thanks for sending Joyce."

"Anytime." His gaze shifted back to the street.

"You could have just left me. That way I'd be out of your hair. So why didn't you?"

"Nathan has a lot of connections. The mayor, cops, some high-powered Vegas businessmen. I figured you'd be safer with me than inside."

Her heart did a nosedive. She wasn't sure what she'd expected to hear. Maybe that he cared about her?

"But one thing I don't get is why Nathan had you arrested when he planned to have you killed tonight?"

She crossed her ankles. "To show he's in control. He knows how important my career is to me. And his plan worked."

"Why? What happened?"

She looked at her hands and fiddled with her fingers. "My contract was terminated. I was canned."

The hell with Mike Wildell and WBNN. No one could be as good as her father. He was one of a kind. But once she broke the cloning story, she would have her pick of stations to work for.

Blake rested his hand on her knee drawing her attention back to him. "I'm sorry."

"Don't be. It was bound to happen sooner than later. Now I know for sure that the station had been grooming Cliff for my position."

"Speaking of Peterson, airport security was forced to release him. He has a room at the Golden Gate."

"Lovely." That was the last thing they needed. *Cliff, the pariah, getting in the way, screwing up everything.* "We have to stop him before Nathan gets a hold of him."

"We'll pay him a visit, stop him from doing anything stupid. The hotel's only a few blocks from the Cyber Hub. We need to find out who Andrew West is."

In other words, her life was more important, and Whitney couldn't agree more. A whistle of air snuck through the partially open window and tickled her face. She gazed out the window amazed at how unattractive Vegas looked in the daylight. Concrete and bland.

After Blake parked the truck, they walked past the Aladdin Hotel and Casino. A young man shoved a flyer into Whitney's hand. A sense of uneasiness filled her. She glanced at the colorful glossy paper advertising a seedy strip club. Blake raised an eyebrow and grinned. She crumpled the ad into a ball, determined to toss it the first chance she got.

At the Cyber Hub, Whitney paid the clerk ten dollars for an hour of Internet use. The high-tech haven was much larger than she'd expected and tastefully decorated. The walls and floor were bathed in muted earth tones. Brightly colored Vegas show posters hung above each of the desks. She heard the steady flow of traffic outside and the occasional clickity-clack of the rollercoaster at the Boardwalk Casino across the street, the sound unnerving.

She and Blake took a seat at one of the dozens of wooden computer workstations. For the first time since she'd jumped into this whole mess, she felt a glimmer of hope. When WBNN's welcome message filled the screen, Whitney swallowed the dry lump in her throat and punched in her user name and password. Another window popped open.

Your attempt to sign in has failed. Login and password denied.

"That can't be right." She tried again. Same message. Her optimism vanished. "Damn it."

"What's wrong?"

"I've been blocked out of stations computer network. If I can't login, I can't access my personal files or search the databases." Clenching her hands into fists on her lap, she shook her head. "I don't believe this."

Blake stood. "Well, let's go. We'll have to come up with another plan."

"No, wait. I have an idea. Give me your cell phone."

Blake handed her the phone and sat down again.

Whitney dialed her assistant's private line at WBNN. After four rings, the young woman picked up.

"Caroline Price."

"Hi, Caroline."

"Whitney. I'm so sorry about George. I miss him."

"Yeah, me too. Listen, I need your login info to access the network. Mine won't work."

"I can't. I'll get fired too. I've got kids to feed."

Good news traveled fast. At this point, Whitney had nothing to lose. "I know. If anyone asks, just tell them I stole your info. Okay?"

"I'm sorry, I can't. I have to go."

Whitney jumped to her feet and almost knocked

the chair over. "Wait. Please. George died because of this story, and a small child is involved. I'm begging you."

A long beat of silence passed, which Whitney wasn't sure was a good sign.

Then, "Rugrats. All lowercase. Password, Four-two-six-zero. I have to go."

The line went dead.

Blake shifted in his chair. "Did you get it?"

"Yes." Whitney sat back down, typed in the information, and hit enter. A new window spawned the stations blue and silver call-letters. She was in. *Thank you, Caroline.*

Whitney bit her lower lip and keyed the name Andrew West into the search box. Less than a minute passed. Her hand flew to her mouth. "Oh, my God."

CHAPTER TWENTY-SIX

Whitney stared at the computer monitor. A familiar tingle raced through her veins. The same adrenaline rush she experienced dozens of times when she'd uncovered a smoking gun that could make or break a story. For a moment she'd forgotten Blake was sitting next to her.

He touched her shoulder. "Hey, are you going to fill me in, or keep me guessing?"

"Oh, sorry." She turned in the chair and faced him. "In 1999, a confidential source with the Miami-Dade police department contacted me about the disappearance of millions of dollars' worth of cocaine from the department's evidence locker. Before the story ran, I'd uncovered evidence that a Detective Ramon Sheppard and two other veteran detectives had stolen the haul and sold the drugs on the street. After I testified at Sheppard's trial, he was sentenced to four years at Everglades Correctional Institution."

Blake arched an eyebrow, clearly confused. She continued. "About six months ago, Sheppard was found dead in his cell. He'd hung himself."

"Okay. But what's the connection between Sheppard and West?"

"This." She pointed to the legal document on the screen. "Look who was the executor of Sheppard's will."

Blake leaned forward. His jaw gaped open. "I'll be damned. Andrew West—his son."

"But get this. I personally ran background for the story. I swear Sheppard was a widower with no children." Whitney shook her head. "I don't get it."

Her stomach did a quick roll. She couldn't have possibly missed such an important detail. Could she?

Blake put his hand on her knee in a comforting gesture. "At this point, what's it matter? West is a cold-blooded killer hell-bent on taking you out."

He didn't understand. It mattered to her. Whitney bit her lip feeling her career unravel completely. The truth hit with a belly punch of realization. Had she been so preoccupied with wanting to win the Peabody award, she'd missed vital information? Prickles of panic chased up and down her spine. What else had she missed?

"He blames me for his father's death, doesn't he?"

"Looks that way. So how the hell does Nathan fit into this?"

Whitney shrugged. "It's a mystery to me, but I have every intention of finding out. Even though I know who and why it doesn't make me feel any better or safer."

Blake rested his arm protectively on the back of her chair. "We have one thing in our favor; West doesn't know we're on to him. For now, we have the upper hand."

For how long, though? "It would help if we at least knew what the guy looked like. He could be anyone, anywhere."

Blake's gaze flicked over her shoulder toward the front door. Before Whitney had a chance to see what he was looking at, a rasping female voice called out.

"Blake? Is that you? It is. I thought I saw you through the window."

He stood. "Marlene?" The chair creaked and jerked behind him, forcing heads to turn.

Six-inch heels clicked on the ceramic floor. A long-haired redhead ran straight into his arms. She kissed him and left a glittery red lip imprint on his cheek. "Where have you been? I haven't seen you around the casino lately."

The woman was a vision of beauty right down to her rainbow colored mini-skirt. Whitney clutched the computer mouse and remained seated in her "fresh out of jail" jeans and a wrinkled T-shirt.

Blake awkwardly shoved his hands into his jeans pockets. "I've been busy."

Marlene looked down her perfect little nose and gave Whitney a once over. "So I can see."

Whitney reminded herself that her partnership with Blake was business and nothing more. So they'd had sex once. It didn't mean anything. Who was she fooling? She stood, squared her shoulder and stuck out her chest. *At least my breasts are real.*

Blake took her cue and interjected. "Marlene, this is Whitney. She's a reporter."

The woman smiled at her as if dealing with a temperamental child.

Whitney returned a fake smile. "Oh, are you a dealer at one of the casinos?" Like she really cared.

"God, no. I work at the Riviera. I'm part of the Wild Girls Topless Revue." Marlene winked at Blake. "Hottest ticket in town." Her gaze slid to Whitney. "Have you seen the show?"

Was this woman for real? Whitney forced herself not to roll her eyes. "Maybe next time I'm in town."

Blake checked his watch, and then glanced at Whitney. "How about you print out what we need while I walk Marlene out?"

Whitney nodded, pleased to see the woman go. One thing was certain, Blake and Marlene were more than just friends. Their body language said it all, the way he placed his hand on the small of her back as they walked away. Well, Blake could have her. There were more important things to worry about. Like staying alive long enough to expose Nathan's dirty little secret to the world.

When the printer finished, she stuffed the pages into her purse. Through the bank of windows partially covered by vertical blinds, Whitney eyed Blake and his gal pal talking. Marlene's mouth moved a mile a minute. Blake grinned and shifted from foot to foot.

Not wanting to deal with Marlene again, Whitney waited five minutes before walking to the front of the Internet café. She put her hand on the door handle for a moment, then, taking a deep breath, opened it.

To her surprise, Marlene was already wiggling her way through the crowded sidewalk with her designer shoulder bag bouncing from her hip.

At first, Blake didn't make eye contact with Whitney.

He reached to take hold of her hand.

Whitney jerked it away, and plucked a tissue from her purse and handed it to him. "You might want to wipe the lipstick off your right cheek."

"Thanks." Looking sheepish, he took the tissue and wiped his face. "Listen, about Marlene—"

She held up her hand. "Don't, okay? There's no need to explain. What you do in your life is none of my business. We need to get to Cliff before he goes to Nathan."

While they walked the next four blocks in silence, Whitney scanned the hectic six lanes of cars, cabs, and buses. A shiver whispered through her. "Do you think he's following us?"

"West? I doubt it. Finding the GPS put a huge kibosh into his plan. I'd sure as hell like to get my hands on Norm. He's the last person I thought could be manipulated by Nathan."

"Well, he was. Money's a powerful motivator." Was that what it took to convince Andrew West as well?

Outside the Golden Gate Hotel and Casino, tourists congregated under the canopy of the mall filled with one-of-a-kind shops. A young woman dressed in a knee-length white wedding dress and long beaded veil, snuggled against a man dressed in a turquoise Hawaiian shirt, black suit jacket and jeans. Newlyweds. Sin City was full of them.

Once inside the hotel, Blake waited in the lobby while Whitney went to the concierge desk and asked a staff member to buzz Cliff's room. After two attempts, it was clear he wasn't there.

Her stomach knotted. Fearing the worst, that Cliff might already be on his way to ShawBioGen to see Nathan, she used the hotel's courtesy phone to call his cell phone. When he didn't answer, she left a voicemail.

Damn it, Cliff. "Hi, it's Whitney. If you want the cloning story, it's all yours. I'll give you everything I have." She looked at the address Blake had scribbled on a piece of paper. "Meet me at the Starz Motor Inn, 1853 Las Vegas Boulevard, room seven, at nine-thirty tonight." The knot in her stomach tightened more. She hung up the phone.

"Did you get a hold of him?"

Whitney turned at Blake's voice and shook her head. "No. I had to leave a message. I hope he shows up tonight."

Then the most horrifying thought hit her. She forced down the lump in her throat. "Would Nathan harm the child if he felt his back was against the wall?"

A long beat of silence.

Blake's gaze met hers. "Of course, he would."

❋ ❋ ❋

Blake drove with the window rolled down, grateful for the cool air on his face. He still had a difficult time believing a cloned kid existed, let alone hidden somewhere inside ShawBioGen. But the kid had to exist. Why else would Nathan resort to such extreme measures? Blake had no doubt Nathan would destroy all evidence, human or not, to save his ass from a lifetime behind bars. And if he did, Blake might never ever know if there was a connection between Nathan and his sister's death. They had to get into that lab tonight.

"What's Nathan's motive? I mean why would a man in his position risk everything for this cloning experiment?"

At first, Whitney seemed startled, the way her body jerked at the sound of his voice. "I don't know. Greed? Power? Insanity?"

"Nathan's far from being insane. He's an eccentric oddball and a genius. The man knows exactly what he's doing. He does everything for a reason." Blake peered in the side-view mirror, mentally listing the makes and colors of the three vehicles behind them. "This whole situation reminds me of that religious sect a few years back, had claimed they'd produced the first cloned baby."

"The Raelians. I interviewed their leader in 2001. A real kook. He believed he was created by extra-terrestrials, and planned on building some sort of embassy in Jerusalem to welcome the return of his alien clan. One of the strangest interviews I've done in my...career."

Sadness and loss echoed in her voice. She wasn't taking the thought of unemployment very well. Who could blame her? Her job was her life, and so was his. He wished he could say everything would work out, but he couldn't. They'd be lucky if they survived the night.

Blake sucked in a deep breath and released it slowly. Lying, and leading a double life defined him. Who he'd been for over a decade. So why the sudden overwhelming urge to tell Whitney the truth?

Never compromise your cover.

The words had been drilled into his head since he'd joined the Bureau. He couldn't remember the last time he'd taken a woman out on more than two dates in a row. That's what working undercover got you. No real life. His job was his life.

Shaking off the familiar wave of guilt that came with leading a double life, he glanced at Whitney, then back to the road. She hadn't questioned him about Marlene. Must be killing her, especially after her inadequate attempt to hide her jealousy at the Cyber Hub. Considering how dangerous things could get tonight, some things needed to be said.

His palms grew damp. His gut tightened as he re-positioned his hands on the steering wheel for a better grip. Jesus. Nothing like feeling like an eighth-grader ready to proclaim his feelings to the girl of his dreams.

It's now or never.

He cleared his throat. "For the record, Marlene and I are friends. Nothing more. We've never even dated. She's not my type."

Whitney shifted in the seat and chuckled. "Miss Gorgeous isn't your type? Yeah, right. Come on. A Pam Anderson look-a-like is every man's dream."

"Not mine." Blake flicked on the left-hand turn signal and stopped at the red light. He looked down at Whitney's legs. Even in a pair of jeans, man, she had incredible legs, shapely and strong.

"I prefer a feisty blonde, turned brunette, with sexy ankles." His voice dropped a fraction. "Look, what I'm trying to say is I like you, like you a lot. I wanted you to know."

There, he said it. If by some vicious twist of fate things went terribly wrong tonight, he'd have no regrets.

Whitney turned and looked at him. His gaze held hers. She was as worried about tonight as he was.

"You make it sound like I'll never see you again. We'll pull this off. We have to." She leaned over and kissed his cheek. "I like you too."

The whisper-like contact of her lips on his skin seeped to his groin and gave him an instant hard-on. *You have no idea what you do to me, woman.*

A horn squawked repeatedly behind them. The light had turned green. Blake stepped on the gas and turned the corner. Daylight faded an hour earlier, replaced by a half-moon.

He pulled into the Starlight Motor Inn parking lot and shut off the truck. "Here we are."

Whitney wrinkled her nose and shot him her famous, 'you've-got-to-be-kidding' look. "Nice place."

"It'll have to do." After removing the keys from the ignition, he reached under his seat and pulled out his gun.

He sure as hell wasn't taking any chances. Not this time.

When Whitney opened the door and got out, she seemed to stagger, fighting to keep her footing on the pavement.

Blake hopped out and bolted to the other side of the pickup. He grabbed her arm, concerned she'd collapse. "Hey, you okay?"

In the diffused white light, her skin looked pale and her hands trembled slightly. He was worried but didn't let on. They would need every ounce of physical strength to get into the lab, and right now he wasn't sure if she had it in her.

"I'll be okay. I'm just a bit light headed. We haven't eaten a thing all day."

"Well, I'll have to fix that, won't I? Once you're settled inside, I'll go and pick us up some dinner." His departure for food would give him the needed opportunity to check in with his Bureau contact. Thanks to Whitney's growling stomach, he wouldn't have to dream up yet another excuse to leave—wouldn't have to lie again.

"There's a great little Italian take-out a few blocks from here. They make one mean veal scaloppini. Sound good?"

Her eyes widened and lit. "Sounds absolutely delicious. Maybe a salad. Oh, and something cold to drink."

"You got it." Blake guided her to the motel room, unlocked and opened the door.

The second he flicked on the light, Whitney's forehead creased, and she frowned.

Smoke-stained walls. Worn-out furniture marked with cigarette burns and the overpowering stench of ammonia. *Gross.*

"Lovely place." He'd met informants in better rooms than this. "Think of it this way." He shut and then locked the door. "We'll only be here for a few more hours. Eat, and go over the plan for tonight. Then we're out of here."

"Thank God." She set her purse on the worn bedspread next to their clothes and personal items he had dropped off before picking Whitney up at the police station.

He gathered Whitney tightly against his chest, her soft curves molded to his body. As he held her, he felt her uneven breathing against his cheek. "You sure you'll be okay while I'm gone?"

"I'm feeling better. I'll be fine. I'm going to take a quick shower and get ready for tonight."

He ran his hands down her back and firmly over her ass. "You know I'd rather stick around here and help wash your back."

A smile ruffled her mouth. "I'm sure you would. It's a nice thought, but feed me, please. I'm starving. It's going to be a long night."

If he kissed her on the lips, he'd never leave. After a long pause, he pressed his lips against her forehead instead. "I won't be long. Under no circumstances do you open the door. If there's a problem, my gun is on the nightstand. Use it."

CHAPTER TWENTY-SEVEN

Andrew West smiled, satisfied he'd done everything right. Stayed on the opposite side of the street at least eight feet behind her. Stopped and looked in a window or two using the reflection to keep his eye on the reporter. Then he'd tailed the pickup, kept no less than two cars between them, and changed lanes often, invisible in a river of rental cars.

Dad's cardinal rule of surveillance: *Never lose sight of your subject, Andy.*

Sitting in the rented Toyota Corolla at the end of the motel parking lot, he opened his canvas overnight bag and pulled out the 9 mm Glock pistol, courtesy of Nathan's treasure trove of unlimited assets.

Payback is a bitch.

The reporter and Neely had stopped at the Golden Gate Hotel earlier. No clue why.

Not that it matters—we're all here now for the grand finale.

Glancing through the windshield at room seven, he twisted the silencer into place at the end of the gun. Tonight, he preferred a handgun, loved the shorter radius between the front and rear sight more than with a rifle.

Up close and personal.

His attention flicked to the digital clock on the dash. His palms itched with anticipation.

Not much longer. Nathan would have his alibi.

He peered in the rearview mirror and grinned. This won't take long, not long at all.

Surprise. Kill. Leave.

❊ ❊ ❊

Whitney ducked under the shower one last time. Lukewarm water spurted and rushed over her head, soaking her hair until the shampooed strands turned into wet silk on her neck and back. She tried not to look or think about the numerous rust stains spotting the tub beneath her feet, but she couldn't. Goosebumps erupted under her skin and sent a chill through her body. She shut off the water and got out.

The Fiesta Gardens Motel had been a palace fit for a princess compared to this place. What a dump. After drying with a dingy, thin towel the color of dirty dish water, she put on a pair of black panties and matching bra, navy track pants and a navy V-neck top. As she bent over and towel dried her hair, her stomach twisted and rumbled with a mixture of hunger and worry.

Getting into the lab tonight would be dangerous, possibly deadly. They only had one chance. They'd either find the cloned child or die trying. The Las Vegas bookmakers would put Nathan as a two-to-one favorite. Okay, the odds sucked, but they had one thing in their favor. Surprise. Nathan had no clue as to what was about to go down while he faked his way through the Man of the Year awards dinner.

As scared as she was about not knowing the outcome of tonight's mission, Whitney knew one thing. She'd fallen in love with Blake. For the first time in her life, she'd met a man who truly cared for her, didn't feel threatened by her independence, didn't resent her job —well the job she'd had a day ago.

A cynical voice sliced through her thoughts.

He'll hurt you.

Blake had better be for real, 'what-you-see-is-what-you-get'. Her heart couldn't take another disappointment in the romance department, especially after her disastrous relationship with Mason.

She paused to catch her breath, her fears stronger than ever. Afraid to love Blake, afraid not to. Terrified they'd be dead by morning.

* * *

Andrew's pulse pounded in his ears. Scrunching down in the driver's seat he watched Neely's pickup speed out of the parking lot. Adrenalin surged through his fingertips to his toes. When the truck was out of sight, he climbed out of the rental car. In the distance, a sticky valve in a vehicle's engine ticked and caught his attention.

Get the room key.

After a quick scan of the half-empty lot, he walked briskly to the motel office, keeping the gun out of sight, tucked snug against the right rear pocket of his jeans.

Through the office window, he saw the weighty clerk, leaning on the counter reading a girlie magazine. Overhead bells jangled as Andrew opened the door. He stepped inside and did a quick inventory of his surroundings. The walls were bare, except for a clock, the furnishings sparse, and the air hot and stale.

The male clerk laid down the magazine, his ample forehead slick with sweat. "You need a room?"

Not likely. Andrew whipped the gun out from behind his back and jabbed the barrel into the man's cheek.

The guy's eyes bulged with fear. "Hey, mister. I don't want no trouble. The money's in the register. Take it, okay?"

Thanks, but no thanks. Andrew waved the gun. "Go on. Get in the back."

"Please don't kill me." The clerk turned and shuffled down a hallway where the motel jutted to the right. At the end, Andrew eyed the storage room filled with supplies.

Perfect. Even has a dead bolt on the outside of the door.

He shoved the gun into the clerk's back. "Now go on. Get in there. If you make any noise, I'll blow your fucking head off. Understand?"

The guy nodded and walked into the room. Andrew stepped back, closed the door three-quarters of the way and positioned the semi-automatic at the back of man's head.

No witnesses.

He squeezed the trigger.

A fine mist of blood sprayed from the exit wound. The clerk dropped forward like a toppled tree to the linoleum floor. As blood pooled around his head, a stream of red inched toward a mop and bucket in the corner. Without a second thought, Andrew shut the door and secured the lock. Before leaving the office, he located the duplicate room keys hanging inside a metal cupboard and snatched the one he wanted.

Outside, nothing moved except a light breeze. Giddy with excitement, Andrew sauntered along the motel's façade, ducking between the windows until he stood in front of room number seven. On the other side of the door, a television rumbled.

The twenty-four-hour news station, more than likely.

He gritted his teeth at the thought of her, how she'd ruined a good man's life—his father's.

Your time is up.

With the gun clutched in one hand, Andrew eased the key into the lock.

CHAPTER TWENTY-EIGHT

I nside Crispinos, a cubbyhole of a restaurant that smelled of Italian spices, garlic bread, and cheese, Blake sat and waited for his order. He stretched his arms above his head, trying to ease the stiffness in his shoulders.

Once he returned to the motel, he and Whitney would eat, and go over the plan for tonight one last time before heading to the complex.

Nathan had no idea how much his life was about to change. No more three-hundred-dollar cigars. No booze. No freedom. Only a six-by-eight cell. And when this mission was over, Blake could tell Whitney the truth. He had worked hard to keep his secret hidden, his real identity buried. How would she react? She had to understand. Not much different from reporters protecting their sources. All part of the job.

When his order was ready, Blake paid for the food and left. Outside, under the restaurant's green, white and red flag, he stopped on the pavement and stared at the Toyota Corolla parked behind his pickup. Something clicked in his mind. He'd seen that same model of rental car before, following them to the motel. Then a second time parked in the motel lot when he had left.

Could be just a coincidence... What if it wasn't?

"Shit." Blake hopped in the truck, dropped the bag of food on the seat next to him. Shoving the key in the ignition, he revved the engine and swung the truck out onto the street.

He tapped his fingers on the edge of the steering wheel. "I should never have left her alone."

Was he overreacting? Hell, there were thousands of that make and model rental cars in Vegas. Then why were his insides shaking with worry?

✳ ✳ ✳

Whitney thought she heard the motel room door close. Blake had returned. As if on cue, her stomach growled. She needed food. A headache pounded at her temples. She flung open the bathroom door and walked into the main area of the motel room.

"I can't wait to eat. I'm starving."

Her heart seemed to stop. Every sound in the room faded. A dark-haired man with a 9mm clutched in his right hand faced her, the gun aimed at her chest. His gaze locked with hers.

Andrew West. He'd come to kill her.

His black eyes held an expression intense with hatred. A sardonic smile twisted the corners of his mouth. "You know who I am."

"Yes." Whitney risked a glance to the nightstand and wished like hell she could get to Blake's gun obscured by clothes.

Six feet away.

Too far.

I am not dying in this dump of a motel room.

If she could just edge closer. Did the guy believe

she'd stand there and allow him to shoot her? An offensive move was better than a defensive one, her Sensei always said.

"You killed my father, you bitch. Now I get to kill you. And it will be an absolute pleasure." His muscles twitched in his bare arms as he slowly raised the gun.

Her pulse sped. Now was her chance. The only one she might get.

God, please let me live.

Adrenaline ripped through Whitney's veins, fueling her muscles making her limbs light and fast. She pivoted on her left leg, lifted her right leg high and struck Andrew's hand with the ball of her foot with such force, bones cracked and crunched. He never knew what hit him. The gun flew out of his hand. A white-copper flash exploded from the muzzle. Cordite filled the air. The round discharged and dug in into the smoke-stained stucco below the window. The weapon dropped behind the dresser.

Andrew clutched his right hand to his chest and barreled toward her with clenched teeth. "You bitch! I'll kill you!"

His booming threat jolted her heart rate into third gear. Her roundhouse kick caught him square in the jaw, spun him sideways and slammed his right shoulder into the door. A defined crack, like a branch snapping in two. A small victory for now, but he'd make another move yet. The only question was whether Whitney could get to Blake's gun before it was too late.

Andrew shook off the hit, recovering quicker than she anticipated. He fixed her with an icy glare that made her heart stop, again. If she didn't move now, she'd die.

She belly-flopped diagonally across the queen-sized bed and clawed her way to the nightstand, reached for the gun and missed. The lamp toppled to the carpet. The light bulb popped. The room darkened. The only light came from the bathroom. Barely able to catch her breath, a strong hand closed around her ankle.

"Where do you think you're going? We're not done. Not until you're dead." He grunted and worked to yank her off the bed. He outweighed her by a good eighty pounds.

She gasped small breaths and kicked at him with her free leg. Sweat rolled down her forehead. They tumbled to the floor. The sateen bedspread and ammonia-smelling sheets heaped around them.

"Get off me!" Whitney shoved and thrashed against his chest with her fists. "Help!"

Would anyone hear her? She attempted to ram her knee into his stomach, but couldn't.

He was too close.

He was gaining control.

His knee slammed under her ribcage.

Air exploded from her lungs. She clamped her mouth shut to kill the scream of pain erupting from her throat.

He had her pinned.

Help me. One huge hand seized her throat and squeezed. Hot breath touched her ear. "Now you die."

Steel bands of panic tightened around Whitney's chest.

Fight. Can't give up. She slapped and clawed at his face. Beneath her nails, a long welt opened down his cheek. Something else he wasn't expecting. Blood dripped on her collarbone.

Eyes wild, Andrew let go of her neck. "You cut me, you fucking bitch."

She wheezed and gulped a breath, and then another. He raised his hand. His fingers curled into a fist, ready to punch her face. Three loud, sharp raps on the door stopped his hand in mid-air. He turned his head toward the door.

"Whitney, are you in there?"

It was Cliff. He was early.

"Help me, Cliff." Her words never came out any louder than a strained whisper. She twisted and squirmed under Andrew's weight until she freed a leg. With every ounce of strength, Whitney jammed her socked heel into his larynx. His unbroken hand immediately went to his throat. He stared at her, wide-eyed, for one brief second before the blow sent him hurtling backward into the dresser. She rolled to her feet, scurried around the bare mattress, and retrieved Blake's gun, determined to stop her attacker.

Andrew continued to grip his throat. Pain distorted his face. Then he lunged forward.

"Go straight to hell." She fired the gun.

The acrid scent of gunpowder filled the space between them. His head snapped back from the impact of the bullet. Blood, bone fragments and brain matter scarred the wall behind him. For a few brief seconds, his body jerked and twitched. His knees caved beneath him, folding him into a lifeless heap next to the wastebasket. A fitting end for a piece of garbage.

The strength that had carried her through the last horrible minutes vanished. Her legs wobbled. She sat on the edge of the bed and kept the gun on her lap.

Blake burst through the door and hurried to her.

Cliff was right behind him. He stopped, looked at the body on the carpet, then cast her a questioning glance, but didn't ask what had happened. For the first time since Whitney had met her co-worker, he was speechless. Completely out of character. She wondered how long his silence would last.

Blake sat next to her, took the gun from her lap, and put his arm around her shoulders.

Sweat stung her eyes. She blinked and stared at him. "I killed him. I had to."

"I know, honey. It's over."

Whitney's voice lowered to a whisper. "For now."

"Yeah, for now. Are you hurt?"

She lowered her head and examined the bruises and red welts on both her arms. "No. Just sore."

Cliff finally spoke. "I'll call the police." He pulled his cell phone from his shirt pocket.

"No. I'll look after it." Blake removed his arm from her shoulders and stood. "Cliff, stay with her while I make the call."

Blake's abrupt instructions turned softer when he bent and gently kissed her forehead. "I'll be right back, okay?"

Whitney nodded, somewhat confused. What difference did it make who called the authorities? Something wasn't right. For the life of her, she had no idea what.

CHAPTER TWENTY-NINE

After Blake brought his SAC, Trent Chambers, up to speed on what had transpired, he had a brief conversation with Mike and then ended the call. They had a body that needed to be processed, and little time to waste dealing with the local cops. Nailing Nathan was still priority one.

Tell Whitney the truth. Time's running out.

The thought struck Blake with icy certainty. How to tell the woman he was in love with he wasn't who he claimed to be. He was nervous. He'd never been in this position before. The news might not go over well.

With the Bureau's field office less than ten blocks away, Mike would arrive soon to handle the cops, allowing Blake and Whitney free to leave. In less than four hours, Nathan would return from his awards dinner and learn that Andrew West was dead. No telling what the wide-eyed weirdo would do next. Kill the kid? Flee the country? Blake hadn't spent close to a year undercover to let the slimy bastard slip through his fingers. Shaw had something to do with his sister's death. Blake bet his life on it. His gut instinct had never steered him wrong before.

Under the weak glow of the parking lot lights, Blake

opened the car door and conducted a visual search of the green Toyota Corolla. Fast food wrappers littered the back floor, a canvas duffle bag sat on the passenger seat. As much as he wanted to know what was inside the bag, he didn't want to destroy any possible evidence that might link Nathan to West. Blake popped the glove box, and carefully removed a clear vinyl envelope containing the rental agreement. His suspicions were confirmed. The vehicle had been rented to Andrew West. Before closing the car door, he set the agreement back where he'd found it. With the shrinking timeline looming like a rain cloud ready to explode, he high-tailed it to the motel office.

He'd move Whitney to another room where they could talk in private, away from the hustle and bustle about to descend on the crime scene.

Inside the compact office, Blake found the front desk area empty. Behind the counter, a computer monitor sat atop a dusty shelf with its screen turned from the public eye.

Too damned quiet. He didn't like it. Uneaseness gripped his gut. He reached under his T-shirt and pulled out his weapon. After unlatching the safety with his thumb, he peered around the corner. "Hello? Anyone here?"

When no one answered, he crept down the narrow hallway, gun readied, his rubber-soled shoes silent on the aged green linoleum. To the left, a small bathroom. Further down on the right, a room secured with a padlock. Blood seeped beneath the door.

Shit.

He lifted his leg and kicked open the flimsy, wooden door. The rancid stench of death eased up his nostrils.

"Jesus."

A male body lay face down on the tile floor. A halo of crimson encircled what was left of his head. Blake turned away. He'd experienced this type of scene before. Hellish images no human could ever get used to, not even a veteran agent. A single shot to the back of the head where the skull met the spine. That's all it took. The clerk was dead before he hit the floor. Quick and painless. Executed by Andrew West.

After getting the key to the room, Blake hurried out of the office. Across the parking lot, three curious onlookers gathered on the sidewalk, pointing, and talking amongst themselves. Unlike most crime scenes, at least he didn't have to contend with a mob of bystanders. The familiar low growl of a motor cut the night. The '69 cherry-red Camaro rumbled into the parking lot. Just like his personal vehicle, his Bureau contact wasn't someone you forgot easily. At six-four, Mike was stocky and as intimidating as hell. He looked more like a hulking bounty hunter or an undercover cop than an FBI agent.

Mike pulled up next to Blake, shut off the car and hung his head out the window. "Hey, man. Good to see you. It's been a while. Where's the body?"

Blake knelt to window level and smiled, happy to see his ex-marine buddy. "Room seven. There's another one in the motel office storage room. I'll move Whitney next door into room six. I need to talk to her alone."

Mike climbed out of the car and shut the door. A moment of silence passed between them before he spoke again. "You going to tell her?"

"I have to." Blake forced his voice to sound optimistic. "She needs to hear the truth from me." He noticed the tense look on his friend's face.

"You must really have it bad for this one." Mike patted him on the shoulder. "Good luck, man."

Luck was what Blake needed. As they walked to his pickup, sirens shrieked, louder, closer. Not much longer and they'd have a full house.

You have to tell her.

Blake shook the thought away and changed his train of thought. "Make sure the crime scene guys also sweep the green Corolla." He pointed to the west edge of the motel property.

"Looking for anything in particular?"

Blake opened his pickup door and grabbed the bag of take-out from the front seat, then he closed the door. "Anything that can put the final nail in Nathan Shaw's coffin."

"Gotcha." Mike handed him a key. "Here. Everything you need for tonight is at Portal Storage. Unit thirty-four. You sure you don't want any backup?"

"Thanks, but no. Christ, Chambers is already pissed off enough at me. He gave me a ten-minute verbal ass-chewing. The fewer agents involved the better. I need to handle this one personally." In other words, the Bureau would only lose one agent if the plan went south.

"I had Allison run a check on Erik Friklin. Seems he came into some cash recently. Two deposits of five grand, each a week apart. Small enough to fly under the bank's radar no-questions-asked."

Blake rubbed his chin now prickly with stubble. "So, Andrew West paid Friklin to kidnap George Raines."

"Looks that way."

"Makes sense. I bet Friklin thought he'd really hit

the jackpot when he met West. All he had to do was exchange George for Nathan's precious videotape. A heart attack would've been the furthest thing from the guy's mind. Anything else?"

"So far there isn't any evidence linking Nathan Shaw to West or Friklin. Shaw's done a good job covering his ass."

The news, or lack of, didn't surprise Blake one bit. "Nathan's too smart to leave a trail that could lead back to him."

But Blake also knew from past cases, even the most brilliant minds eventually screwed up, and he was counting on that fact.

"If you change your mind about backup, you know where to find me. Otherwise, I'll meet you at Nellis Air Force Base." Mike shoved his hands in his jeans pocket. "Nail Shaw's ass to the wall. And stay safe, man."

Blake smiled. "Safe is the only way to be."

Inside the motel room, Blake found Whitney exactly where he'd left her, sitting on the bed. Cliff stood by the window with his suit jacket slung over his shoulder. You couldn't cut the tension in the room with a machete.

Blake held out his hand to Whitney. "Come on, we'll go next door."

She eased to her feet. Her face twisted in pain.

"I'm coming with you." Cliff took a step ready to follow them.

Mike moved in front of Cliff and blocked the doorway. "Whoa there, slick. You're not going anywhere. You're a witness to a crime. We'll need your statement."

Cliff groaned, and stepped back, his cocky demeanor diminishing quickly. "You've got to be kidding. I was held at the airport for hours, now this. I didn't witness anything. You can't hold me."

Blake cut in. "They can and will."

Cliff turned to Whitney. "Whitney, tell them—tell them who I am. You know I didn't see anything."

Whitney shot Cliff a 'I-don't-give-a-shit-look.' "Sorry, Cliff. You're on your own. Believe me, it's for your own safety."

Cliff jabbed a finger at her. "Ungrateful bitch."

Blake gritted his teeth. He'd known Peterson for less than ten minutes and already he'd had enough of the jerk. He shoved him against the wall, held him there with an arm pressed hard against the guy's chest. "Now, apologize to the lady."

A few beats of silence passed. Blake forced his arm harder into Cliff's chest. Cliff's eyes bulged as he squeaked and choked. "I'm—sorry."

Blake smiled to himself and lowered his arm. "That's better." He escorted Whitney to the door.

As they left the room, Mike leaned against the door-jamb and smiled a goofy grin. Blake was confident his buddy would keep Peterson out of their hair, even if Mike had to handcuff him to the bumper of his beloved Camaro.

❋ ❋ ❋

Settled in the room next door, the air felt thick and murky, much like Blake's courage. As minutes ticked by, he ran a hand over his tired eyes. Exhaustion had set in hours ago and there was still a long night ahead. While moonlight spilled through the room's thin cur-tains, he studied Whitney as she inhaled the lukewarm veal he'd picked up earlier.

He wasn't hungry. His appetite had disappeared when he realized he had no choice but to tell Whitney the truth. Her hair was mussed; dark wisps fell across her forehead. Reddish-blue bruises formed the outline of a hand imprint around her neck. A protective need washed over him. He wanted to hold her and kiss every part of her body that West had hurt. Never had Blake been so relieved when he'd opened their motel room door and found Whitney alive and that piece of scum dead on the floor. In the end, West got what he deserved. And Whitney deserved to know the truth. She'd more than earned the right.

"Feeling better?"

She put down the plastic fork and knife next to the Styrofoam takeout container. A paper napkin fluttered to the carpet. "Quite a bit. But we need to leave soon."

He glanced at the clock radio and contemplated the tight timeline. An hour to prepare. Two hours to drive to the complex, which left less than an hour to get in and out alive with the kid. Alive being the key.

"I know." He inhaled a deep breath and released it slowly, his gaze never wavering from hers. "First, we need to talk." He reached and touched her arm.

She flinched. "Don't you dare say I'm not coming with you, because I am. I want to see Nathan behind bars as much as you do. Probably more."

Her adamant tone amused him. One of the many traits he loved about her. But that amusement disappeared.

Get it over with.

Every sound in the room washed away, except for his heartbeat thudding in his ears.

"Don't worry. You're coming with me." He noticed his voice had taken on a somber tone. His courage faltered again.

Tell her.

There would be no turning back.

He cracked his knuckles. "I'm an FBI agent."

* * *

Every nerve ending in Whitney's body went numb. She couldn't believe her ears. She stared at Blake, mouth agape, not knowing what to say. The man she was in love with had lied to her. Her mind raced. Everything clicked and finally made sense. His short and vague answers to her questions, hiding the fact he was a sky marshal, and those secretive phone calls. How could she trust him now? A realm of unanswered questions ran rampant in her mind. What else had he lied about? His feelings for her? Then reflexes took over. She raised her hand and slapped him across the face.

Blake ran his fingers over his left cheek. He didn't appear surprised by her physical reaction.

"You should have told me. I'm a reporter. I protect sources every day. I keep secrets. That's what I do."

"Whitney, of all people, you should understand. It's my job. I couldn't jeopardize the mission to bag Nathan. You know damn well we're both on the same team."

I thought we were. "Clearly, we aren't. Who the hell did you think I'd tell?"

"It's not like that."

Not only did she feel hurt, she felt used. Her voice quivered slightly. "Then explain it for me."

"I took an oath, just like you. I'm sorry I couldn't tell you until now. I'm still the same person, and my feelings for you are real."

Yeah, right. *Do you really think I'm that gullible?* "I don't believe you." She took a sip of water and slammed the bottle down on the dresser.

He was no better than Mason. Why couldn't Blake have been truthful, especially when he'd known how she felt about Mason's lies? Her heart squeezed hard. How could she have fallen for another liar? This was the unkindest cut of all. She should have stuck to her plan when it came to men. No feelings, no promises, equalled no hurt, ever.

Blake slid off the bed onto his knees. "Talk to me."

She stood, placed her hands on her hips and narrowed her eyes. "Is your name even Blake Neely?"

"No. It's Robert Blake Barnett. I go by Blake. I promise I'll answer all your questions on the way to the complex."

Claire Barnett's obituary whirled through Whitney's mind. Obviously, Blake hadn't been mentioned as Claire's brother to protect his cover. Disbelief swelled. Being with him this past week felt so right, so natural as if they'd known each other for months. Only now did she realize she knew nothing about him. Who was she angrier with? Blake for lying, or herself for falling for him? What kind of reporter was she? Part of her job involved, following up on tips, cultivating sources, and sifting through information. Blake worked for the FBI. How had she missed the signs? Investigative reporting 101. *Be pro-active.* She'd become too emotionally involved and didn't do her job. Damn him. She clenched her hands into fists and stalked to the door.

Blake hopped to his feet, caught her arm, and stopped her. "You're not leaving without me. We need each other, and you know it."

I thought I needed you in more ways than one. I was wrong. She glared into his brown eyes. All she saw was betrayal. A long moment passed, and he released her. Thank God. The comfort and familiarity of his closeness stabbed at her heart.

Angry and hurt, she sat on the bed and crossed her arms over her chest. She needed him. Needed his expertise and skills to get into the lab. On a personal level, to hell with Blake. Forget about him. She couldn't allow him to continue to affect her this way. The man was nothing more than a distraction from her real purpose—the story of a lifetime.

A fury of rapidly moving footsteps outside the room caught her attention. Three sharp raps at the door followed.

Blake's gaze met hers. Although he tried to hide it, Whitney saw a flash of hope in his eyes. Hope that she could get past his deception—that things would be okay between them. She slammed the brakes on her thoughts. Another unguarded moment and her heart broke again.

"Blake, wait. There's something I need to say." Whitney lowered her head. God, she couldn't even look him in the eye. "We can only be friends. Nothing more."

He turned to answer the door, his voice tinged with concern. "We'll talk about this later."

"I'm not changing my mind." *I can't.*

The man, who had stopped Cliff from following them, stepped inside. Blake closed the door. "Whitney, this is Mike Jacobs. He's—FBI too."

Through a haze of stifled anger, Whitney's muscles tensed and she forced herself to speak. "Hi."

The man smiled. "Hi."

He appeared to be about the same age as Blake, with brown hair to his shoulders and a silver stud in his right ear. Mike didn't look like your stereotypical FBI agent, but neither did Blake. No Brooks Brothers suit, no FBI jacket with his credentials hanging around his neck like in the movies. Instead, faded blue jeans, cowboy boots and a black shirt.

Mike leaned against the chair next to the window. "You're cleared to leave. Everything's looked after." He handed Blake what appeared to be a badge. "You're going to need this."

Blake took the wallet style ID, and slid it into the back pocket of his jeans. "I haven't seen this baby in months. Feels good to have it back."

Whitney eyed Blake's gun, tucked in his waistband. No wonder he looked so at ease carrying a gun. He'd been carrying one for years.

Mike placed his hand on the doorknob. "McBride and Cally are at the convention center keeping tabs on Nathan. McBride will contact you the moment Shaw leaves the site."

Blake nodded.

As the two men continued to talk, Whitney tried to imagine what it would be like working undercover for months, sometimes years, living a lie to nail the bad guy. A lonely, yet noble job. Noble or not, that still didn't excuse the fact he had lied to her. She could understand not telling just anyone he was an agent, but hell, she thought they'd shared something special. Stupid. Stupid. Stupid. Blake glanced over Mike's shoulder and smiled. Desire curled in her stomach. She wanted Blake in her life. Now all she needed to do was convince herself to forgive him.

CHAPTER THIRTY

*F*riends. A word Blake didn't want to hear. Okay, so she hadn't counted on falling in love. That wasn't part of his plan, either.

He sat at the foot of the bed with his elbows resting on his knees, his hands steepled. As Whitney walked to the bathroom, deep lines etched her forehead. Was that a glint of uncertainty flickering in her eyes? He could only pray she'd change her mind.

He hopped to his feet and paced the length of the room. Hell, maybe she was right. Maybe they should be just friends. Leading a double life was part of who he was, who he'd always been. His life was complicated, and his job was demanding and secretive. Enough with the excuses. You love her, don't you?

"Yes."

Then fight for her.

Blake plopped back down on the bed and raked his fingers through his hair. He could push her. However, pushing could very well backfire in his face. On the other hand, he could let the subject slide, give her time to forgive and forget, but right now time wasn't on their side. He wanted her so badly he could still smell her perfume. He'd like nothing more than to hold her, kiss her...

His gaze drifted to the clock. He quickly dismissed

the thoughts. He had to. Thanks to Andrew West, they'd lost a good two hours, which prevented Blake's plan of hang gliding into the facility. There wouldn't be enough time before Nathan left the awards dinner. They'd have to go in with guns blazing.

The risk factor had just quadrupled.

When Whitney emerged from the bathroom, a bit of color had returned to her face, far from the healthy pink glow she'd donned earlier. The bruises around her neck had transformed to a deep bluish-black. The breath burned in Blake's throat. Good thing Whitney had shot the bastard. If he had gotten a hold of West, he would've made him suffer long and hard before putting a bullet in his head. His hands balled into fists. Damn it! He should've been there to protect her.

Between his deception, and West's twisted revenge kick, the woman had to be a total mess inside. He wondered how she was coping because he knew first-hand killing another human was difficult to deal with. Guilt could suck the life out of you if you allowed it to. Just another chapter in his own life he'd have to come clean about if he had any chance with Whitney. All she wanted was honesty. Could he give her what she needed? Christ, he wanted to more than anything.

Tense silence hung in the air for several moments before their gazes met.

Blake stood. "You ready to go?

She glanced at her watch. "Yes."

When she said, "Time to take care of *business*," with the emphasis on business, he knew he had his work cut out for him. Forgiveness wasn't going to be easy. This was one battle he intended on winning.

❋ ❋ ❋

Whitney stepped outside the motel room. A bevy of flashing blue lights swirled and forced her to squint. Yellow crime scene tape stretched the edge of the parking lot. Inside the cordoned off area, three police cruisers flanked the sidewalk. An ambulance sat unattended with its back doors open in front of the room where Andrew West's body lay. She grimaced and bit her bottom lip, trying to suppress the realization of what she'd done.

She had killed a man. What choice did she have? It was her life or Andrew West's. If she had no other option, then why did she feel so guilty?

The shrill blare of a siren cut through her thoughts. A second ambulance swooped into the parking lot and pulled up to the motel office.

A shiver drove up her spine. Whitney froze in mid-step and turned to Blake. "What's going on? Was someone else hurt?"

"West shot the desk clerk."

The words tumbled from her lips even though she knew the answer. "Is he—"

"Yeah, I'm afraid so."

Her stomach clutched with anger. It was hard to believe how many lives Andrew West had destroyed. Whitney knew she wasn't responsible for his father's death. Suicide was Ramon Sheppard's choice. When she had broken the story, her facts were correct, and a jury found Shepard guilty, not her. Still, there were so many unanswered questions. Was Andrew West adopted? Did he kill Mason? Had he played a part in Blake's sister's death as well, or was that Nathan's doing?

Blake's hand wrapped around hers, and damn if her stomach didn't quiver from his touch. Why did he do that? Act as if things were fine between them. Everything she thought she knew about him was a lie. Damn him. She snatched her hand from his grasp and quickened her step.

After getting into his truck, Whitney fastened the seatbelt. Blake slid into the driver's seat. He secured his seatbelt and started the engine.

Mike crossed in front of the truck's headlights.

Blake rolled down the window. "What's up?"

"Thought you should know. Nathan's cell phone logs turned up empty. So did West's home phone and work line."

Blake smacked his hand down on the steering wheel. "Sonofabitch."

Even with the Bureau's high-tech spy device, the Carnivore, which scanned private messages through Internet providers, not one incriminating email had been intercepted. Nathan had covered his tracks well. Too well.

Blake rubbed the bridge of his nose. "We've got nothing worthwhile to get an arrest warrant."

Mike nodded. "Looks that way."

Whitney sat forward in the seat. "Maybe they used disposable cell phones."

Blake looked at her. "Could be, but without the actual phone or number, it'll be next to impossible to locate the communications company that transmitted the calls." He turned back to Mike. "Find out where West was staying. He had to have had a room somewhere in Vegas. Take Jimmy Velez with you."

"Will do." Mike poked his head inside the truck and gave Blake a stony look. "Don't let that slimy piece of crap walk."

Gooseflesh broke out on her skin at the thought of Nathan getting away with murder. "Not a chance in hell."

"She's right. Shaw is going down. We'll get the evidence we need. You can bet on it, Mike."

"Hey, I almost forget. I have a message from Chambers."

Blake rolled his eyes. "What's the message?"

Mike smiled. "The boss told me to remind you that you're, and I quote, 'skating on fucking thin ice.'"

Blake grinned as he put the vehicle in drive. "Hell, when aren't I?"

❋ ❋ ❋

At Portal Storage, Whitney waited by the truck as Blake loaded the second of two black canvas backpacks containing aerosol cans of tear gas, pepper spray and other items they would need, into the trunk of the Chevy Cavalier.

Changing vehicles might give them a slight advantage. At least security would be looking for Blake's pickup, not a car. Part of her was also relieved to learn she wouldn't be hang gliding in the middle of the night. The other part of her was nervous as hell. Blake's revised plan was extremely risky. Could they actually pull this off?

Whitney schooled herself to stay calm even though her heart pounded against her ribs. "This is going to work, isn't it?"

"It has to." He walked to the other side of the car and handed her a bulletproof vest. "Put this on."

She took the vest and slipped the protective gear over her head.

He stood behind her and helped tighten the Velcro straps, his breath warm on the side of her neck. "It has to fit snug for maximum protection."

Her pulse jumped by his nearness. Her breathing grew shallow, and her blood seemed to heat. Too close for comfort. *Change the subject.* "Were you really in the Marines, or was that a lie as well?"

He turned her to face him, his eyes narrowed. "No, I was in the Marines." Then he stuffed his hands into his pockets like a first-grader and stalked to the car.

Behind her, Whitney heard him swear before the car door slammed shut.

* * *

Whitney watched the inky blackness of the desert speed by her window. She pushed the button to unroll her window a crack and welcomed the rush of fresh air. They hadn't said two words to each other since they'd left the outskirts of Vegas over an hour ago. Out of the corner of her eye, lights from the console illuminated Blake's set jaw.

"So how long are you going to stay pissed at me?"

She switched her gaze from the window to the chipped nail polish on her fingernails. "Forever."

He removed one hand from the steering wheel, and gently stroked the side of her face with his fingers. "Forever could be an awfully long time, Whitney. Can't we start over?"

No. She looked at him. Her voice hardened. "Why?"

"Because I'm in love with you."

The words wrapped around her like a warm blanket. Her hand clutched the strap of her purse. Why should she believe him? She'd trusted Mason and look where that got her. Cheated on and divorced.

However, Blake wasn't Mason. Not even close.

God, she wanted to believe Blake.

Remorse quickly quieted her tone. "Friends. That's the way it has to be."

She knew he turned his head, so she couldn't see how much her answer affected him.

Several minutes passed. Blake abruptly swung the car to the side of the road and threw the vehicle into park.

He flicked on the interior light.

She blinked in the sudden glare. "What are you doing?"

"You want honesty. It starts right here, right now. But you might not like what you hear."

His lips tightened. "About eleven years ago, I killed a man. He had figured out Mike and I were agents and threatened our undercover mission to bag his twin brother, a major Colombian drug and arms dealer. I'm not proud. I did it out of necessity. And I'd do it again."

His what-do-you-think-of-me-now admission took her by surprise and her face probably showed it. He stared at her, his eyes searching. For what? Confirmation? Empathy? Acceptance? For a long moment, she was speechless. How could she judge him, when she was no better? She too had killed out of necessity—simply under different circumstances.

"Why are you telling me this now?"

Blake flipped off the interior light, hit the gas, and pulled back onto the road. "Because I might not get another chance."

The bulletproof vest felt heavy as lead as if it was squeezing the breath out of her. The full horror of what they were about to do hit her.

❊ ❊ ❊

The hair on Whitney's arms stood on end. At the south corner of the facility, Blake parked the car, popped the trunk and got out. When he closed the door, a tinny echo sliced through the silence. She climbed out of the car and scanned the darkness. Nothing but barren desert for miles. No traffic. Even the desert animals appeared to be snoozing.

She took a long, deep breath, and let it out slowly. "Can I help with anything?"

He lifted the cardboard box containing the dynamite from the trunk. "No. Stay here. If you see a vehicle, let me know."

The clouds drifted apart and the moon emerged. That's when she noticed the disappointment he tried to hide in his eyes. Guilt pinched her. She nodded before looking away.

While Blake set the explosives, Whitney's mind drifted. At one point during the week, she really wanted to get to know Blake, every detail of him. Something about being in his presence lured her in—made her body weak.

Get over him. You have to. She blew out an angry breath and cursed the effect he still had on her.

"I'm done. We have to get moving." When Blake tossed the empty box back into the trunk and closed the lid, Whitney had no idea how much time had passed.

They jumped back into the car and drove about two miles before stopping again.

"We've got less than fifteen minutes before the explosives blow. Then all hell is going to break loose. Security will be hopping. That's when we'll slip through the main gates on foot." Blake handed her a gun. "Keep this handy and be prepared to use it."

A stinging burn flooded her stomach. With a shaky hand, she took the weapon. She didn't want to kill again. Once was more than enough.

"Remember, stay close. Keep your earpiece in at all times. No one will be able to hear our conversations."

"What about the cameras? They're everywhere."

"I'll look after that problem once we're in."

When his cell phone rang, Whitney almost jumped out of her skin.

He grabbed the phone from the dash and answered the call.

Her muscles tensed.

"McBride, what's his ETA?" Blake's eyebrows twisted. "Shit. Yeah, thanks, man." He shut off the phone, tossed it on the seat between them. "Nathan is just getting ready to leave the convention center."

"Oh, no. Not yet." She eyed the clock on the dash.

Nine minutes...

As they neared the facility, she peered to the east. Even from a distance, the huge structure of concrete and steel dwarfed everything around it.

Blake shut off the headlights and slowly pulled over to the ditch.

Six minutes...

In the near darkness of the vehicle, his gaze locked onto hers. Whitney knew what had to be done. She wouldn't see him again after tonight. The thought squeezed at her heart. She'd get the story, then immediately head home to Florida and forget Blake Barnett had ever entered her life. Of course, that was if she didn't get herself killed tonight.

They got out. Opened the trunk. Put on the backpacks and black ball caps.

Two minutes...

Blake raced along the fence. Whitney followed, her legs heavy from fatigue and the strain of fighting off Andrew West. A hundred feet from the entrance, Blake held out his arm to stop her, directing her attention to the two cameras mounted on either side of the towering gates.

One minute...

Suddenly, he tilted her chin and kissed her. Her knees weakened by the softness of his lips. She thought for sure she'd collapse like a pile of warm mush to the ground.

He broke the kiss and looked into her eyes. "In case I don't ever get the chance to do that again."

The first explosion rocked the desert floor with a deafening roar. Yellow and orange flames leaped high into the night sky. Sparks rained down through a plume of gray-white smoke. Several seconds later, another blast, and then another.

CHAPTER THIRTY-ONE

Blake crouched between the cement pillars. While the facility's alarm howled like a tornado warning system, beads of sweat slid down the side of his neck and pooled at the edge of his Kevlar vest. He sucked in a big gulp of air. He smelled and tasted nothing but smoke.

As the final explosion pierced the night, Blake yanked on Whitney's arm, pulled her to her knees beside him. "Stay down. It won't be long now."

His limbs tingled with anticipation and fear. The risk was high, the unknowns, countless. The chance of dying—Christ, he didn't want to think about it.

Being the head of security did have its privileges. He knew the company's protocols inside and out. Hell, he'd redesigned those months ago. He dropped his backpack, reached in and grabbed his night vision goggles. After pulling them on, Blake poked his head around the pillar and peered through the fence, training his gaze to the main entryway. Sweat stung his eyes. He blinked to clear his vision.

Through the green glow of the goggles, he watched employees pour out the revolving front door in controlled chaos. Some hurried. Others walked to their living quarters, exactly where they were supposed to go during a "situation." A situation had never happened in the past—only numerous practice drills.

Three hundred feet from the entrance, Bravo team had gathered, fully armed, ready to use any means necessary to protect Nathan's dynasty. Norm Camaron appeared to be missing from the mix. Blake clenched his jaw. Norm should be with them directing the team, but he wasn't. What was he up to?

The team dispersed and packed into three Humvees.

Whitney's voice squeaked in Blake's earpiece. "What's happening?"

Headlights flicked on simultaneously. Blake crawled backward behind the column, collected his backpack and slung it over his shoulder.

"They're coming." After removing the goggles, tossing them in his pack, he squeezed Whitney's hand. "Be ready to move."

She nodded her eyes wide beneath the peak of the ball cap. Her gaze darted back and forth. The woman looked terrified. Who could blame her?

Headlights splashed bouncing shadows across the road. Seconds ticked away. The steel gates opened.

They wouldn't have much time.

He retrieved his gun tucked in the waistband of his jeans and kept the weapon at his side.

The security vehicles charged by and left a massive dust cloud in their wake. Once the last Humvee's taillights were no longer visible, he hopped to his feet, forcing Whitney to hers.

It was now or never.

They slipped behind the cameras, through the gates

and ran like hell.

While they ducked behind a boulder and waited for the last of the employees to trickle out of the building, thunder rumbled, and for a few moments drowned out the wailing alarm. The weather echoed his thoughts. What was the connection between Nathan and his sister? Would he ever know the truth about Claire's death?

Blake looked at Whitney. "Get your weapon out."

Without hesitation, she pulled the gun from her backpack. As the wind picked up, lightning spidered across the sky. A millisecond later, another vicious snarl of thunder bit the air.

Her thumb flicked off the safety. "How long before security realizes the explosions were only a diversion?"

Not long enough. "If we're lucky, maybe fifteen minutes."

The same sinking feeling he had in the pit of his stomach mirrored in Whitney's eyes. He redirected his gaze back to the entrance just as Norm stepped out the door, stopped, and lit a cigarette. Then he hurried toward the security parking lot.

After a quick scan of the area, Blake grabbed Whitney's hand. As they ran fast and low, gravel sprayed beneath their shoes. Careful to stay out of view from the numerous cameras positioned throughout the area, they zigzagged through the gardens filled with rocks and thorny plants.

Stopped at the northeast corner of the building, Blake watched Norm. What he noticed next made his heart skip a beat. Norm stood next to a black Chevy Camaro parked in the last slot.

"Son of a bitch." *That's the car that tried to run me*

down at the airport. Blake's pulse hammered in his ears.

"What is it?"

He ignored Whitney's question and sprinted across the parking lot. His hands landed on Norm's shoulders. He shoved the man backward against the trunk of the car. "You asshole!"

Norm let out a painful grunt when his lower back slammed into the vehicle.

"How much did Nathan pay you?"

Norm avoided eye contact with him, and finally answered through a raspy cough. "Twenty—thousand. I had to. My son—needed money."

From past conversations, Blake knew Norm's thirty-something kid had a chronic gambling problem. Still didn't give the guy an excuse to try to kill him.

"What's the connection between Shaw and Claire Barnett?" When Norm didn't answer, Blake wrapped one hand around Norm's neck and squeezed. "Answer me, damn it!"

Perspiration trickled down the man's temples. He jerked his head back and forth. "I don't know."

"Bullshit. You know, and you're going to bloody well tell me."

Whitney's hand clamped down on Blake's shoulder. "Stop it. We don't have time for this. We need to get inside."

He gritted his teeth. As much as he wanted, needed answers right now, she was right. They had to keep moving. Blake removed his grip from Norm's neck and jabbed his gun under the man's ribs. "Give me the keys."

Norm slipped a hand into his pants pocket, pulled out a key ring and handed it to him.

Blake passed the keys to Whitney. "If something

happens and we can't get out together, take his car. Head north on the highway. Mike and the rest of the team will be waiting at Nellis Air Force Base."

She held out her hand, her fingers trembled. "But—"

"No buts, Whitney." His gaze roamed her pale face. "That's the way it has to be. Understand?"

Her gaze lowered. "Yes." She finally took the keys, slipping them into her jeans pocket.

His attention shifted to Norm. The guy didn't know it yet, but he'd be their ticket in and out of the complex, a bargaining chip if needed. Blake removed Norm's employee keycard hanging around his neck, and then swiped the card through the scanner. The service entrance door buzzed open.

He pointed his gun at Norm's head. "Now you're going to take us to the kid. And don't pretend you don't know anything about her either."

❊ ❊ ❊

The helicopter turned sharply right. Nathan white-knuckled the weighty glass statue he balanced in his lap. He leaned back in the seat, loosened his silk tie and undid the top button of his white shirt. Why hadn't he heard from Andrew West? The man had proved to be more than reliable in the past week. He should have checked in by now.

Nathan adjusted his headset. "How much longer?"

"About twelve minutes, sir." His female pilot glanced at him, and then ahead to the instrument panel. Her shiny white helmet vibrated a rainbow of colors and reflected off the instrument panel.

There was no point in cracking open one of his treasured bottles of Krug, Clos du Mesnil, at least not yet. He smiled to himself. Champagne would flow the second he heard the reporter and Neely were dead.

* * *

Aching muscles and exhaustion were history. The frigid coldness of the stainless-steel walls seeped into Whitney's bones. She tightened her grip on the gun and crept down the corridor behind Blake and Norm. With each careful step, her heart pounded triple time. Regardless of what Blake had said, she wasn't leaving without him. They had come together. They'd leave together. Saying goodbye would come soon enough. Too soon.

A few feet ahead, she watched the two men disappear around the corner and out of sight.

Her earpiece crackled. She heard Blake draw in a sharp breath, followed by, "Don't move."

Whitney's heart jumped. She stopped, held the gun tight to her chest and waited. Finally, he gave the "all clear."

Shaking inside, she steadied her legs before proceeding down the hall. What the hell was she doing? She had to be insane to think they could pull this off. Even if they found the child, would they get out of the complex alive? Too late to turn back now. She firmed her grip on the weapon and met up with Blake and Norm at the service elevator.

Blake dug Norm's cell phone out of the man's jacket pocket.

"Call security. Inform Jackson a bomb threat was just called in. Tell him to evacuate the area immediately."

He handed the phone to Norm and lowered his

voice. "If you do anything to screw this up, I'll put a bullet in your gut and leave you here to die. Got it?"

Norm's eyes widened. He snatched the phone and made the call.

Whitney knew by the worried expression on Blake's face they were running out of time. She broke out in a cold sweat. "How long to clear the security room?"

"Less than four minutes. They know the drill." Blake stared at his watch. "This way no one will be physically monitoring the cameras. Buys us some private time to high-tail it to the lab."

Minutes passed. Silence tightened with tension. The fluorescent lights in the corridor flickered half a dozen times.

Whitney's gaze snapped to the ceiling. "That can't be a good sign."

"Definitely not. It's an electrical problem that should have been resolved months ago." He stopped looking at his watch and pressed the elevator button.

When the doors opened, the three stepped inside. As she jostled her backpack to shift its weight, her body pressed against Blake's side. He slid his hand around her waist and squeezed. For a moment, she actually felt safe. The feeling disappeared, three floors down when the elevator came to an abrupt stop.

The doors opened, revealing yet another maze of endless sterile hallways. Before exiting, Whitney took a deep breath.

Norm's cell phone rang. Blake pulled out the phone and checked the caller ID. His gaze shifted to hers.

Whitney's body stiffened. It was Nathan.

❋ ❋ ❋

In the south corridor, Blake bent down on one knee and glanced up at Norm. "Who's watching the kid?"

"Dr. Vanderzee and his assistant."

Whitney leaned against the wall. The tense lines on her face tightened even more. "Do you think Nathan's already here?"

"I don't know. If he isn't, he will be soon." The bastard wasn't far. Blake could feel it.

He dropped his backpack and opened the flap. He knew there would be two security guys posted outside the lab. They were only doing their job, probably had no clue as to what was really going on.

"Okay, Norm. How many guys inside?" He handed Whitney four sets of handcuffs and a roll of duct tape.

"Only one." The man's bushy eyebrows twisted. "You'll never get him to open the door."

"But you will." Blake left the backpack on the floor and stood.

He raised his gun and inched the weapon slowly toward Norm's left temple. "Time for you to make a choice, Camaron. Either you're with us, or you're not. Which is it?"

"Okay. Okay. I'll help you."

Blake smiled to himself. "Good."

Whitney placed her hand on Blake's arm. "You can't possibly trust him after what he tried to do to you."

"You can trust me. I don't wanna to go to jail. I'll tell you about the boss and Claire."

For a second Blake wasn't sure if he really wanted to know the truth, but he needed closure. "I'm listening."

Norm paused, and then said, "They were lovers. Had been for quite a while."

CHAPTER THIRTY-TWO

*W*hen I get my hands on Nathan, I'll kill the little prick. Acid burned in Blake's gut and threatened to slither up his throat. Was Claire the kid's mother? Christ, Whitney had been right all along. The man Blake despised had been involved with his sister. He'd just refused to believe such an unlikely possibility. He clenched his fist so hard, his knuckles turned white. What had his sister been thinking? Unfortunately, he would never know.

"There's more." The left corner of Norm's mouth twitched as he continued. "She carried the kid. A surrogate. That's what I heard."

Blake's jaw dropped open. All he could do was stare at the older man. A surrogate? Why? For who? This didn't make sense, but other things did. Like why he hadn't seen much of Claire during the past few years. It also cleared up the mystery notation in her autopsy report, "...autopsy evidence she bore at least one child." A detail he hadn't revealed to anyone, not even his parents.

When he looked at Whitney, her eyes were huge. Her horrified expression said it all. She was as stunned as he was by the news. "Then who does the kid belong to?"

"Don't know." Norm's gaze shifted to the east corridor, then back to Blake. "If you want to keep your job, you don't ask questions."

A fact Blake knew all too well. He bit back the urge to know more, ripped the flap open on his backpack and pulled out a Taser gun. *Focus.* He needed to force the craziness he'd heard to the back of his mind. He'd have his chance to deal with Nathan, his way.

"You take the guard on the right." *You'd better not screw me over, buddy.* Blake hesitated for a moment before handing the weapon to Norm. "I'll look after the other one."

Norm inspected the chunky black gun. His bloodshot eyes lit. "This thing could incapacitate a damn bear."

That was the idea. Blake spoke to Whitney loud enough to ensure Norm heard every word. "Keep your weapon on him at all times. If he looks like he might double-cross us, shoot him between the eyes."

She nodded. "I will. I'm sorry about Claire. You have no idea how much I wanted to be wrong about her and Nathan."

You and me both. Blake pretended to check his watch again, his mind still trying to accept the most improbable couple of the century—his sister and Nathan Shaw.

Blake stood behind Norm and waited for him to aim the Taser. The red laser sight landed on the guard's upper thigh. The fluorescent lights in the hall flickered, again.

The guard looked down. "What the f—?"

Norm fired.

Two probes attached by wire, shot out of the

gun's muzzle. Fifty thousand volts crackled, exploding through the guard's central nervous system. He let out a sharp scream. His body slammed to the floor. Then the man curled into a fetal position, rocked from side to side, and whimpered. A split second passed. The other guard eyed Norm. He reached for his gun. Blake snuck behind him and whacked the man on the base of his skull with the butt of his weapon. The guard spun around, dropped to his knees, but not before he rammed his fist under Blake's ribs.

Air swooshed out of Blake's lungs. Explosions of white light flashed behind his eyes. He gasped for air and fought to keep from doubling over. Blinking, he tried to re-orient himself. Through watery eyes, he watched Norm race to retrieve the handcuffs from Whitney. Old Norm had proven himself. By the time Blake had caught his breath, both guards were cuffed, their mouths duct taped.

Whitney placed her hand on Blake's forearm. "Jesus, are you all right?"

Clutching his gun, he ran his hand along his ribs. "Yeah, I'll survive."

Her gaze moved to the guard hit by the Taser. "What about him? He doesn't look very good."

Blake looked at the man bound and gagged sitting on the floor. A layer of sweat glazed his pale forehead. "He'll be fine. Probably pretty sore for a few days, but we can't leave them here." Blake pointed down the corridor and quickly led the way.

After securing the guards in a washroom stall, he passed the cell phone to Norm. "Same scenario. A bomb threat. Tell them Nathan wants everyone moved to the heliport."

Norm shrugged. "Don't know if it'll work."

Blake cursed under his breath. His voice transformed into a low growl. "Just do it. We don't have all night."

By his calculations, they had less than fifteen minutes. More than enough time to get into the lab, not enough time to flee the facility. The thought sent a chill through his veins.

While Norm used the phone, Blake and Whitney took positions on either side of the lab door, guns readied. He couldn't help but notice the way her bottom lip quivered. She was trying so hard to stay tough. They needed to get through this because he wanted her in his life, at least have another chance to change her mind.

Norm shut off the phone. "I think they bought it."

Blake sucked in a breath of relief. "Good. Stay put."

Seconds dragged on. The lab doors opened elevator-style.

The guard emerged with a confused expression on his face and walked toward Norm. Blake rushed behind him and pressed his gun into the man's spine.

The guy flinched when the weapon touched his body. "What the hell is going on here?"

"Where's the kid?"

The man didn't answer.

Blake raised his voice above the facility's alarm still echoing in the hall. "Where is she?"

"The doc's getting her ready to move."

So far, so good. Almost too easy. If Blake knew one thing from experience, luck would run out. It always did.

They had to move and quick since all the doors in the complex were set by timers, a security feature he'd added less than a month ago.

He glanced over his shoulder at Whitney. "We'll restrain him inside."

She managed a weak smile and trailed Blake as he convinced the guard into the lab using the tip of his gun. Norm followed. The doors closed and locked behind them.

❊ ❊ ❊

Nathan stood in his office and stared at John Sawyer, the head of Bravo Team. *Useless fool.* The reporter and Neely should never have been allowed to get this far. Andrew West also proved just as ineffective. Nathan had heard via a contact at the Las Vegas Police Department the man had died from a single gunshot wound to the head, put there by the reporter.

Sawyer rattled on. "The intruders used explosives to take out about two hundred and fifty- foot stretch of fence in the southwest corner. Apparently, they snuck through the gates when the team was dispatched."

Nathan removed his tuxedo jacket, folded it lengthwise, and laid it neatly over the back of the chair. "Don't shut off the alarm. Make them believe they're safe. The element of surprise is a definite advantage. And John, this situation is critical. You do know what I mean, don't you? In other words, shoot to kill."

Sawyer nodded. "I understand, sir."

"Now get Russell. Meet me at the elevator in five minutes." Nathan heard the office doors shut. He unclipped his gold cufflinks, placed them in his pants pocket, and then rolled up the sleeves of his white shirt.

Above the retractable bar, he punched the combination into the wall safe's electronic keypad. The door clicked open. He pulled out a handgun. Billions of dollars, decades of research, more than twenty failed attempts. Angel—the perfect specimen. Genetic perfection at its finest. He wasn't about to spend the rest of his life in prison. The outside world couldn't find out about her. He inserted a magazine, pulled back the semi-automatic's slide, released it, and chambered a round.

He knew what needed to be done.

CHAPTER THIRTY-THREE

Long fluorescent bulbs covered the lab's ceiling and reflected off the white walls, forcing Whitney to squint.

Between the brightness, her battered body, and the aggravating sound of the facility's alarm, she'd be lucky if she didn't end up with a killer headache. That is—if she lived long enough to develop one.

She could tell the news about Claire and Nathan weighed heavy on Blake's mind, because of his set jaw, and the lines creasing his forehead as he and Norm finished binding the last guard to one of the lab's workstations.

A surrogate? Could Claire not have children of her own? Whitney's stomach knotted. More unanswered questions. Only one person knew the truth. Nathan.

Norm's raspy voice pierced her thoughts. "Hey. What are ya doing?"

She turned to see Blake handcuff Norm next to the guard. Huh? Clarity clawed through the fog. Blake didn't trust him anymore than she did. How could she, after he'd tried to run down the man she loved? Whitney stopped herself. This wasn't the time to allow her emotions to take over.

Blake ripped off a strip of duct tape with his teeth. "I appreciate what you did back there in the hall. But this is where we say goodbye." Before Norm had a chance to protest, Blake pressed the tape over the man's mouth.

Whitney checked her watch. Time wasn't on their side. While the alarm continued to wail, she crept further into the lab. Her mind recorded each shadow, hum, and beep coming from various strange-looking machines and abandoned computer terminals.

The area was downright creepy. Would they make it out of the facility alive? Adrenaline mixed with exhaustion and uneasiness pumped through her. God, they had to. Too much was at stake. Not only a child's life but the world needed to know the truth about Nathan Shaw so he could never pull a stunt like this again. And she was the only reporter who knew enough to stop him.

The hairs on her arms stood on end. Her attention snapped to the right. A few feet ahead, a door flung open.

Her heart jumped into her throat.

Reflexes flattened her back against a frosted Plexiglas partition. She waited and watched. A woman wearing a longer than usual white lab coat skidded to a stop and made eye contact with Blake. Dr. Vanderzee's assistant.

The woman tilted her head to one side. "You're not allowed in here. Leave now."

After a quick visual acknowledgement from Blake, Whitney tiptoed sideways until she was close enough to reach and snatch the woman's wrist.

The assistant twisted and tried to yank free.

"What? Let go of me."

Surprised by the petite woman's strength. Whitney tightened her grip. "Stay still for heaven sakes." She was about to raise her weapon, but Blake beat her to it with his gun.

The woman froze.

Nothing like staring down the barrel of a gun to make you stop and think. Confident the woman wasn't going anywhere, Whitney released her arm and stepped back. She checked her watch, again. Her stomach knotted tighter. Six minutes had passed since they'd entered the lab.

They were taking too much time. "Blake, we need to hurry."

His forehead glistened with sweat. Uncertainty etched his face. He waved his weapon at the assistant. "Lead the way."

The woman shuffled toward the door she'd exited moments before. "You're going to scare the child with those guns."

The last thing Whitney wanted to do was upset the young girl. She'd be distressed enough being rushed away by two strangers. Whitney looked at the weapon clutched in her right hand, then up at Blake.

Reality jolted her as if a rubber band snapped against her skin. His preoccupation and quietness scared her. She needed Blake at his best, strong and focused if they had any chance for success. They didn't have a backup plan.

They'd either survive or die.

She leaned over his shoulder and whispered. "Are you okay?"

His voice was odd, robotic-like. "Yeah, fine. We've

got to move."

No, he wasn't fine. That much she did know. What would he do to Nathan? Kill him? That thought terrified her as they traveled down an extensive hall. Whitney stopped at the end in front of an unmarked door and peered through a small glass window. In the corner, she eyed a man she assumed was Dr. Vanderzee then the young child. Without thinking, Whitney slid her weapon into her bulletproof vest, out of sight.

The massive room looked like a typical little girl's room drowned in pastel paint and fabrics. A rainbow mural plastered one wall. The blonde-haired girl sat on the edge of an ornate canopy bed with her tiny legs crossed at the ankles. A pink stuffed bunny lay across her lap. Whitney's heart squeezed. Had this room been this poor child's life? God, had she ever been out of the facility?

Nathan, you pathetic monster. Whitney turned to Blake for direction.

"I'll take care of the doctor. We'll tell him Shaw wants us to get them to the helicopter. You get the kid." He pressed his gun against the assistant's ribs. "And you're staying right here, understand?"

A glint of fear flashed in the woman's eyes. She nodded and swallowed.

Whitney drew a deep breath and adjusted her backpack digging into her shoulders. Blake opened the door and she followed his lead.

He rushed to the corner of the room where Doctor Vanderzee stood. "Nathan wants us to escort you and the kid up to the heliport."

The doctor's eyes widened. "What? Why wasn't I told about this? I had better talk with Mr. Shaw." The man reached for the phone on the wall.

Blake stepped in front of him. He flashed his weapon. "Don't do anything stupid."

The doctor's eyes widened. "You won't make it out of here."

Blake inched closer and nudged the doctor with his gun. "That's a chance I'm more than willing to take."

Whitney stopped at the bed and looked at the child. "Hi there. What's your name?"

The little girl smiled, her blue eyes round. "Angel." She held the stuffed animal out to Whitney.

Whitney inspected the toy. "That's a very nice bunny." She sat on the bed for a moment. "How would you like to come with me for a while?"

"Okay." Angel climbed on Whitney's lap.

The immediate trust surprised Whitney. "But you have to be very quiet. Can you do that for me?"

The child nodded, yes, and wrapped her arms around Whitney's neck.

Now ready to leave the area, Blake lifted his hand to the electronic keypad in the lab and raised his gun with the other. "What's the code?"

Fear jumped in the man's eyes. Dr. Vanderzee hesitated for a moment, and then blurted out, "Seven-six-eight-nine-one."

Blake punched in the numbers. The doors slid open.

Holding the child on her hip, Whitney did a quick visual sweep of the corridor. All clear—for now. But for how long?

❊ ❊ ❊

Fire brewed in Nathan's veins. He stared at the main monitor in the security room. "Under no circumstances can they be allowed to remove the child from the premises."

Sawyer looked at Russell, then back to Nathan. "I can have the rest of the team come in."

"No." Nathan had other plans. The fewer people in the building, the better.

He turned to Sawyer. "Shut off the alarm. Don't let anyone back into the complex until I say so."

What idiots! This was perfect. Hell, he didn't want to spend twenty years in jail, did he? Get them to do his dirty work, and then eliminate them. He'd be home free.

And the child?

Guilt squirmed in his belly. No point in being sentimental at a time like this.

❈ ❈ ❈

Whitney held Angel close and stopped in the hallway. The alarm had been shut off.

Panic crawled up her throat.

Nathan knows we're here.

She looked at Blake. Sweat beaded his scalp. Concern filled his eyes. Suddenly it felt like they were prisoners heading to their execution. She forced herself to keep it together for the child's sake. They had to make it out.

After they dumped their backpacks on the floor, Blake led, weapon raised, sweeping corridor after corridor. Whitney stayed close behind him and re-checked each hall. No way was Nathan going to let them simply walk out of the facility.

Shadows fleeted at the end of the south corridor. Her pulse pounded out of control. Whitney sidestepped the open area and flattened against the wall.

"Stop," she whispered in her headpiece.

Blake stopped. "What is it?"

Whitney pointed around the corner.

Blake turned. "Can you see anyone?"

Whitney shifted Angel to her other arm and cautiously poked her head around the corner. Nothing. No shadows. Had she imagined them? She stepped out a half foot for a better look.

She caught a flash of movement. An arm. Then a gun.

Whitney wheeled back against the wall. A bullet sliced past her shoulder.

Two more shots rang out.

"Get to the stairs. I'll hold him off." Blake fired his weapon.

"But—"

"Go!"

Whitney held Angel tight and ran down the hall. She almost swallowed her heart. Jesus!

One of the facilities security men stood eight feet away with his gun pointed at Whitney's head.

Angel let out a high-pitched scream.

A hand clamped down hard on Whitney's shoulder. She felt a gun jab her ribs. The hall lights flickered.

She froze.

Warm, cigar-laden breath. Nathan.

"Miss Steel. A pleasure as always."

Without a word, he leveled his gun and shot his security man in the head. What the hell?

The man dropped into a bloody heap on the floor.

My God! What kind of animal would do such a thing in front of a child? Possibly his own child? Angel whimpered and cried. Whitney hugged and tried to console the child. It wasn't working.

Blake had his weapon trained on Nathan. His eyes narrow, full of hatred. "Let them go, or I'll blow your fucking head off."

"You see, that's where we have a problem. I can't do that."

Nathan's gaze shifted past Blake.

"Behind you, Blake," Whitney yelled.

Blake turned slightly, kept his gun on Nathan. "Sawyer, this isn't your fight."

"I'm doing my job," Sawyer said in a calm voice.

"Nathan will kill you, just like he killed Russell. You want to end up like that?"

The man appeared confused, unsure of what to believe. But he didn't back down.

Blake kept trying. "Did you know your boss had my sister, Claire, killed because she knew too much? And the bodies keep piling up. You have to believe me."

The man shook his head. "I don't understand."

"Sawyer, I'm an FBI agent. I've been working under-cover to nail your boss' ass."

Nathan's voice grew loud. "Enough of this." He shot Sawyer. The young man bounced off the wall and hit the floor.

Whitney squirmed unable to escape Nathan's grasp.

He positioned the gun against her temple. "Now, drop your weapon, Blake. Slide it over to me."

Blake bent and placed the Glock on the floor, and did what Nathan asked. "Why did you kill Claire?"

"Ah. Claire. It's too bad." He hesitated for a moment. "Let's say after a while she didn't pass my loyalty test. She was going to take off with the child. You know I could not allow that to happen."

Whitney choked back her anger. "She's a human being, a little girl, not some twisted experiment."

"I agree she's human, Miss Steel. Genetic perfection at its finest. An identical copy of dear Claire, replicated by technology that I've spent a lifetime developing and perfecting. The first cloned human."

If Nathan was telling the truth, which she believed he was, Blake now had the answers he desperately needed.

"Hand over the child, Miss Steel. We really don't have time for this idle chitchat."

She glanced at Blake. "Don't do it, Whitney."

"Put the girl down, or I'll shoot your friend here. You wouldn't want that, would you?"

Whitney's legs trembled. She didn't know what to do. Seconds dragged on.

"Whitney, don't. As long as you have the kid—"

Nathan's hand moved from her temple. He fired another round.

The bullet hit Blake in the left side of his shoulder under his bulletproof vest. The blow knocked him sideways. He kept his hand pressed against his upper chest to stop the bleeding.

"No! You bastard." Whitney fought back the tears. She noticed Blake easing his other hand toward his extra gun stuffed in his sock.

The lights flickered again. The complex went black.

Blake's voice choked with pain. "Run, Whitney!"

She did. And didn't look back. Flashes of gunfire lit the corridor. The stairs. She had to get to the stairs.

CHAPTER THIRTY-FOUR

Whitney burst outside and ran across the security parking lot. She glanced over her shoulder. Relief and dread kicked in. No one had followed her. With Angel clutched in one arm, she fished in her pocket for the car keys Blake had given her earlier. His words played over in her mind.

"If something happens and we can't get out together, take the car. Mike and the rest of the team will be waiting at Nellis Air Force Base."

She unlocked Norm's Camaro, yanked the door open, and got in. Quickly she placed Angel in the passenger seat and belted her in. The child continued to hug her stuffed animal.

"Everything will be okay, small one. I promise."

Whitney shoved the key into the ignition and turned it. The engine roared to life.

The little girl pointed out the window. "Go."

"Yes, we're going."

Whitney backed up. The tires squealed as she accelerated out of the lot. The car had more power than she'd estimated.

She eased up on the gas pedal. The last thing she needed was to draw attention.

There was only one way out, through the gaping hole in the fence line they'd blown apart hours ago. From there, she'd hit the highway, and head to the air force base.

She wanted so much to go back and help Blake. She fought to shake the image of him on the floor bleeding.

He could be dead for all I know. No! Stop thinking that way. Stay focused and get to safety. That's what he wanted.

She drove around the corner to the front of the complex and kept her eyes on the small pockets of employees still gathered at the main entrance. If they only knew what hell had gone on inside.

Whitney passed the circular gardens and living quarters without incident. A mile or so and they'd be free, away from this horrible place and out Nathan's deadly grip. But her thoughts returned to Blake. Would he make it out? He had to.

The car's headlights bounced across the uneven road slicing through the darkness. Not much longer. She could do this.

At the northeast corner, she spotted two sets of headlights. Security vehicles. Her heart pounded. Wait. This was Norm's car. So they'd think she was Norm... unless Nathan had already tipped them off.

A security man stood right in the middle of the escape area, waving his arms for her to stop. When he realized she wasn't, he pulled out his gun.

"Damn it!" She'd have one chance to get through.

She gripped the steering wheel and tromped the gas pedal to the floor. The car jerked forward. Gravel spit out behind the tires.

Angel twisted in the seat. She giggled. "Go, fast like on TV."

"Hang on." Whitney gasped. *Get out of the way. I'm not stopping.*

The man continued to hold his ground.

A couple of yards away now. For God sakes move!

He raised his weapon, aimed it at the car.

No. She wasn't stopping.

She clenched the wheel tighter. For a split second, she closed her eyes. When she opened them, he jumped out of the way and rolled to the ground. The right fender grazed the fence. Whitney cranked the wheel hard to the left.

The car fishtailed onto the highway. A tanker truck sped by in the north lane. A sickening fog of diesel fumes waffled through the car's vents. She swiped the hair out of her eyes and checked her mirrors. Taillights disappeared in the distance. The security vehicles weren't moving. Thank God.

In less than an hour, they'd arrive at Nellis Air Force Base. Worry overpowered relief. *Blake, please be alive.*

"I'm hungry," Angel said, holding the bunny on her lap.

"Okay, sweetie. I'll get you something to eat and drink soon."

Whitney couldn't stop now. Couldn't take the chance.

With the speedometer pushing eighty-five, she'd traveled a good two miles before the adrenaline rush left her. She slowed the car. Her fingers relaxed around the wheel, even though she checked her mirrors every few seconds to see if they were being followed.

No one. Not a soul on the road.

The pain in her left shoulder where Nathan had grabbed her hurt like heck. She rubbed the ache and fought the terrifying realization that Blake was still out there. She had no clue if he was alive or dead.

❋ ❋ ❋

A pair of F15's thundered across the gloomy early morning sky. Whitney moved away from the window and paced the empty office located in Area 1 of Nellis Air Force Base. Down the hall and to the right, the rest of Blake's FBI team had gathered in private.

Her stomach winced. The waiting was killing her. She checked her watch for the fiftieth time. Where was Blake? He should have been here by now. Two hours had passed since she'd left him at the facility, bleeding. *I didn't have a choice. I had to leave you.*

She rushed to Mike the moment he walked through the door. Immediately, she noticed the somber expression on his face.

Her body trembled. "Any word?"

Mike shook his head. "Nothing yet. We should know something soon."

She had to ask even though the thought was unbearable. "You don't think he's dead, do you?"

"No. He's too damn tough."

That may be, but Whitney had seen how much blood he'd lost. More than she thought humanly possible. Anything could have happened after she had fled with Angel. That poor child would have nightmares after what she'd witnessed. Right now the little girl was being looked after at the hospital on base.

Whitney jumped, startled by the ring of Mike's cell phone.

She held her breath as he answered the call. *Please be good news.*

Mike's expression changed...but she couldn't read him. "Yeah, thanks." He shut off his phone.

"They just brought Blake in. He's unconscious, lost a lot of blood. Things don't look good, Whitney."

She exhaled. A lump formed in her throat. As long as he was alive there was hope.

"I have to see him, Mike."

"Yeah, me too. Let's go."

❊ ❊ ❊

Whitney arrived at the base hospital, terrified, not knowing what to expect. When she saw Blake through the window, her breath caught in her throat.

He looked pale, his skin yellowish-gray under the bright lights of the trauma room. Blood everywhere. A doctor was busy inserting a chest tube. She wanted to look away but couldn't.

Whitney felt Mike's hand on her shoulder. "He's going to make it."

The thought of not having Blake in her life ripped at her heart.

"I hope you're right." She pressed her hand against the window. "What about Nathan?"

"The locals are bringing him in. He can't hurt anyone again."

But he'd already hurt the most important people in her life...Mason, George, and Blake.

The trauma room doors swung open. A weary looking male doctor greeted them.

"How is he, Doc?" Mike asked as if he knew she couldn't find the words.

"Your friend is lucky to be alive. He received a serious gunshot wound. He's stable for now. We'll know more once he's in the operating room. "

Remain strong for Blake. He needs you. Her voice strangled with emotion. "Can we see him?"

"Yes, of course. He's still unconscious, though."

Whitney and Mike followed the doctor into the trauma room. She was only an arms length away.

Monitors beeped.

"He's in v-tach!" One of the two nurses working on Blake pushed Whitney aside.

A male voice said, "He's not responding."

Someone else yelled, "I can't find his pulse."

Whitney shoved forward trying to reach Blake. "No! Fight damn it. I love you."

CHAPTER THIRTY-FIVE

Blake felt like he was floating. Fragmented voices and sounds swirled in his head, muffled as if he was under water.

At one point, he'd even thought he'd heard Whitney's voice but couldn't make out what she was saying. Garbled words that didn't make any sense.

Why couldn't he see her?

Rushed footsteps. Commotion. Something poking at his arm.

What the hell was going on? And why did his shoulder and chest hurt like hell? Think. Think. Then he remembered.

Nathan shot him.

Open your eyes.

Bright lights forced them closed.

The faint smell of rubbing alcohol and ammonia.

Dizziness. Queasiness. Crap. The hospital. That's where I am.

He tried to talk. A moan escaped, nothing more. Something was stuck in his throat.

An unfamiliar female voice said, "Dr. Millbank, he's coming to."

Had he been unconscious? God damn it. His chest

hurt...heavy, sore and burning.

Blake pried his dry eyes open, blinking trying to focus.

"Welcome back, Agent Neely," a male voice said.

Apparently, he'd gone somewhere. That didn't sound good. Nope, he didn't want to know.

"You have a tube down your throat. Don't try to talk. Just nod. You're in the recovery room. We had to go in to stop the bleeding. Touch and go there for a bit. But you pulled through just fine. Are you in pain?"

Blake nodded.

The same male voice said, "I'll have the nurse increase your pain medication. There are a couple of people who want to see you."

Whitney. Blake wanted to see Whitney.

He heard Mike's voice first. "Hey, buddy. Damn, glad to see you."

Yeah, happy to see you too, man. Glad you're here.

Whitney's face came into focus. She smiled. "I thought I was going to lose you."

I'm not going anywhere. I promise. He lifted his hand. Her hand was warm in his. He wanted to say so much. Damn tube. He'd have to wait.

She lowered her head and kissed his cheek. Then her lips brushed his ear. "I love you. Get some rest."

He held her hand tight. *No. Please don't leave. You have no idea how much I love you, honey.*

She patted his hand. "Don't worry, we'll have plenty of time when you're back on your feet."

Time. Yes, lots of time. Her hand slipped away.

A warm, fuzzy feeling flooded his body. His eyelids grew heavy and started to close. Only then did he remember...Nathan was in custody. He'd got the murdering bastard.

CHAPTER THIRTY-SIX

Through his prison-issued jumpsuit, Nathan rubbed his sore right shin. The rough material irritated the area where Blake shot him. A superficial wound, the doctor said. An annoyance more than anything.

Nathan stared at the concrete walls. He felt a sick tug at his gut. For twenty-three hours a day, he was stuck in his cell. Then there were the humiliating daily body searches which always ended with, "Squat twice and then spread those cheeks."

He lifted his shoe and squashed a large bug skittering across the cement floor. He may be stuck in prison hell, but at least he had the best lawyers money could buy. Nathan also had time, a large amount of money hidden, and contacts on the outside that could be bought at a moment's notice.

In the cell across from him, his new-found friend, Pablo Sanchez, sprawled across his cot on his stomach, reading a ragged paperback. Every now and then, Nathan heard the man laugh. The chilling cackle-like sound echoed off the cellblock walls.

During the past few weeks, their conversations in the concrete prison yard had been to the point, and

Pablo had less than twenty-four hours left on his ten-year conviction.

At one time, he'd even bragged about being on the FBI's "10 Most Wanted" list for years before the law had caught up with him. The man's future had been decided the second he had been nabbed.

Revenge for his twin brother's death.

Nathan smiled because they had a common interest. To make one FBI agent's life hell.

Just a matter of time.

CHAPTER THIRTY-SEVEN

"**H**ave I told you how much I missed you?" Blake slid his left arm around Whitney and pulled her close.

"Only a dozen times since I brought you home from the hospital this morning. "I missed you too, very much so. Bet it feels good to be home."

He never realized how much he missed his two-bedroom condo. Might be sparsely furnished and lacking in decorating, but it was home.

"More than you can imagine." Blake grabbed his mug of coffee from the kitchen counter and downed the last swallow, placing the empty cup next to the sink. "Even better knowing you're sticking around."

"Well, I have to." She winked. "Someone needs to keep you out of trouble. Besides, I've decided to take the reporting position at News3. I start in four weeks, which gives me just enough time to tie up some loose ends in Florida and have the rest of things moved here."

He noticed a trace of sadness in her eyes and in her voice. Nathan Shaw and Andrew West had taken so much from her. Mason, George, and almost him. Blake hoped that after the memorial service in Florida for George, the sadness would begin to disappear.

"You sure about cohabitating in Vegas?"

"I'm positive. I'm looking forward to a new start."

He admired her. She'd forgiven him for lying about his identity, which couldn't have been easy. Made him love her even more. "Looks like we have lots to celebrate today."

"Definitely we do. And there's more."

"Really?" He watched her fill the coffee maker with water, add coffee, and flip on the switch for the second time. The cutest little grin crossed her face.

Blake smiled. *God, you're beautiful.*

"When you were in the shower, I received a phone call." Her eyes lit and sparkled. "My cloning story is nominated for an Emmy."

"That's great, baby. Congratulations." Blake was thrilled for her. She'd been waiting years for this award.

"Thank you." She took a sip of her coffee. "Tell me something. What happened after I left the complex with Angel?"

"Everything is still pretty fuzzy. Apparently, Norm saved my life."

Her eyes widened. "How could that be? I watched you handcuff him in the lab?"

"I didn't do up the cuffs, told Norm to stay put if he knew what was good for him. I'm damn glad he didn't listen. He heard the gunfire and he stepped up."

"Wow."

"He secured Nathan after I shot the bastard in the leg. *Wished I'd shot that sick sonofabitch in the head.* "I don't remember much after that."

"Well, I'm extremely grateful. Norm really came through for you in the end."

"Yeah, only to save his sorry ass from a prison sentence. But if it weren't for him, I wouldn't be standing here—aching to make love to you."

"Whoa. Slow down, cowboy. We have a house full of company due in an hour and a half. Or did you forget about your welcome home party?"

"Forget the party." He slid his hand up her top, her breast warm against his palm. Her nipples hardened at his touch. "You have far too many clothes on."

❋ ❋ ❋

Whitney stared into Blake's eyes and laughed, softly.

She wanted him as much as he wanted her. "We don't have much time. Someone is sure to interrupt us."

"The world can wait." Her pulse sped up as Blake slipped her top over her head and let it drop to the floor.

He unhooked her bra with one hand, and gently pushed her back against the kitchen counter, his body hard against hers. Before she knew it, her jeans and panties were off.

His mouth grazed her lips, her throat, slowly moving to her nipples, teasing each one, and then back to her mouth. When he held her close and kissed her long and hard, the intoxicating combination of Drakkar cologne and his kiss made her dizzy with passion. His hardness pressed against her naked body.

Her heart pounded in her throat. Her skin tingled. *Everything and everyone* can *wait.*

She carefully raised Blake's arms and removed his baggy T-shirt. Her heart ached at the red and purple, jagged scar on his upper chest where Nathan had shot him. She shoved away the horrible images of that day; not wanting to remember how she'd almost lost the man she loved. They'd both lost so much.

"Are you sure you're up to this?"

"Oh, yeah," he murmured while nibbling her ear lobe.

Whitney unsnapped his jeans, tugged them down. He kicked them off and left them in a heap at his feet.

Downward his mouth traveled, over her breasts, her stomach...

His fingers slide between her legs, moving gently in and out. He lowered to his knees and spread her legs apart.

She tossed her head back, and moaned, raking her fingernails across the taut muscles of his shoulders.

He shuddered. His tongue moved faster and he pushed his fingers deeper inside her.

Whitney bucked and squirmed. Hard ripples of spasms shook her body as she came. Time stood still. The small waves of spasms continued to assault her body. Never had she experienced such a powerful orgasm. One of love, need, and hope.

Blake rose to his feet, turned her around, and bent her over the kitchen table. "You have the most incredible ass."

Her breathing quickened. The anticipation of having him inside made her even wetter.

He pressed against her, his hands on her hips, and he slid inside. His breath tickled the back of her neck. He ran a finger down her spine.

She shivered and gasped.

He stirred inside her, finding his rhythm, slowly, slowly. In and out, in and out...

Nothing in this world could possibly be this good. His voice, his touch. He was so hard, so hot. The grip on her hips tightened. He thrust hard once.

She moaned and shoved against him, hungry. Sweat formed between their bodies.

He picked up the pace, plunging deeper.

Pressing her hands on the table, she arched. Her legs trembled. "Oh, God!"

Suddenly, her body locked in a hard shudder as she came again.

Blake thrust one more time and exploded inside her. He held her tight, trembling against her for a long moment.

Still, inside her, he leaned against her back and kissed her neck. "I love you, Whitney."

"I love you, too." *More than I can ever tell you.*

Blake straightened and pulled out.

She stood, grasped the edge of the table, her legs wobbly.

He wrapped an arm around her, gently turned her around to face him. "A little jelly-like below the waist, eh?"

"Yeah, just a bit. Well worth it, though." She glanced at the clock above the kitchen sink. Their guests would be arriving in forty-five minutes. "We'd better get showered, again."

Blake gathered his clothes from the floor, balling them up in his arm. "You never know, we might have a few extra minutes for a little soapy fun."

Whitney laughed. "There is no slowing you down, is there?"

"Nope. Not until I'm six feet under."

CHAPTER THIRTY-EIGHT

After they showered and dressed, Whitney kissed Blake, her tongue teasing his. "Looks like your guests are starting to arrive. If you're good, I'll show you how much I love you tonight."

"Tease. I can't wait." He looked past the living room, through the open patio doors to the community pool area. A colorful "Welcome Home" banner fluttered in the breeze.

The doorbell rang. "I'll be right back." She disappeared to answer the front door, leaving Blake hard, and more than a little bit uncomfortable.

When he spotted Mike, and their SAC, Trent Chambers, he side-stepped behind the kitchen island to hide how aroused he was. Damn it. The woman was driving him crazy, again.

Mike entered the kitchen first. "Welcome home, man. See you still haven't done much with the place."

Chambers was a few steps behind him, his gray hair freshly cut army style.

Blake opened the refrigerator and grabbed a couple beers, passing one to Mike, the other to Trent.

Chamber's opened his bottle. "Can't say I hate to

lose you guys, wish you the best with your new business venture. Gets you the hell out of my hair." He took a sip of his beer. "If you guys ever need anything, don't call me. Actually, after today, I never want to hear from you two again."

Believe me, Trent, the feeling is mutual. Blake burst out laughing and so did Mike.

The week before, both men had resigned, more than ready to leave the FBI. Starting their security-investigation company over the next few months had been discussed numerous times over the years. The timing was perfect. The Nathan Shaw case was their last. The one Blake wanted to forget.

Whitney walked into the kitchen holding a small package in her hand.

"It's wonderful to see both of you." She gave Mike a hug, and then Trent.

Both men had silly boyish grins on their faces and Blake knew exactly what they were thinking.

Whitney looked hotter than hell in that tight white top and black short skirt: all legs and beautiful.

Blake smiled to himself. He was the luckiest man in the world.

Mike snatched a handful of potato chips out of a bowl on the counter, popped a couple in his mouth. "We'll be outside, buddy. Looks like Cally and McBride just showed up."

"Great. I'll be out in a bit."

"Oh, this is for you." Whitney handed Blake a small, padded manila envelope. "It came special delivery."

"Today, the world can wait." He placed the envelope on top of the refrigerator.

She grinned. "I couldn't agree more, because more

guests have arrived. I'd better get out there and greet them."

"Okay, baby."

After Whitney left the kitchen, he started to pile a large platter with steaks. His mind wandered.

Important decisions still had to be made. Right now, a little girl's future lay with Nevada's Child Welfare system until Blake could figure out what to do. Was he prepared for a long battle down the road if he chose to adopt Angel? The little girl was happy, comfortable and thriving with her foster parents. Whitney and his parents had visited her numerous times while Blake was in the hospital.

How would Whitney feel about having Angel in their lives twenty-four-seven? Christ, he wasn't even sure how he felt at this point adopting a child who looked identical to his sister.

Blake turned with the plate in his hand. A buzz of apprehension tickled his spine when he spotted his father making his way toward him.

"Son, you look well considering."

Up until now, Blake had never noticed how much his father had aged since Claire's death. His gray hair almost white, once smooth skin wrinkled and tired looking.

"Dad, glad you and Mom could come." He placed the plate of meat down on the counter. "I'm feeling pretty good. Chest is still a bit sore yet. Beer?"

"Sure."

Blake opened the refrigerator, pulled out a beer for himself and handed a bottle to his father.

Long beats of uncomfortable silence passed between them, until his father said, "Your mother has taken a real liking to Whitney."

From the kitchen, Blake saw his petite mother giggle as she chatted with Whitney. "I can see that."

"Whitney's an incredible woman. She cares about you a lot. Going to marry her?"

Not like the thought hadn't crossed Blake's mind. At least a half dozen times especially during the last few days in the hospital. When the time was right, he'd ask and hope like hell she'd accept. "We'll see, Dad."

"Look, son. I know I've never been very supportive when it came to your career with the FBI. Had always hoped you'd become a career marine like your old man, but—son, I'm proud of you. Always have been."

Blake almost choked on his drink. He forced down the mouthful of beer.

Those were the words he had waited for years to hear. He finally had his father's approval. Too bad, it had taken so long.

His father set his drink down and gently hugged him.

Blake froze. "Um, thanks, Dad."

His father released him and awkwardly cleared his throat. "Guess I should see what kind of trouble your mother is getting into."

Blake nodded. "Probably a good idea. I see Whitney's feeding her wine."

"Great. You know how she gets when she's had more than a glass."

"Yeah, quite tipsy." Blake patted his father on the back.

After his dad joined the others outside, Blake went to light the gas barbeque. Even though gray clouds raced east to west across the afternoon sky, there was nothing gloomy about today.

He had everything he wanted, everything he needed. Whitney, his friends and family, and the satisfaction of knowing Nathan Shaw would never hurt anyone again.

❊ ❊ ❊

Whitney held a glass of white wine in her hand and watched Blake through the living room window.

He looked so happy, smiling and laughing. His color had returned. A huge difference from a few weeks ago, when he was lying in the ER, deathly pale, and unconscious.

Whitney was happy too. The happiest she'd ever been.

After years of trying to prove herself to her male colleagues, she had finally realized acceptance means nothing without the one you love.

She was elated by Blake's decision to leave the FBI. She'd almost lost him once, and couldn't imagine going through that again. Today they were starting their new life together. She couldn't wait to cuddle him all night long.

In between songs playing on the stereo, Whitney heard the doorbell ring again.

She went to answer the door.

Kate Leathham, the Senior District Attorney, looked stylish as always dressed in a tailored navy jacket and knee-length skirt. Her straight, auburn hair hung an inch above her shoulders.

"Kate, I'm glad you could make it. Come on in."

A sudden sense of foreboding dread hit Whitney. Her palms began to sweat.

The DA stepped inside. "Unfortunately, this isn't a social call. I need to speak with you and Blake in private."

Whitney's stomach clenched. "Umm...yes, of course. Let me get him."

She rushed through the house. Possibilities sprung up in her mind. Was there a problem with the Nathan Shaw case? Was something wrong with Angel?

Before going outside, she took a gulp of her wine to calm her nerves. Guests stood around the pool socializing. A half dozen had changed into their bathing suits and where playing a feisty game of water volleyball. Every now and then water splashed.

Blake was sipping a beer, talking to Mike and another agent, Paul McBride.

She calmly walked over to them and forced a smile. "Sorry to interrupt, boys. But I need to steal Blake away for a few minutes."

"Sure thing. I'll take over barbecue duty for you. McBride here can help," Mike said.

"Hey, just don't burn my steak, buddy." Blake set his beer down on the table next to the grill.

Whitney looped her arm around Blake's and weaved through their guests toward the house.

She kept her voice down. "Kate Leatham's inside. This isn't good news, Blake."

In the foyer, Blake stared at the district attorney. Her expression appeared pinched with concern. "What's wrong?"

Kate looked him straight in the eye. "I just received word Joanna Hurst has been murdered."

The name took a few seconds to register in Blake's

mind. *Angel's foster mother.*

Whitney's hand flew to her mouth. "Oh, my God."

His chest throbbed where Nathan had shot him. "What about the little girl?"

He couldn't lose Angel, not after everything that had happened.

"The authorities are still searching the area. Nothing yet. There is a possibility she may have been kidnapped. A command post has been setup inside the Hurst's home in case Joanna's husband, Peter, is contacted."

Who the hell would kidnap her? It just didn't make sense to Blake.

Any information about Angel had been buried deep. Only a handful of FBI agents and high-up officials in the Justice Department knew about the girl. And Nathan Shaw, of course.

Blake's chest suddenly hurt more.

Kate's gaze moved from Whitney, back to him. "Has anyone tried to contact you?"

"No."

Whitney turned to Blake. "The package that came earlier."

Today, the world can wait. "God damn it." He sprinted to the kitchen, grabbed his cell phone off the counter, and called Mike outside. "Mike, gather Chambers, McBride, and Cally. We have a problem. Don't look too obvious. We don't want to spook the guests."

"Done."

Blake ended the call and let his phone drop on the counter.

He snatched the package from the top of the refrigerator and tore it open. Inside he found a DVD. In the spare bedroom he used as an office, Blake sat behind his desk and powered up his laptop. He put his cell phone on his knee.

Whitney stood beside him. Kate, Chambers, McBride, Cally, and Mike stood behind him waiting for the DVD to play.

What Blake saw ripped at his heart.

The three-year-old girl lay on what appeared to be the back seat of a vehicle. She looked like she was sleeping.

A male voice said, "Such a pretty little chica."

Mike peered over Blake's shoulder. "Christ, that sounds like—"

"Pablo Sanchez. No fucking way." But it was. Blake could never forget that voice. He clenched his fist.

"When did that asshole get out of prison?" Chambers asked.

"We should have been notified," Mike said.

Blake's thoughts exactly. Someone in the Bureau had screwed up, and Blake wanted to know who. He shook his head and continued to stare at the laptop screen.

With his back to the camera, a man ran a stubby finger down Angel's cheek. "Doesn't take much cocaine to keep her quiet."

Blake felt Whitney's hand squeeze his shoulder. Her voice was shaky. "He's giving her drugs. Dear, God."

Every muscle in Blake's body tensed. Curly hair— brown eyes—scar over the right eyebrow—serpent tattoo running down his neck.

Definitely, Sanchez. Older, tougher looking, and Christ, he was feeding the kid coke.

You're dead, you sonofabitch.

The lens zoomed in until the screen filled with the man's face.

Sanchez licked his cracked lips. His voice hardened. "Remember my brother, Manuel? You slit his throat like a pig and left him to die."

His voice lowered to a whisper. "*Un ojo para un ojo.*"

McBride translated before Blake had a chance to. "An eye for an eye."

"You will bring me, someone, you love. Whitney Steel. A fair exchange, don't you think?" Sanchez grinned. "Only then will I spare the child's life."

Blake's mouth went dry. He swallowed hard. *This can't be happening.* He reached for Whitney's hand and held it tight.

Not a chance in hell was he using the woman he loved as a pawn.

Kate spoke up. "I'll see what I can find out through my connections."

"I'll contact our friends at Immigration and Customs. Have them pull everything they have on Sanchez." Chamber's said.

"Good idea." Blake paused the DVD. "Mike, find out when Sanchez was released, then we'll know how much time he's had to plan this."

Mike patted Blake's shoulder. "You got it, buddy."

Before Mike had a chance to make the call, his cell phone rang. Blake's went off at the exact same moment, followed by Trent Chambers.

It was clear. They weren't the only ones who knew about the kidnapping.

CHAPTER THIRTY-NINE

While the DA was busy working in the living room, Trent and Mike worked in the master bedroom. Cally and McBride found a corner in the kitchen. So far, Whitney had been running back and forth checking on their guests and talking with Blake.

She walked into the spare bedroom. Blake sat behind his desk. Perspiration beaded his forehead revealing how much he was suffering as well. The happiness she'd experienced earlier was long gone replaced with worry and anger.

Whitney took a deep breath and fought to force down the bile crawling up her throat. Her legs went weak. An uncontrollable numbness drove to her ankles.

Blake jumped out of his chair, caught her by the arm before she lost her balance. "Are you going to be okay?"

She was worried sick about Angel. "No. How could this have happened?"

He shook his head and rubbed his chest. "I don't know. But I *will* find out."

Whitney was also concerned about Blake. Was he physically strong enough? The gunshot wound was healing well, but it probably wouldn't take much to reopen, if he overdid it.

She pushed the thoughts from her mind. If she didn't, she'd fall apart. Strength was what they needed if they were going to get through this.

"I just got off the phone with Ned Ford at the Justice Department." Blake picked up a piece of paper from his desk and read it.

"According to Ford, there were only three other members beside your ex-husband on the task force to nail Nathan. Senator John Warmark, Bob Tilman, a lawyer, and Trish Vargus, a biologist with our DNA Analysis Unit."

"Would anyone else within the FBI know about Angel?"

Blake paused for a moment and rubbed his chest, again. "Other than our team, Director Forsberg would be aware of the situation."

"What about Dr. Vanderzee and his assistant? Or Norm Camaron? Maybe they told someone."

"Vanderzee and his assistant are in protective custody until Nathan's trial. No one can get to them. And I sure as hell can't see Norm making the same mistake twice."

Actually, neither could Whitney. Not after the man had saved Blake's life.

"Chambers is sending an agent to question the social worker in charge of Angel's case. Pablo got that confidential information from someone."

Whitney couldn't agree more. "I think it's time to get our guests out of here. A few have been asking questions. I'll tell them you aren't feeling well."

"Good idea."

She recognized the undeniable strain in Blake's voice.

"Have my parents stay, though. I want to fill them in on what's going on."

"Okay."

He kissed her cheek. "We'll get her back, baby. I promise."

For a long moment, she looked at Blake. She believed he would. Nothing would stop him. But at what cost? Her life? His?

* * *

Blake winced. Another spasm erupted across his chest. His shoulder throbbed. He yanked open the desk drawer, found the bottle of Ibuprofen and popped two into his mouth and swallowed them dry.

The stress was getting to him. It was wearing on everyone involved.

His fax machine beeped. Pages began to roll out. He grabbed the first one. Information Chambers had requested from Immigration and Customs on Sanchez.

One thing kept eating at him. They should have been notified of Sanchez's release. Chambers would have been notified first. A missed memo? Or had it conveniently disappeared?

Blake really didn't like where this was going. He checked his watch. One-thirty.

He focused on his laptop and played the DVD one last time, frame by frame, looking for anything that could lead him to Sanchez before the exchange tonight at eleven.

Something caught his eye. A hand came into view for about four seconds then disappeared. He noticed a small tattoo of a serpent at the base of the thumb. The same serpent Sanchez had on his neck. Blake stopped the DVD. Only one person had that same tattoo, Pablo's cousin, Alberto Guerrero.

Mike walked into the room.

Blake swiveled in his leather chair to face him. "What did you find out?"

"The Department of Corrections said Sanchez was released yesterday morning. He didn't report to his parole officer today. Get this. He was transferred out of Nevada State Prison due to overcrowding and moved to Ely—the same cell block as Nathan Shaw."

The name slammed into Blake's chest with the force of a bullet. "God damn it!"

He wanted to pick up the paperweight on his desk and hurl it across the room.

Even behind bars, Shaw was pulling strings, continuing to screw with their lives. Obviously, there were more people involved, bought and paid for.

"Hey, I need you to have someone quietly check into Chambers' financial information."

Not once in all his years with the Bureau, had he ever suspected any of the agents he trusted his life with as "gone bad."

Why now? Why Chambers?

Mike raised a brow. "You don't really think he's in on this, do you?"

"Let's hope not. Also, have the locals put out an APB out on Alberto Guerrero. Looks like Sanchez's cousin is involved too."

"I'll get on it." Mike turned and rushed out of the room.

Now with Shaw's involvement as well, more than

ever Blake knew everyone in his life were targets, including his parents. He'd make sure they would be safe.

Afterward, he'd pay a visit to Nathan, and it would take all his willpower not to kill the bastard.

❊ ❊ ❊

Blake watched his father's jaw tighten.

"I refuse to be run out of my home."

A typical response from Colonel Frank Barnett.

Blake swore under his breath, his patience growing thin. "Dad, you don't have a choice. You're going to the safe house. This is not up for discussion."

His mother's voice trembled. "Frank. For once, listen to your son."

Emotions were high. The news of the kidnapping had hit everyone hard.

She sat on the couch in the living room, buried her face in her hands. "That monster has that sweet little girl. No telling what he's doing to her."

Blake didn't want to think about it. He couldn't. If he did, he'd lose focus. He pushed back his emotions. All he could do was pray Angel was still alive.

His father turned away and stared out at the pool, unsure how to comfort his wife. A scene Blake had witnessed many times during his childhood.

Blake crossed the room and sat beside his mother. "Mom. Why don't you go and finish your tea in the kitchen with Whitney?"

She slowly raised her head, wiped her nose with one of the tissues clutched in her hand. "Yes. That's a good idea."

After his mother left the room, Blake followed his father outside.

His father pulled a cigarette out of his shirt pocket and lit it. After taking a drag, he exhaled and narrowed his eyes.

"You were a Marine, son. Once a Marine, always a Marine. Let me come with you tonight." He took another drag. "I'm still in pretty good shape."

Blake had to admit for a sixty-two-year-old, his father was in better physical shape than most men half his age. Lean and muscular like a runner.

"Thanks, Dad, but I can't." He couldn't put anyone else in harm's way. "It's too dangerous. Besides, Mom needs you."

He recognized a flicker of disappointment in his father's eyes. He also saw what he thought might be a hint of understanding.

"Do you really believe this Pablo character will try to get to us?"

Blake felt the muscles in his neck tighten. "There's no doubt in my mind."

He hadn't told his parents about Nathan Shaw's involvement or the fact Sanchez wanted Whitney in exchange.

"Joe Cally, you met him earlier, will take you home. Get packed as quickly as possible. Once you're at the safe house, two US Marshals will look after you and Mom. You'll be in good hands."

Blake wasn't taking any chances. No telling who Shaw had paid off. He had chosen two men he'd known for years and knew they could be trusted.

"Guess you can't tell your old man all the details."

"Believe me, the less you know, Dad, the better."

After a couple more quick drags, his father butted his cigarette in the ashtray on the patio table, and then placed his hand on Blake's shoulder. "Bring that sweet child back safe, son. We can't lose her too."

He was right. They couldn't afford another emotional loss.

CHAPTER FORTY

Blake had made the five-hour drive in just under four hours and twenty minutes. His shoulder and chest ached. At least he knew his parents were secure at the safe house.

Ahead, he spotted one of the two guard towers at Ely Maximum State Prison. Razor wire ribboned the perimeter fence of the prison.

There was no reason why Shaw couldn't be calling the shots from his prison cell. The bastard still had influence, the ability to manipulate, and unlimited resources to buy anything or anyone.

The DA's office dropped the charges against Shaw related to illegally cloning humans. Sure, they had the evidence, a mountain of research, and of course, they had Angel.

It had been decided not to put the child through anymore. She'd been hidden away in ShawBioGen for the past three years, suddenly exposed to the real world, and then placed in emergency foster care before being sent to stay with the Hurst's. That was more than enough for the child to handle.

Even the media didn't know she was the first cloned human and Blake prayed they never would. The last thing Angel needed was a media circus invading her life.

Nathan had enough charges against him. If convicted, he'd receive the death sentence. Two counts of first-degree murder, attempted murder of a federal agent, numerous counts of conspiracy to commit murder, weapon charges, and the list went on and on.

Blake's hands tightened around the steering wheel.

If anything happens to Angel.

His knuckles turned white. He wanted to kill the man. Wrap his hands around the bastard's neck and squeeze the life out of him.

I can't. I need him alive.

Blake parked and then checked in with the Visitor Center staff. When he had spoken to Warden Dykes earlier, the man had been more than accommodating. Told him he'd make Shaw available to Blake anytime.

After showing his identification, he was searched and photographed. A prison officer escorted him to one of the private conference rooms.

The room was typical. Bright, not too small, with a scratched up brown table and four chairs. The walls were painted two putrid shades of green. Voices sounded outside the door.

He drew a deep breath. *Keep your cool or you'll end up here too.*

The door opened.

Nathan Shaw shuffled in with his ankles shackled, hands cuffed in front. His two thousand dollar suits had been replaced with a twenty dollar orange prison-issued jumpsuit.

The guard behind him guided the prisoner to a chair.

Nathan sat.

Then the guard left the room. Blake heard the loud

click of the door automatically locking.

Across the table, Blake remained standing. He cracked his knuckles trying to keep his anger under control.

Nathan smirked. "Blake Barnett. I see you still have that annoying habit."

Blake gritted his teeth. "I'm not here to discuss my habits. Where is Pablo Sanchez keeping Angel?"

"I have no idea what you're talking about. By the way, how is Miss Steel?"

"Don't change the subject. I know Sanchez was moved to your cell block. Only a handful of people know about Angel's existence."

Shaw lowered his head and picked at a fingernail.

"If you help me, maybe the judge will take that into consideration during your sentencing." That was the last thing Blake wanted, but he had to try for Angel's sake. The man deserved nothing less than a death sentence for all the lives he'd destroyed.

"I'm surprised at you, Blake. You have me convicted before my trial has started. Isn't Whitney supposed to testify sometime? How is the lovely woman?"

Blake slammed his fist on the table. "Enough of the games. You told Pablo Sanchez about Angel. Supplied him with the resources to pull off the kidnapping. Who the hell else is involved? I want names."

"You have an active imagination, very much like Miss Steel." Nathan stretched his legs and leaned back in the chair.

Blake heard the blood rush to his ears. He kicked the empty chair beside him. "You're a fucking liar. If anything happens to that little girl, I'll make sure they stick a needle in your arm and you can kiss your ass goodbye."

Nathan stood, hobbled to the door, and knocked. "Guard, we're done here."

Before he left the room, he turned and grinned. "I have a very strong suspicion our Miss Steel won't be available to testify. What a shame."

❈ ❈ ❈

Whitney's stomach felt queasy. Blake's news of Nathan's involvement fresh in her mind.

Hadn't they endured enough?

Damn it. Why couldn't you have left us alone? So many wasted lives. Haven't you done enough?

They'd been so happy today, looking forward to their life together.

Nothing could happen to Angel. Not now. Blake would be destroyed if he lost her. He'd gone to question Nathan. Whitney wouldn't expect anything less from him.

She tried not to think about tonight, the exchange, and what could possibly go wrong.

Her mouth went dry. She picked up a glass from the counter, filled it with cold water and took several small swallows. Then re-filled the coffeemaker and flipped on the switch for the third time.

With Blake at the prison, she was grateful not to be alone. Trent Chambers had left a few hours ago to update his superiors. McBride, Kate, and Mike sat around the kitchen table eating cold cut sandwiches and salads made for the welcome home party. The steaks Blake had started to cook earlier ended up burned beyond recognition and tossed in the garbage.

The coffee maker stopped gurgling. "It's ready. Who

wants a fresh cup?"

Kate wiped her lips with her paper napkin. "Please. Just a half cup, though."

"Yup. Me too," Mike said. He popped the last bite of his sandwich in his mouth.

McBride nodded. "No, thanks. I'm full and coffeed out. I think I'll slip out for a smoke." He stood, and then left the room.

Whitney re-filled the DA's mug. "When do you think Nathan's trial will start?"

"Probably not for another few months." She felt Kate's hand on her arm. "You're not having second thoughts about testifying, are you?"

"Oh, God, no. I want to see Nathan Shaw get what he deserves. Even more now. The death sentence."

Mike pushed his empty plate aside and leaned back in the chair. "We all want to see that."

"The physical evidence against him is weak. He covered his tracks like a pro. Since his alleged paid hit man is dead, and pretty well anyone else involved, our case hangs heavily on eyewitness testimony. Mainly yours and Blake's."

Whitney's stomach clenched. She swallowed hard. She had to know. "Is there a chance he could be acquitted?"

The DA paused for a moment before answering. "Honestly, that's a possibility with any case. Do I think it will happen with this one? No. We'll get him."

After Kate finished her coffee, she stood. "I should get back to the office."

Mike returned to the spare room to make some more phone calls.

The women walked together to the front of the

house.

Whitney opened the door. Late afternoon sunlight splashed across the foyer floor.

For some reason, she glanced up and down the street, as if looking for a something or someone that didn't fit into the neighborhood. The DA's black Lexus was parked on the other side of the street under a huge tree.

"I'll call you and Blake if I find out anything about Pablo Sanchez." Kate swung her purse over her shoulder. "Good luck, tonight."

"Thanks for everything."

She walked across the street to her car.

McBride stood on the front lawn smoking a cigarette. By the grin on his face, he was clearly enjoying the DA's long legs and shapely figure. Whitney couldn't help but smile.

A little boy about six years old flew down the sidewalk on his bicycle, his mother ran behind, trying to catch up.

Kate waved and then got into her car.

Whitney raised her hand and waved back. She turned to close the front door as an ear-splitting explosion rocked the neighborhood.

CHAPTER FORTY-ONE

F ear sucked the breath out of Whitney's lungs. She found it hard to catch her breath, her body paralyzed.

Next to the fire-engulfed Lexus, birds scattered from the tree to escape the shooting flames. Branches split and crashed to the ground igniting the grass on fire.

Through billowing thick black smoke filled with the sickening smell of gasoline, a twisted car sunroof and bumper had rained down into the middle of the street.

Whitney had watched McBride drop to the ground the moment the Lexus had exploded. He jumped to his feet and sprinted to the DA's car. A wall of flames and heat pushed him back. He paced in front of the vehicle, hands on his head.

There was nothing he could do. Nothing anyone could do.

Kate Leathham was dead.

Whitney's attention shifted to the young boy up the street on his bike. His mother was on her knees hugging him. He was pointing and crying.

Thank God they weren't hurt. Whitney trembled.

Mike grabbed her arm. "Are you okay? You're not hurt, are you?"

Tears welled up in her eyes. "No, but Kate…"

He stared, wide-eyed at the carnage in the street and rubbed his forehead. "Jesus Christ. This is unbelievable."

The street was littered with charred car parts, some still flaming, shattered glass and one of Kate's black high heels.

Sirens wailed in the distance.

Neighbors gasped and pointed. Some gathered on their front lawns, others were too terrified to leave the security of their homes.

Her voice quivered. "Mike, I have to phone Blake and tell him…the DA is dead."

❈ ❈ ❈

Blake sped down US 93. He slammed his right hand down on the steering wheel. "That God damn lying bastard."

He glanced over at the copy of Nathan's visitor and phone logs Warden Dikes had provided to Blake before he'd left the prison.

One way or another he'd prove Nathan and Sanchez were working together.

A little girl with big brown eyes and a contagious smile was depending on him.

Before he'd left the prison, he'd also called to make certain his parents were secure at the safe house.

They were.

One less thing to worry about. He had enough on his mind with the exchange going down in less than three hours.

Sanchez had made it clear on the DVD. If he saw anyone other than Blake and Whitney, he'd kill Angel.

He had chosen an abandoned Chevron gas station about forty-five minutes east of the Las Vegas Motor Speedway.

Blake didn't like it.

For one, the exchange was taking place at night. Certainly not the best time of day. Two, the area provided no protection, no place for possible backup. Basically, they'd be in the middle of nowhere. Too many things could go wrong.

His cell phone rang. He put the call on loud speaker. "Hello."

"It's Agent Lois Reimer. Mike Jacobs asked me to look into some financials for you."

Christ, with the exchange weighing heavy on his mind he'd almost forgotten about Trent Chambers' financial records.

Blake clutched the wheel. "What did you find out?"

"There's nothing out of the ordinary. He's clean." A short beat of silence. "This had better not come back on me. I can't afford to lose my job."

"Don't worry. If Chambers finds out, you were following my orders. You have my word. I take full responsibility."

"Okay."

"Thanks for your help." He ended the call.

He was wrong about Chambers. Blake was actually relieved. The guy would be pissed when he learned they'd been snooping through his finances. Not as if the man could fire Blake, he'd already resigned.

His phone rang, again. This time Blake checked the caller ID.

It was Whitney. She was probably calling to see when he'd be back.

He pressed the talk button. "Hi, baby. I'll—"

"Oh, God, Blake. Something's happened. Kate's dead. Her car blew up."

"What? You've got to be kidding me?"

"I'm not. I wish I was."

His chest began to ache again. "I love you. Put Mike on the phone."

"I love you, too."

A short pause of silence.

He heard Mike's voice. "Hey, you wouldn't believe the mess over here."

"What the hell happened?"

"I just spoke to the locals. Looks like a car bomb, detonated by remote control. She never had a chance, man. Not a chance."

Remote control? Whoever had planted the device had been waiting and watching. Sanchez or his cousin, under the direction of Nathan Shaw.

Christ. The house could go next. Mike's Camaro or Whitney's SUV. They weren't safe.

His hands began to sweat. "Mike, have the bomb squad sweep your car, then get Whitney the hell out there. Meet me at the field office. Contact Cally, and have him meet us." Blake glanced at the clock on the dashboard. "I'm still about an hour away."

"Okay, I'll see you there."

Blake disconnected and tossed his phone on top of the prison log files. "God damn it."

Another innocent life, gone. When would it end? The answer was simple.

Not until Nathan Shaw was executed.

CHAPTER FORTY-TWO

At nine-fifteen, Blake steered the Suburban into the field office parking lot on Lake Mead Boulevard. Through his headlights, he spotted Mike's Camaro parked at the back under a lamp post. Blake parked beside him, shut off the vehicle, and got out. Mike, Whitney, and Cally climbed out of the Camaro.

Blake nodded to Mike and Cally. He hugged Whitney and whispered in her ear. "Missed you."

"I missed you too." She kissed Blake on the cheek. "How did it go with Nathan?"

"Typical. The bastard acted like he didn't know anything. A big waste of time."

Mike shook his head. "Oh, man, Chambers is irate. He found out about the financial check."

"I'll deal with him later." Blake rubbed his chest.

"Umm...too late." Mike pointed over his shoulder. "He's stalking this way."

Blake turned.

In the light, the man's face was red. His eyes narrow. Both arms were at his side, his hands clenched into tight fists.

"Shit," Mike said.

"Shit is right." Blake didn't have time for this.

Chambers stopped and faced him. He loosened his tie. "How dare you run a financial check on me. What the fuck do you think you're doing? Last I checked, you and Jacobs resigned last week. You're off this case. I'm sending another agent to meet Sanchez."

Not a chance in hell.

Blake had had enough. He was tired and sore. "Fuck you. You saw the DVD. You know Sanchez's terms." He gritted his teeth. "I might have had to put up with your bullshit for thirteen years, but you are not putting that little girl's life in jeopardy. Now, get the hell out of my way." He pushed Chambers to one side.

Everyone was speechless, including Chambers, who stood with his mouth gaping open. He never said another word.

Blake turned to Cally. "Contact the locals and have them cancel the APB on Alberto Guerrero. More than likely he's with Sanchez anyway. We sure as hell don't need any surprises that could put Angel in any more danger. Oh, I need a Crown Vic, one of the armored ones, and about a foot of rope or cable." Cally raised an eyebrow questioning the request for rope but never asked. He knew better. "Okay, I'll get on it." He headed toward the back door of the field office and disappeared inside.

Mike leaned against the front of his car and crossed his feet. "What's the plan?"

Blake put his hand on his shoulder. "You my friend, are joining us. Your view will be from the trunk of the Crown Vic. Sorry, man. It's the only way I can have you back us up without Sanchez knowing."

Mike grinned. "Thank God I'm not claustrophobic."

❈ ❈ ❈

Blake sat in the Crown Vic and adjusted his earpiece. "Can you hear me?"

He heard Mike say, "Yup, loud and clear."

In the rearview mirror, he watched as the trunk slowly raised, and Mike crawled out. He went to his car, grabbed a rifle, and his Kevlar vest from the back seat. He put it on.

Blake checked his watch. They had to leave in ten minutes.

He looked at Whitney. She sat next to him in the passenger seat with her head tilted back on the headrest, her eyes closed.

"Everything will be okay. We'll get Angel."

"I hope so." Whitney opened her eyes and looked at him. "I'm scared to death. I almost lost you once. I can't go through that again." He saw weeks of pain and loss collect in her eyes. And tears.

He knew tonight was risky. There were no guarantees. He would do everything in his power to make sure everyone came out of this alive.

Blake reached for her hand and planted a kiss on her palm. "Just remember, this car is armored and has bullet proof glass. Don't get out unless I give you the signal, okay?"

"Okay."

Blake started the car.

A few minutes passed.

He glanced in the side-view mirror at Mike at the back of the car.

He saw the trunk open then close. "Ready?"

Mike's voice echoed in his earpiece. "Let's roll."

❉ ❉ ❉

Blake shifted in his seat, trying to get comfortable. The weight of the bullet proof vest made his shoulder and chest burn and throb like hell. Every few minutes, he glanced in the side-view mirror to make sure they weren't being followed.

He wouldn't put anything past Sanchez. Blake had no idea what they were about to walk into as it was.

He grasped Whitney's hand and laced his fingers through hers.

She held on tight as if she never wanted to let go. He didn't want to let go either, but he knew he had to soon.

As they passed the sprawling Las Vegas Motor Speedway, Blake flipped on the windshield wipers to clear the light rain that began to fall.

"Mike, we're just on the other side of the LVMS. You okay back there?"

"Uncomfortable as hell, man. You owe me big time for this little adventure."

Blake smiled to himself and kept his focus on the road ahead.

Tense silence in the car stretched on and on.

He spotted the tall, blue, red and white Chevron sign coming up on the left. He shut off the wipers happy to see the rain had stopped.

His insides vibrated with adrenalin and fear.

Whitney drew a shaky deep breath and then exhaled.

He gave her hand a squeeze, then let go. "Mike, five minutes."

"All right, I'm ready."

Blake flicked on the turning signal, slowed the car and turned into the abandoned station. He glanced at the clock on the dash.

Ten-fifty-eight.

His heart beat thundered in his chest. He popped open the glove box, grabbed his gun and rested it on his knee.

On the other side of the row of gas pumps, a dark colored van turned its headlights on.

Sanchez.

Blake wheeled the Crown Vic around and stopped on a slight angle, hoping to give Mike the best possible position to raise the trunk without tipping Sanchez off.

"Showtime, buddy." He put the car in park.

Whitney leaned forward in the seat and pointed. "Is that him?"

Sanchez sliced through headlights dressed in blue jeans and a white T-shirt. Blake immediately spotted the colorful serpent tattoo on the man's neck. Rage and hate swirled through him. His body tensed. "Yes."

Then he spotted the gun clutched in Sanchez's hand. He unhooked his seatbelt, and picked up his weapon, making sure the safety was off.

"Be careful," Whitney whispered.

He opened the car door and stood there, using the door as a partial shield. "Where's the girl?"

"The chica you get when you hand over Whitney Steel." He raised his gun and aimed it at Blake.

Blake raised his weapon. "No, Sanchez. Not until you show me the girl is alive. Then we trade."

A few tense seconds passed that felt like forever.

Sanchez's face twisted. He took a few steps backward and waved toward the van.

The side van door opened. His cousin, Alberto, jumped out. He grabbed Angel and lifted her out and placed her on the ground beside him. He kept his hand on her shoulder.

Please don't move, Angel.

Blake prayed Mike was ready. He'd only have one chance.

"Take Alberto out," Blake whispered.

He held his breath and waited.

"See she is well. Now we trade." Pablo stepped forward.

Take the shot.

"Sure." Blake was not getting Whitney out of the car no matter what.

Come on. Shoot, Mike.

Blake heard the rifle fire. The shot hit Alberto square in the stomach. He doubled over, fell to one knee, and then crumpled to the ground.

Angel let out a scream. She started to run toward Blake.

Pablo pivoted.

Blake squeezed the trigger. The bullet got Pablo in the arm. He sprinted to the van.

Mike was out of the trunk and rushed to Angel. He scooped her up in his arms and ran.

An engine growled. Tires screeched.

Pablo floored it.

"Oh, God. No!" Whitney screamed.

The van was racing straight at Mike and Angel.

Blake stepped out from behind the car door and aimed. The shot shattered the van's windshield.

The vehicle swerved away from them toward the highway.

Blake ran.

He fired off another round. The bullet missed the back tire and took out one of the taillights instead.

Sanchez had made it to the highway. The van veered in and out of traffic and tunneled out of sight.

"Damn it." Blake stopped to catch his breath.

He pulled his cell phone out of his pocket and hit speed dial.

"Cally, I need an APB out on Sanchez. Dark blue Chevy van. Nevada plate, F-r-e-r-i-d-e, heading west on Las Vegas Boulevard. He's injured, gunshot wound to the left arm. Have the hospitals be on the lookout."

"Got it. Did you get the child?" Cally asked.

They did. But Blake knew it would never be over as long as Pablo Sanchez was out there.

"Yeah, she's safe." Blake ended the call.

Bent over, with both hands on his knees, he took a long deep breath and then exhaled. He was getting too damn old for this crap.

EPILOGUE

Seven months later...

I n the living room, Blake sat beside Whitney on the couch. "I just got off the phone with Chambers. The good news is they arrested Angel's foster care case worker. Apparently, Sanchez had paid her twenty thousand dollars in return for a copy of Angel's file. That's how the bastard knew where to find her."

"My God. It amazes me how money can be such a powerful motivator. To choose dollars over a little girl's life. I'll never understand that." She looked at Blake. "And the bad news?"

Whitney noticed he swallowed hard before he spoke. "Sanchez somehow got out of the country. Sources say he's back in Colombia."

It was as if the air had been suddenly sucked out of the room.

"Can't the authorities pick him up there? For goodness sakes. The man killed Joanna Hurst, Kate, and kidnapped Angel."

Blake shook his head. "It'll never happen. Sanchez and The Sur del Calle cartel have been lining the pockets of the Colombian National Police for decades."

He wrapped his arm around her shoulder and cuddled her. "Don't worry, he's on every U.S. watch list.

We're safe. He wouldn't risk coming back here."

But would he try if he knew his cousin had survived? She didn't want to think about it. She couldn't. There were so many happy things to think about instead, like house hunting tomorrow.

They'd outgrown the two bedroom condo as soon as Whitney had moved her things from Florida. Cramped space was an understatement.

They were also looking forward to the day when Angel officially became part of their family. The adoption papers had been filed. In the meantime, they'd continue to visit the child twice a week at her new foster home.

Blake kissed her on the cheek and then stood.

Whitney stared at his face. He had a silly little grin on his face.

His brown eyes sparkled. "Have I told you how much I love you today?"

She smiled. "You have. Want to tell me again?"

The man could tell her a thousand times a day and she'd never get sick of hearing those beautiful words.

"I love you with all my heart, body and soul, baby."

He dropped to one knee.

The breath caught in Whitney's throat.

Blake held out his hand.

Then she saw it. A diamond ring. The most beautiful princess cut, white gold engagement ring she'd ever seen.

"Whitney Steel. I need you. I want you. Will you marry me?"

He slipped the ring onto her finger.

Tears pooled behind her eyes. There was no chance of stopping them from running down her cheeks. She didn't even try.

"Yes, I'll marry you. I love you." She slipped her arms around his neck and kissed him.

His face beamed. "You just made the happiest man alive." He stood back up. "I think this calls for a drink to celebrate."

"I couldn't agree more."

A wedding. She was getting married. Whitney couldn't stop smiling.

While she waited for Blake to return to the living room, she thought about the other changes that had taken place over the past few months.

She liked her new job at News3 where she was respected by all her colleagues. The first time ever, and it felt incredible. Blake and Mike had started their investigation-security firm and she loved the fact Blake was home every night, not putting himself in harm's way anymore.

Nathan Shaw's trial was in full swing after a new district attorney had been assigned to the case following Kate Leatham's death. Whitney and Blake would be called to testify, and she was confident Nathan would receive the death sentence.

The scar on Blake's chest would always remind them how close he came to dying.

Whitney wiped the tears from her cheeks with the back of her hand. She looked down at the ring on her finger.

A new beginning. And eventually, they'd be rid of Nathan Shaw, a man who had taken so much from them but at the same time given them so much.

Each other and Angel.

AUTHOR'S NOTE

I'm always asked what inspired me to write *Reflection*. The story evolved after Clonaid (a company founded by the religious sect called the Raelians which views cloning as the first step in achieving immortality) announced the birth of Eve, the "first human clone" in 2002 using the similar technique to clone, Dolly the Sheep.

About 160 nations in the world have yet to outlaw the birth of human clones and others are allowing the creation of human clones as long as they are not put into a woman's womb (how do we know they *aren't* implanted?), add a kick-ass investigative reporter, a sexy FBI agent, and thus, *Reflection* was born.

If you enjoyed reading *Reflection*, I have great news! Blake and Whitney's story isn't over yet!

Buy *Retribution* (A Whitney Steel Novel – Book Two)

Buy *Resurrect* (A Whitney Steel Novel - Book Three)

Watch for *Redemption* (A Whitney Steel Novel - Book Four) coming soon!